# CITY of BETRAYAL

## BERKLEY PRIME CRIME TITLES BY VICTORIA THOMPSON

### Gaslight Mysteries

MURDER ON ASTOR PLACE

MURDER ON ST. MARK'S PLACE

MURDER ON GRAMERCY PARK

MURDER ON WASHINGTON SQUARE

MURDER ON MULBERRY BEND

MURDER ON MARBLE ROW

MURDER ON LENOX HILL

MURDER IN LITTLE ITALY

MURDER IN CHINATOWN

MURDER ON BANK STREET

MURDER ON WAVERLY PLACE

MURDER ON LEXINGTON AVENUE

MURDER ON SISTERS' ROW

MURDER ON FIFTH AVENUE

MURDER IN CHELSEA

MURDER IN MURRAY HILL

MURDER ON AMSTERDAM AVENUE

MURDER ON ST. NICHOLAS AVENUE

MURDER IN MORNINGSIDE HEIGHTS

MURDER IN THE BOWERY

MURDER ON UNION SQUARE

MURDER ON TRINITY PLACE

MURDER ON PLEASANT AVENUE

MURDER ON WALL STREET

MURDER ON MADISON SQUARE

MURDER ON BEDFORD STREET

### Counterfeit Lady Novels

CITY OF LIES

CITY OF SECRETS

CITY OF SCOUNDRELS

CITY OF SCHEMES

CITY OF SHADOWS

CITY OF FORTUNE

CITY OF BETRAYAL

# CITY
 of
# BETRAYAL

## VICTORIA THOMPSON

BERKLEY PRIME CRIME
NEW YORK

BERKLEY PRIME CRIME
Published by Berkley
An imprint of Penguin Random House LLC
penguinrandomhouse.com

Library of Congress Cataloging-in-Publication Data

Names: Thompson, Victoria (Victoria E.), author.
Title: City of betrayal / Victoria Thompson.
Description: New York: Berkley Prime Crime, 2023. |
Series: A Counterfeit Lady novel; book 7
Identifiers: LCCN 2023031471 (print) | LCCN 2023031472 (ebook) |
ISBN 9780593440605 (hardcover) | ISBN 9780593440629 (ebook)
Subjects: LCGFT: Cozy mysteries. | Novels.
Classification: LCC PS3570.H6442 C575 2022 (print) |
LCC PS3570.H6442 (ebook) | DDC 813/.54—dc23/eng/20230713
LC record available at https://lccn.loc.gov/2023031471
LC ebook record available at https://lccn.loc.gov/2023031472

Printed in the United States of America
1st Printing

Book design by Kristin del Rosario

*With thanks to Elaine Weiss, whose book*
The Woman's Hour *was both an inspiration and*
*an invaluable resource for this book.*

# CITY of BETRAYAL

# CHAPTER ONE

"I KNEW IT WOULD BE DIFFICULT, BUT I NEVER DREAMED IT would be impossible," Elizabeth Miles Bates said, staring at the letter she'd been reading.

Her mother-in-law looked up from her knitting. "Are you talking about passing the amendment, dear?"

"Yes, I am. I'll never understand those people who are so dead set against allowing women to vote."

"What does Miss Paul's letter say? And I'm sure she doesn't say it's impossible."

Alice Paul was the leader of the National Woman's Party, the more radical of the two organizations that had been working for Woman Suffrage. Their demonstrations outside the White House had gotten many of their volunteers jailed. Elizabeth and her mother-in-law were among them.

"You're right, she doesn't say it's impossible," Elizabeth admitted, "but it is going to be *nearly* impossible. I thought that since thirty-five states have already approved the amendment, we could easily get the one more state that we need to make it the law of the land, but Miss Paul makes it clear that there is only one state left that might actually approve the amendment, and that state is Tennessee."

Mother Bates frowned. They both knew that almost every other Southern state had already rejected the amendment, and Tennessee was likely to join them. "Why is she so sure it comes down to Tennessee?"

"Since eight states have already rejected it, that leaves just five states that could approve it. We know North Carolina and Florida will never approve it, and the governors of Vermont and Connecticut have refused to call a special session of their legislatures even to vote on it. That means Tennessee is the only possible state left."

"If only we hadn't lost in Delaware," Mother Bates said sadly.

"That was such a disappointment. We were so sure . . ."

"Then we must be sure we will win in Tennessee. Is that what Miss Paul advises?"

Elizabeth looked down at the letter she still held. "Not exactly, but she is calling on all her volunteers to help in whatever way they can."

Mother Bates stopped her knitting needles and stared at Elizabeth. "Did she ask you to go to Tennessee?"

"Yes, she did," Elizabeth said with a sigh.

"That's a great honor. She knows how effective you've been in convincing legislators to vote for the amendment."

Elizabeth and Mother Bates had traveled to several other states to help lobby for the amendment. "Not in the South, though," Elizabeth reminded her.

"Then Tennessee will be the exception."

Elizabeth looked at the letter again. Miss Paul was quite eloquent in her praise of Elizabeth's ability to convince reluctant officials to support Woman Suffrage. If only she knew that Elizabeth's skills came from being raised by a con man to become a con artist herself. She could lie without blinking and charm even the most unappealing gentleman. When she had married Gideon Bates, she had thought her days of conning marks was over, but she had found her skills could come in handy in getting justice for people who could never get it any other way. She had used those skills several times to help her friends.

It had been almost a year since she'd run a con, though, unless she counted lobbying politicians for Woman Suffrage, which she probably should.

"I don't know what Gideon will say," Elizabeth murmured.

"What I'll say about what?" Gideon asked as he came into the parlor.

"Darling, I didn't hear you come home," Elizabeth said, jumping up to give him his welcome-home kiss. Mother Bates tactfully averted her eyes. "How was your day?"

"Boring as usual." Gideon was an estate attorney, so he rarely did anything exciting. "And don't change the subject. What is it you think I'll have something to say about and is that a letter you're holding?"

"It's from Alice Paul," his mother said helpfully.

Elizabeth sent her an exasperated look, which she ignored.

"Ah, I see. Where does Miss Paul want to send you now?" he asked, taking a seat on the sofa and pulling Elizabeth down beside him.

"Tennessee," Elizabeth said.

"In the summer? It gets awfully hot down there in the summer."

"It gets awfully hot in New York in the summer," Elizabeth countered.

Gideon shrugged. "I'm just warning you. Why does she need you in Tennessee?"

"Because it's our only hope." Elizabeth and Mother Bates took turns explaining the situation and how dire it now appeared.

"Does Miss Paul really believe Tennessee will approve the amendment?" he asked when they finished.

"We don't know, but I think we can all agree that they must," his mother said.

"I hope they know that," Gideon said with a grin.

"They will when we tell them," his mother said.

"*We?*" Gideon echoed.

"You can't think I'd let Elizabeth go to Tennessee by herself when I could help, too."

Elizabeth gave her a grateful smile.

Gideon frowned. "You need to know what you're getting into."

"We've done this before," Elizabeth reminded him.

"Yes, but not when it was down to the wire like this. Some of the other fights have been hard, but the Antis will bring out all their dirty tricks for this one," Gideon said, using the nickname for those who were anti–Woman Suffrage. "Politics can be an ugly business, and when so much is at stake, it gets even uglier."

His mother smiled a little. "Surely, you don't think those Southern gentlemen will do anything unpleasant."

"Oh no," Gideon said. "They'll be smiling very sweetly as they stab you in the back."

"But we have to go," Elizabeth said. "After all we've done for the Cause, we can't sit by now and just watch. What if we lose in Tennessee? I'd never forgive myself for not doing my part."

"I'm not saying you shouldn't go," Gideon said.

"And I'm very happy to see that you also aren't telling her she *can't* go," Mother Bates said with some satisfaction.

"I wouldn't dare," Gideon replied with a smirk.

Elizabeth knew her father had warned him that forbidding her to do something only guaranteed that she would do it. "Then we'll go."

"And I'm going with you, too," Gideon said.

"Do you think we need your protection?" Elizabeth said in surprise.

"Let's hope it doesn't come to that, but I'm sure the Suffs can use some male help. Those legislators can be difficult to track down, and they go places that ladies can't go. As a member of the Men's Ratification Committee, I feel it's my duty to volunteer."

"What about your law firm?" Elizabeth said. "We don't even know how long it will take."

"Mr. Devoss will insist that I go when I tell him I'm needed to protect my mother."

"Gideon," Mother Bates scolded, but Elizabeth noticed her cheeks were pink. Mr. Devoss was very devoted to her mother-in-law.

"Do we know Mr. Devoss's stand on Woman Suffrage?" Elizabeth asked.

"I believe Mother convinced him to support it," Gideon said.

His mother glared at him, but he ignored her.

"Then he will certainly let you go to Tennessee," Elizabeth said. "It shouldn't take very long, should it? Surely only a few days. It will be a special session of the legislature and they'll only be considering the amendment."

"Do we know when it will be held?" Gideon asked.

"Not yet. Miss Paul isn't even certain the governor will call it. He's afraid if he shows he supports Woman Suffrage, he won't win his primary on . . ." Elizabeth glanced at Miss Paul's letter to verify the date. ". . . on August fifth, so it will be after that."

"Tennessee in August," Mother Bates said with a mock shudder.

"Another reason the legislators won't want to linger," Gideon said. "But won't they need people there ahead of time to get the legislators to pledge their votes?"

"According to Miss Paul, the Tennessee chapter of the Woman's Party is sending their members out across the state to find the men at their homes and get their pledges."

"So they'll know how many votes they have even before the session starts," Mother Bates added.

"What if they don't have enough?" Gideon asked.

"Then they'll start trying to convince those who wouldn't pledge or who seemed undecided to vote to approve," Mother Bates said.

"And keep those who did pledge to vote for it from changing their minds," Elizabeth said.

"No easy task, I'm sure," Gideon said. "Don't forget that very powerful forces are determined to stop the amendment from becoming law."

"How could we forget?" Elizabeth said. "The railroads and the whiskey men and the textile manufacturers. They're all afraid that if women get the vote, they'll want to end things like corruption and child labor."

"The whiskey men can't still be worried that women would insist on Prohibition since we already have it," Gideon argued.

Elizabeth smiled wisely. "It seems they're worried women will insist that the laws are *enforced*."

"Ah, I see," Gideon said. "But Tennessee was already dry for years before Prohibition."

"I hope you aren't too surprised to learn that law wasn't really enforced, either," his mother said.

"I can see I should have gone with you on these trips sooner," Gideon said. "I'm hopelessly naïve."

"Not hopelessly," Elizabeth said, patting his arm. "We'll make sure you're properly educated by the time we go to Tennessee. We have a few weeks, if the governor isn't going to call the session until after his primary."

"Maybe he'll schedule it for later in the year, when it will be cooler," Mother Bates said hopefully.

"Oh no, we want it as soon as possible so women have time to register to vote in the November elections," Elizabeth said. "Just think, they'll get to vote for a new president this year."

"But only if we can convince enough of those Tennessee gentlemen to support the amendment," Mother Bates said.

"I have every confidence that the two of you will succeed and all the women in America will be able to vote in the November election," Gideon said.

Elizabeth decided she needed to kiss her husband again, and this time Mother Bates didn't even look away.

Is THERE SOMETHING GOOD IN THE GOSSIP COLUMN TODAY?" Anna Vanderslice asked as she breezed into the Bateses' library to find Elizabeth studying the newspaper.

Elizabeth looked up and smiled at her friend. "I'm sure there is, but I haven't gotten to the gossip column yet. I'm looking for some news about Tennessee."

Anna plopped down on the chair opposite Elizabeth's. "You don't think a New York newspaper will have news about Tennessee, do you?"

"Not usually, but the Tennessee primary election was two days ago, and the governor won his contest, so I'm hoping he'll call the legislature into special session pretty soon."

"That's right. I almost forgot. Are you still planning to go?" Anna asked, pulling off the gloves ladies were required to wear even in summer to protect their hands. Then she started fanning herself with them. "I asked your maid to get us something cool to drink. I hope you don't mind."

"Not at all. It's very warm today, although Gideon keeps warning me it will be much hotter in Nashville."

"You'll be too busy to even notice," Anna predicted. "I should go with you."

"I would love that," Elizabeth said, "but who would look after your mother?"

Anna sighed. "I know. I can't leave her. She's lost interest in just about everything. She won't even see her friends when they call. It's gotten even worse since my classes ended and I'm home all the time now. She is content to let me wait on her hand and foot. I don't know what I'll do with her when I go back to school in the fall." Anna was attending college, studying to be a teacher.

"Does she still . . . ?" Elizabeth started but caught herself.

"Does she still talk about David all the time?" Anna finished for her. "Oh yes. Sometimes I can hardly bear it."

David was Anna's brother who had died in the flu epidemic almost two years earlier. He had also been Gideon's best friend. "I'm so sorry," Elizabeth said.

"Yes, well, let's not dwell on that," Anna said with forced cheerfulness. "Did you find out anything about Tennessee?"

"Not a word, not even in the front section."

"Why would it be in the front section with the real news?" Anna asked with mock amazement. She was as involved in the Cause as Elizabeth was, having been imprisoned with her and

Mother Bates as well. "Everyone knows that news about Woman Suffrage belongs in the women's pages."

"I thought maybe because it involved the governor and politics, they might put it in the front, but no, nothing."

"I'm sure Miss Paul will let you know as soon as she hears. And you can go on short notice since you don't have to . . ."

Elizabeth looked up in surprise when Anna stopped in the middle of her sentence. "Since I don't have to what?"

"Nothing," Anna said sheepishly, not quite meeting her eye.

That was when she realized what Anna had been about to say and why she hadn't said it. "Since I don't have children to worry about," she finished for her friend.

"I'm so sorry," Anna said quickly, obviously ashamed to have brought up the sensitive subject. Elizabeth and Gideon had been married well over a year with no hint of a baby, a lack Elizabeth mourned, albeit quietly.

"That's all right," Elizabeth said with a false smile. "I don't have children yet, so I should take advantage of that freedom. I just hope we have enough time to make our travel arrangements. The Woman's Party is low on funds, so I don't think Miss Paul will be wasting money on long-distance telephone calls or telegrams."

"Low on funds?" Anna scoffed, taking Elizabeth's hint to change the subject. "Won't Mrs. Belmont help them out?" The wealthy Mrs. Belmont was the main benefactor for the Party.

"I don't know, but Miss Paul also asked me for a donation when she wrote to invite me to go to Tennessee."

"She's always asking for donations," Anna reminded her.

"This one sounded a little desperate, though. I know she'll want to go to Tennessee herself so she can direct the volunteers."

"Yes, this is much too important to leave it to anyone else."

"Which is why I sent her some money," Elizabeth said.

"I'll send some, too, although it won't be much. Mother still refuses to understand that we need to economize since we don't have David to support us anymore."

"That's kind of you. I do wish you could go with us."

Anna smiled mischievously. "Yes, we could have a wonderful time with those legislators. Do you think we could run a con to get them to support the amendment?"

Elizabeth gave her a disapproving glare. "I should never have let you kill me." As part of a con, Anna had once pretended to murder Elizabeth, which had ironically saved Elizabeth's life.

"But you did let me kill you, so it's too late now. Do you have an idea for a con?"

"Absolutely not. I can't even think of anything that might work."

Anna did not look convinced. "Just in case you do, and you need help, send for me. Freddie would be happy to come, too, I'm sure." Frederica Quincy was Anna's dearest friend—and perhaps more, but Elizabeth didn't like to pry.

"Isn't she back home with her family for the summer?"

"Yes, but she'd leave in a moment to help."

"I'll keep that in mind," Elizabeth lied. She had no intention of involving Anna and Freddie in any more cons. Besides, a con wouldn't work in this case, would it?

*Would it?*

The doorbell rang, interrupting her thoughts. A few moments later, the maid brought in a telegram.

"Is it from Miss Paul?" Anna asked, leaning over to see it better.

"It's addressed to me, at least." Elizabeth tore open the envelope. "Good heavens."

"What does she say?" Anna asked, snatching the paper from Elizabeth's unresisting fingers. "Yes, good heavens. You have to be in Tennessee by Monday."

"And today is Saturday. That doesn't give us much time."

"How can they get the legislature together so quickly?" Anna asked, handing the telegram back to Elizabeth.

"Telegrams and trains, I suppose. Modern conveniences have made the world a smaller place. Besides, they're all in the same state, so it's not like they need to take a sleeper halfway across the country to get there like we do."

"Is Tennessee halfway across? I would have thought it's closer."

"It doesn't matter. I have to tell Gideon and Mother Bates at once, but they're both out. This doesn't give us much time at all. Luckily, I already got a train schedule."

"Surely, there is a sleeper to Nashville," Anna said. "This is New York, after all."

"Yes, and we should leave tonight. I just hope the Nashville Suffs have got everything organized already."

"Maybe they have already gotten enough pledges to pass the amendment, and it will all be over in just a few days."

"After more than seventy years of working for it, that would be a little anticlimactic, wouldn't it?" Elizabeth asked with a grin.

"I'm sure everyone in the Woman's Party would settle for that. We don't need excitement. We just need the vote. Elizabeth, women can change the world if we get the chance."

"I hope you're right, my dear friend." But Elizabeth wasn't as idealistic as Anna. Changing the world was a lofty goal. She knew too much about greed from her previous experience as a con artist to believe it was possible.

———————

THE TRAIN TO NASHVILLE HAD BEEN HOT AND CROWDED, and they'd hardly gotten any sleep in the stuffy compartment. Gideon's mother had also slept poorly in her compartment next door. Opening the windows offered little relief because of the smoke and cinders blowing in. But they had finally reached their destination. Gideon was looking forward to a cool bath and a nap.

Union Station was swarming with people arriving in trains up and down the tracks as legislators returned to the Tennessee capital and those who wished to influence them arrived in force. To make matters even worse, groups of women were greeting each traveler who stepped off a train and trying pin a rose on them. The Antis had red roses and the Suffs had yellow ones. Woe to anyone who refused both, and even accepting one put a person in the crosshairs of the opposing group. Gideon and his ladies quickly pinned on yellow roses to indicate they supported Woman Suffrage and proceeded to ignore the entreaties of the Antis determined to change their minds.

With much difficulty, Gideon found a porter who loaded their bags onto his cart. "Are you going to the Hermitage Hotel like everybody else, sir?" the porter asked, nodding at the yellow rose on his lapel.

"Indeed, we are."

"I'll have your bags sent over, then. Don't you worry. They'll be waiting for you when you get there."

Gideon smiled. He hadn't expected such good service here. He tipped the porter generously and then directed his women folk to follow the crowd up the steps.

"This is quite impressive," his mother observed when they reached the glass-ceilinged main hall. On one side of the hall was a bas-relief of a gigantic locomotive that appeared to be bursting right through the wall. On another side was a huge clock guarded by two figures representing Time and Progress. Progress held a railroad wheel to his chest. Nothing subtle about that message. Around the room, two dozen female figures with angel's wings were draped over the arched doorways. Each of them held something representing a resource or product of the state. Gideon noticed one of them held a flask of Tennessee whiskey. Would they alter that now that nationwide Prohibition was in force? Somehow, he doubted it.

"Yes, it is impressive," Elizabeth agreed. "Southerners have great civic pride."

"Have you been here before?" his mother asked her.

Elizabeth's life as a con artist had taken her to many different places, so it was a logical question. "Not to Nashville, no."

"My goodness, it is rather warm here," his mother observed.

"I tried to warn you," Gideon reminded them, "although it's even hotter than I expected. I think you could cut the air with a knife."

"I suppose you get used to it," Elizabeth said. "Lots of people do live here all the time, after all."

His mother pulled a fan out of her purse and waved it in front of her face. "Nobody could get used to this."

They made their way out to the street where cabs were lined up to serve the crowd. After a long wait, they took one to the hotel. As soon as they left the chaos of Union Station, the crowds disappeared.

"The city is awfully quiet," his mother said as the cab made its way through the nearly deserted streets. "I thought it would be bustling with all the lawmakers returning."

"I guess the Capitol might be, but it's Sunday, ma'am," the driver reminded them. "Everything is closed and everybody's in church."

Elizabeth caught Gideon's eye. "Not everybody, I'm guessing."

"Oh no, I'm sure Mrs. Catt is hard at work," his mother said, naming the president of the more conservative suffrage organization. "And Miss Paul is probably on her way here, if she isn't here already. I'm sure all the Suffs will be busy, as well as the Antis."

"Are you ladies for or against this woman suffering business?" the driver asked.

Elizabeth and his mother exchanged a glance but somehow managed to keep a straight face, which was more than Gideon could do.

"We're in favor of women having the vote," Elizabeth said.

The driver shook his head in wonder. "I don't know why you'd want to mess around in politics. It's a nasty business."

"We're hoping to make it a bit less nasty," his mother said.

"Good luck to you, then."

"We'll need it," Elizabeth whispered.


WALKING INTO THE HERMITAGE HOTEL WAS LIKE WALKING into a beehive. The enormous Beaux-Arts lobby with its soaring vaulted ceiling and huge marble pillars was filled with people talking in small groups. The murmur of their conversations combined into a cacophony of sound that was like a living thing. Through the haze of cigar smoke they could see that the crowd was composed of both men and women, unusual for a hotel lobby where businessmen gathered to meet with their peers. Or where businessmen went to speak to their legislators, which was why such conversations were called "lobbying." Women would walk through the lobby on their way to shop or visit the home of a friend but would never stop to talk business.

Except when women were trying to convince male legislators

to support the Susan B. Anthony Amendment. Or to talk them out of supporting it. Elizabeth saw many Suffs in the crowd but recognized some of the Antis from her previous trips, too. Virtually all the women and a lot of the men wore either a yellow rose or a red one, making it easy to tell who was who.

"I'll get us checked in," Gideon told Elizabeth and Mother Bates. "Try to find a place to sit down. The front desk seems pretty busy so it might take some time."

He strode off to join the crowd at the front desk.

"My goodness," Mother Bates said. "We got here just in time. Do you see anyone you know?"

"Yes," Elizabeth said, waving to the young woman she had just recognized.

Betty Gram waved back and made her way through the crowd as quickly as she could. She was a pretty thing. She could have been an actress with her stylish dress and perfect makeup, and indeed she had been. She'd left a role on Broadway to demonstrate with the Suffragists at the White House and been arrested for her trouble. She and her younger sister, Alice, had been locked up in the same workhouse as Elizabeth and Mother Bates where they had all participated in a hunger strike. Since then, they had worked together in New Jersey for the very close ratification vote there and then in Delaware where disaster struck and they lost.

Elizabeth returned Betty's hug warmly.

"I'm so glad you were able to come," Betty said. "Miss Paul told us she'd asked you, but we weren't expecting you, too, Mrs. Bates."

"I couldn't let Elizabeth do this alone. Besides, I wanted to be here when we finally get the vote."

All three of them smiled at that, although Elizabeth noted Betty's smile wasn't as confident as she would have hoped.

"I've brought my husband, too," Elizabeth said.

"That's wonderful," Betty said, her eyes sparkling with delight. "We've found the legislators like to go off to the Grill Room downstairs where women aren't allowed."

"I'm sure Gideon will be glad to join them there," Mother Bates said.

"Is your sister here, too?" Elizabeth asked.

"No, she's back at headquarters in Washington City, helping Miss Paul."

"Isn't Miss Paul here yet?" Mother Bates asked in alarm. How could they hope to win without her leadership?

"She . . ." Betty began, then glanced around to make sure no one was listening to them and leaned in closer so she could speak more softly. "The Party doesn't have any money to send her here."

"But I can wire her train fare," Elizabeth said, outraged.

"It's more than that, much more. The Party is in serious debt and the coffers are empty, so Miss Paul can't come until everything is settled. But don't worry. She has put Sue White in charge here in Nashville. Do you know her?"

"I don't think we've ever met," Elizabeth said.

"She's wonderful, and she's from Tennessee so she knows everyone and how to get things done here. She rented a storefront just half a block down the street for our headquarters. She said that's better than a hotel suite, which is what the NAWSA is using, because people can look in the window and see we're ordinary females, not the hideous monsters they claim are the only ones who support Woman Suffrage."

"Miss White is clever, too," Mother Bates said.

"Very clever," Betty agreed. "She assigned three of us, Anita Pollitzer and Catherine Flanagan and me, to different parts of the state. We tracked down all the legislators in their home districts to get them to pledge to vote for the amendment."

"How long have you been here?" Elizabeth asked in amazement.

"In Tennessee? Almost three weeks. I motored hundreds of miles around the state and walked even more, it seemed. I got drenched in thunderstorms and roasted in the heat and stranded by flat tires, but I found all my men."

"Did they all agree to support the amendment?" Mother Bates asked.

"No, some of them are intractable, but I escorted a few of the supporters in on the train this morning. I had Thomas Riddick who was just elected to the House specifically to help with ratification efforts, and Joe Hanover who has pledged to do all he can. I also had the mayor of Memphis who is going to help by talking to the men he knows. We even got Seth Walker to pledge. He's the Speaker of the House, and he has a lot of influence. He also knows all kinds of parliamentary tricks to make the process go the way we want it to."

"Good job!" Elizabeth said.

"Oh, *I* wasn't the one who got him to pledge. He gave me a lot of hooey about the Tennessee Constitution. There's a clause that says a sitting legislature can't vote on a constitutional amendment. The amendment must be announced and then an election held so voters know how the candidates stand on the amendment and they know whom to elect. Then the newly elected legislators vote on the amendment."

"That's horrible," Elizabeth said. "Tennessee wouldn't be able to vote on the amendment until after the November election."

"But the U.S. Supreme Court ruled that section of the Tennessee Constitution was null and void because it contradicts the U.S. Constitution. Sue White finally convinced Seth Walker it would be legal to hold the vote and he signed the pledge."

"That is a relief," Mother Bates said.

"It certainly is. If anyone can bring this home, it's Seth Walker. With him on our side, we have a good chance."

"It sounds as if you ladies have already done all the important work," Mother Bates said. "What can we do now?"

Betty grinned. "Make sure the men who pledged don't change their minds! You would not believe how many people have descended on this hotel to convince them to vote no."

"I did notice a lot of Antis here in the lobby," Elizabeth said, glancing meaningfully around at the sea of red roses.

"Yes, Josephine Pearson and her crew are here in force, but we can deal with *them*. It's the men from the railroads and the distilleries and the factory owners who are the real danger."

"Gideon did mention he thought they might be a factor," Mother Bates said.

"More than a factor because they have money and lots of it. Rumors are flying about job offers and even outright bribes being used to sway the legislators."

"That's scandalous," Mother Bates said, outraged.

Elizabeth wasn't surprised, though. She knew all about greed and how almost everyone could be swayed by their own self-interest, no matter how idealistic they thought they were. "I guess the Woman's Party won't be offering any bribes," Elizabeth said with a small smile.

"Even if we wanted to, we couldn't," Betty agreed. "Of course, Mrs. Catt could, but she's even more of a stickler about those things than we are." Carrie Chapman Catt and the rival National American Woman Suffrage Association she led had received a two-million-dollar bequest from a woman she had hardly known. This allowed the group a financial freedom the Woman's Party didn't have.

Elizabeth knew the effectiveness of a well-placed bribe, but she didn't know any alternatives. "If we can't bribe them, what can we do?"

"We appeal to their better natures," Mother Bates said confidently.

"And what if they don't have one?" Elizabeth countered.

"Then we put pressure on them," Betty said. "We've gotten both of the major presidential candidates, Harding and Cox, to support Woman Suffrage and Tennessee Governor Roberts, too. They're not exactly ardent, but they've publicly committed, so they can't go back without humiliating themselves."

"If they aren't *ardent*, can we really trust them to put pressure on others?" Elizabeth asked.

"The leaders of both parties are putting pressure on them," Betty said, "so I think we can at least hope they'll come through."

Elizabeth turned to her mother-in-law. "I was really hoping this wouldn't be impossible."

"It's not impossible," Betty insisted. "Just very difficult. But surely, America won't let itself be the only civilized country where women aren't allowed to vote."

"If you're hoping to embarrass America into giving women the vote, you're wasting your time," Elizabeth said. "We can surely embarrass a few individuals into it, though."

Gideon had come strolling over, looking like he had accomplished something noteworthy. "I was able to get us a suite. Oh, hello," he added, seeing Betty.

Elizabeth introduced them.

"I've heard your name many times, Miss Gram, and always in admiration," Gideon said.

"I could say the same about you, Mr. Bates. We're very glad to have your help."

"The legislators are fleeing to the Grill Room downstairs where women aren't allowed," Elizabeth explained.

"There's another place they go, too," Betty said. "It started last night, after the Antis had a reception to show off the museum artifacts they have set up in one of the ballrooms."

"What kind of artifacts?" Elizabeth asked.

Betty sighed in disgust. "Lots of old documents reminding Southerners of the way the Yankees forced them to free their slaves and give Black men the right to vote. They will never forgive that, it seems, but even worse, they have a copy of the *Woman's Bible* on display."

"A Bible?" Mother Bates echoed. "What's wrong with that?"

"It's not really a Bible. It's a book written years ago by Elizabeth Cady Stanton. She points out all the ways the Bible oppresses women. It was a scandal when it was published because Mrs. Stanton actually said the Bible isn't the inspired word of God, which offended so many people that the NAWSA had to denounce it even though one of their leaders had written it. The saddest part was that Mrs. Stanton listed the names of women she claimed had helped write the book, even though none of them had, and Mrs. Catt was one of them. The sign on the *Woman's Bible* upstairs says MRS. CATT'S BIBLE."

"How awful," Mother Bates said. "I know we've had our differences with Mrs. Catt and the NAWSA, but she shouldn't have to take the blame for something that wasn't her fault."

"No, she shouldn't," Elizabeth said, "but we've all had to endure being lied about and vilified."

"You're right, dear," Mother Bates said sadly.

"Miss Gram, you were saying the men were going someplace besides the Grill Room that women couldn't go," Gideon said, obviously wanting to change the subject.

"Oh yes, I got sidetracked. The Antis have a suite on the eighth floor. It's invitation only, I'm told, and all the legislators are invited. They serve many kinds of liquor there, but whiskey is apparently the most popular choice, because they're calling it the Jack Daniel's Suite."

"Haven't they heard about Prohibition?" Gideon asked only half seriously.

"They don't *sell* it," Betty said. "They give it away along with lectures on why passing the Susan B. Anthony Amendment would mark the end of civilization in America."

"I don't suppose the Suffs can compete with that," Gideon said.

"Of course not. Most of them in both the Woman's Party and the NAWSA are prohibitionists," Mother Bates said. "Even some of the Antis are, so I'm surprised they are allowing this."

Betty smiled knowingly. "When some of them objected, they were told that in Tennessee, whiskey and legislation go hand in hand."

"I just can't believe a man would sell his vote for a glass of whiskey," Mother Bates said in disgust.

"It sounds like they're holding out for *many* glasses of whiskey," Gideon said with a slight smirk.

"But any pledge made while under the influence cannot be binding," Elizabeth said. "We just have to get to these men when they're sober and convince them to do the right thing."

"Yes, we do. Come to our headquarters when you've gotten settled in your rooms, and we'll give you your assignments," Betty said and gave them the directions. It really was just down the street.

They took their leave of Betty and made their way through the crowd to the elevators. When the shiny brass doors slid open, Elizabeth's heart seemed to stop in her chest because there stood her father. For a moment, the whole world seemed to freeze.

Beside her Gideon stiffened and Mother Bates actually made a little sound of pleasure because she really did like the Old Man and was probably happy to see him.

But he raised a hand to his face and gave them the universal sign that told other con men that he was working so not to let on they knew him. He was chatting with a man, and he spared them not another glance as the two of them went on their way.

"What is he doing here?" Gideon whispered.

"Not lobbying for Woman Suffrage, I'm sure," Elizabeth said.

# CHAPTER TWO

No, he's probably not lobbying for woman suffrage," Gideon muttered, certain Mr. Miles was up to no good. The Old Man never did good unless he was helping Elizabeth in aid of one of her friends and then only if he got paid. But people were still crowding onto the elevator, so they had to wait until they reached their rooms to freely discuss what the Old Man might be up to.

The suite was lovely, with mahogany paneled walls and rich carpeting. The furniture was impressive and comfortable.

"Oh, good, it's on the shady side of the building," his mother said, peering out the window.

"I made sure of that," Gideon said, then turned to Elizabeth, who looked absolutely furious.

"Before you ask, I had no idea he would be here. I didn't even tell him we were coming. There wasn't really time and besides, why would he need to know?"

"He wouldn't," Gideon said. "But he made that sign . . ."

"Which means he's working," Elizabeth finished for him.

"That's so clever," his mother said. "You wouldn't want someone coming up and calling you by another name when you were
trying to con someone, would you?"

"Mother!" Gideon said in despair.

"I'm not admiring con artists, dear, just making an obser-
vation."

Gideon wasn't so sure. His mother seemed fascinated by the
whole science of grifting, and he had no idea if this was as dangerous as he suspected.

"Yes, well," Elizabeth said, obviously trying to distract him,
"con men do read the newspapers in case something that is going
on in the world can present an opportunity for them. Perhaps he
just thought he could find a few marks in all the confusion of
the amendment fight. Judging from the number of people in the
lobby, this city is crawling with men who won't have a lot to do
when the legislature isn't actually in session."

"What kind of a con could he run in a situation like this?" his
mother asked.

"I'm sure that's no concern of ours," Gideon said before Elizabeth could answer.

She gave him what he thought was a grateful look and glanced
around. "Oh, our luggage is already here. Shall we look at the
bedrooms so you can decide which one you want, Mother Bates?"

This successfully distracted his mother. They were all pleased
to note that each bedroom featured a telephone, a private bath,
and running ice water. When his mother had decided which bedroom was hers, Gideon carried the luggage into the proper places.

"If you'd like to rest, Mother Bates, I can go alone to the Party
headquarters," Elizabeth said.

"Aren't you going to find out what your father is up to first?"
Gideon asked. "Better to get him taken care of and avoid trouble
down the road."

She gave him a sad little smile. "How do you propose I take care of him, darling? You saw him give us the signal. I can't approach him while he's working. I could telephone the front desk and ask to be connected to his room, but he probably isn't using his real name."

She was right, he knew. "But still—"

"Don't worry," she said, holding up a hand to stop his protest. "I'm sure now that he knows we're here, he'll contact us. We're using our real names, so we'll be easy to find. Then we'll work out how to behave if we see him."

"I don't suppose you could convince him to move on to another city," Gideon said, thinking how the Antis would react if they found out Elizabeth's father was a con man. She had built a sterling reputation among the Suffs, and he would hate to see the Antis use Elizabeth's past against the Cause.

"I'll have to see what he's doing," Elizabeth said. "With any luck, he's almost finished and will be leaving town soon."

But that didn't seem likely since Nashville had been fairly dozing under the summer sun until the governor called the special session that sent hundreds of people flocking here in the past few days. If the Old Man wanted to find some suckers, he'd probably find more in a big crowd, and the one in Nashville just now was huge.

THEY DECIDED TO GET SOME LUNCH BEFORE DOING ANYthing else, and Elizabeth was pleased to see that in the dining room, at least, yellow roses outnumbered the red. Elizabeth stopped by several tables to greet suffragists she had worked with before.

"Maybe the Antis are too busy to eat," Gideon said with a smile when she mentioned the plurality of yellow roses.

Their waiter had just approached their table. "That's just be-cause they all went out to Mr. Washington's place for a garden party," he said.

"Washington?" Mother Bates echoed in amazement. "I thought the Washingtons were Virginians."

"Maybe our first president was, ma'am, but *this* Mr. George Washington and his wife, Queenie, are Tennesseans. They're rich as all get-out, and four touring cars full of Antis left the hotel a while ago for their party."

"Isn't that interesting," Elizabeth said. As far as she was con-cerned, the Antis could attend all the parties they wanted, but she wondered why they were willing to sacrifice their lobbying efforts for a social event. But perhaps the Tennessee Washingtons had invited some of the legislators to their home as well. That would make sense. "I wonder if Betty and the Party know about this."

"If they don't, they soon will," Mother Bates said. "Shall we order so we can hurry things along? I'm anxious to hear what their plans are."

They ordered and told the waiter they were in a hurry. When they had finished, Gideon went up to their suite to take the bath he'd been craving, and Elizabeth and Mother Bates left the hotel and walked the short distance to the newly established headquar-ters of the Tennessee branch of the Woman's Party.

Only a few women were in the cluttered storefront, as they could plainly see through the windows before they even went inside.

"I was imagining a large group of women busily at work," Mother Bates said.

"I'm sure many of them are still at the hotel, taking advantage of having so many Antis out for the afternoon." Elizabeth opened the door and held it for her mother-in-law to precede her.

The three women who were seated around a table in the middle of the room looked up. Were they a little wary? No one could blame them, since they had all probably been roughed up at one time or another when demonstrating for a woman's right to vote.

"Elizabeth?" one of them said, jumping to her feet and hurrying over to greet her.

"Catherine, I'm so glad you're here," Elizabeth exclaimed, returning the woman's hug. "Mother Bates, this is the great Catherine Flanagan who did such marvelous work in Delaware."

"Not marvelous enough, though," Catherine said. "We lost that one." She was a slight woman, thirty-one years old, with auburn hair, a pale complexion, and a broad, toothy smile.

"But we aren't going to lose this one," Mother Bates said. "Is that a prison pin?"

Catherine reached up to touch the odd pin that had been fashioned to look like a jail cell door. "Yes, and I believe it's just like yours."

Indeed, Mother Bates and Elizabeth were both wearing their prison pins, which signified they had been imprisoned for the Cause.

"Catherine was at Occoquan Workhouse, too, but at a different time than we were," Elizabeth explained.

"You poor thing," Mother Bates said, reaching out to take her hand. Their memories of the workhouse were truly horrible.

The other two women had also risen and followed Catherine, who introduced them as Anita Pollitzer and Sue White. Sue White was a slender woman with a warm smile, and her soft accent spoke to her Southern roots. Today she looked tired but still resolute. Elizabeth hoped she was since she was leading the battle. Anita was younger than the other two women, who were in their early thirties. Anita seemed to be closer to Elizabeth's age, mid-twenties. She was a vivacious brunette whose gray eyes danced with an eagerness Elizabeth recognized from having seen it in the eyes of other Suffragists.

"I saw Betty Gram in the hotel lobby, and she sent us here to get our orders," Elizabeth said. "She also told me Miss Paul had appointed you to head up this fight, Miss White. Congratulations."

"Condolences would be more appropriate," Sue White said with a smile. "But I'm only leading until Miss Paul can get here."

"Then she's coming, after all?" Elizabeth asked in relief.

Sue White and the others exchanged a glance. "She is trying desperately to raise the money, so it's possible."

"Then in the meantime, what can Elizabeth and I do to help?" Mother Bates asked.

"We were just making our plans. Why don't you join us?"

As they all took seats at the table, Elizabeth said, "We just heard that the Antis are attending a garden party this afternoon at the home of someone with the unlikely name of George Washington."

"Yes, we heard that, too. Queenie Washington is a renowned hostess, so I'm sure she has invited a lot of legislators to her party as well," Miss White said.

"Leaving the Hermitage lobby unguarded," Elizabeth pointed out. "The legislators who didn't go to the party are the ones most likely to support the amendment, aren't they?"

"That is exactly what we thought. We already have our ladies at work. That's why we're the only ones here right now."

"When will the legislature actually convene, Miss White?" Mother Bates asked.

"Please, call me Miss Sue. Everyone does. The Senate and the House will convene at noon tomorrow. We'll be up early to decorate the Capitol in bright yellow bunting, so you can help with that, if you like. The Capitol is only a block away."

"We saw it when we arrived this morning," Elizabeth said.

"We'll all attend the sessions. The House and the Senate meet at the same time, so we'll have to split our forces, but we can still pack the gallery in both rooms," Miss Sue said.

"And cheer when we win," Anita added with a grin.

Miss Sue smiled back, but hers was rather wan. "This is going to be a tough fight, ladies, our most difficult yet. Mrs. Catt claims we have enough votes to win, but I think she's exaggerating to encourage the undecided delegates to vote with us."

"Is that wise?" Mother Bates asked. "To exaggerate, I mean."

"It is if it works," Catherine said, "and there's no penalty for being wrong."

"Except that we lose," Miss Sue said grimly. "And if we lose Tennessee, we probably don't have another chance of ratifying the amendment for years to come, so we need to get this one right."

"Have we made any progress in getting Mrs. Catt and her folks to work with us?" Elizabeth asked. She knew most of the women in the Woman's Party had originally been members of the NAWSA. Miss Sue herself had been one of Mrs. Catt's closest aides. But they had become impatient with the NAWSA policy of always being gracious and ladylike, which they felt was not getting them anywhere. When Alice Paul had formed the Woman's Party, those impatient women joined her. Members of the Woman's Party demonstrated, were jailed, and participated in hunger strikes while the NAWSA members remained gracious and polite to those who controlled their futures. This split divided the power and influence of the Cause into two warring camps, but that had eventually resulted in Congress passing the amendment, so perhaps it was for the best.

"Mrs. Catt still doesn't trust us, and we don't trust her, either," Anita said. "We've been asking men politely to give us the vote for over seventy years, and only when the Woman's Party started demonstrating did we finally get their attention,"

"Mrs. Catt is holding a meeting of all the leaders this evening," Miss Sue said. "I would give a lot to know what their strategy is going to be."

"If the meeting is for the leaders, won't you be there?" Elizabeth asked.

Miss Sue shook her head. "I wasn't invited, and I'm sure Mrs. Catt doesn't consider me a leader since I'm not part of the NAWSA."

"That's so shortsighted of her," Elizabeth said, outraged. The others just gave her knowing looks, obviously unwilling to speak ill of Mrs. Catt who, in spite of their differences, had worked so hard for the Cause.

"If their leaders are going to be in a meeting, wouldn't that be a good time for our people to be in the lobby?" Mother Bates said, bringing them back to the matter at hand.

"Oh yes," Catherine said. "We were already planning that."

"May I make a suggestion?" Elizabeth said.

"Certainly," Miss Sue said.

Elizabeth gave the matter one more second of thought and realized she was right. She only hoped these ladies didn't take her suggestion the wrong way. "Since we'll be competing with the Antis and the Jack Daniel's Suite for the attention of the legislators, it would probably be wise of us to send our younger members to the lobby tonight to speak with them. I have observed that men will pay more attention to what a woman says if she's young and charming." She didn't add that it had always worked for her when she was running a con.

The other four women simply stared at her for a long moment in surprise.

For a second, Elizabeth was afraid she had shocked them, and they would send her away with a flea in her ear, but then Miss Sue said, "What a brilliant idea!"

Anita's smile broadened. "Our women are a lot younger and at least twice as charming as the Antis. I can't think of a better way to get the attention of the legislators."

"Be sure to have them wear their finest gowns, too," Elizabeth said.

"We'll ask our Tennessee members to send their young women to the hotel, as well," Miss Sue said. "The NAWSA isn't the only group that can use charm to get their message across."

G IDEON ENJOYED HIS BATH BUT FOUND HE WAS TOO REST-less for a nap afterward. He'd never traveled with Elizabeth to these events, so he hadn't realized how the sense of urgency that pervaded what seemed like the entire city would affect him. When he was dressed, he wandered down to the lobby where he found the buzz of activity had died down a bit with so many of the Antis and their supporters at the garden party. He had pinned on the yellow rose he'd gotten at the train station in hopes of avoiding lectures from both sides, and he picked up a newspaper someone had left lying on a table and settled back in an easy chair to read it.

"Excuse me, sir, but are you a member of the Tennessee legislature?"

Gideon looked up to find a young woman staring at him intently. She wore a yellow rose, thank heaven. He stood up as a gentleman should when speaking to a lady. "No, I'm not. In fact, I'm waiting for my wife who is down at the Woman's Party headquarters getting her assignment."

She smiled at that. "How wonderful that you came with her. We are going to need all the help we can get."

"Are you having any luck with the legislators?"

Her smile disappeared. "It's hard to tell. Some of them are claiming they took an oath to obey the Tennessee Constitution so they can't vote on the amendment until there's another election because that's what the constitution says."

"I thought the Supreme Court decided that rule didn't apply."

"They did, but it still makes a good excuse if a man wants to claim his conscience still won't let him violate his oath, which some of them are doing."

"What other excuses do they use?"

She sighed. "Oh, Woman Suffrage is a dangerous thing. It subverts the plan of the Creator, undermines the purity of women and the chivalry of men, and threatens the home and family. It also . . ." She looked around to see if anyone was listening. No one appeared to be. Then she leaned in closer and speaking more softly said, "It could also threaten what they consider the supremacy of the white race and the Southern way of life."

Gideon just stared at her in amazement. "How could it do that?"

"You're from the North, aren't you?" she said with what Gideon thought might be pity.

"Yes, New York."

She nodded sagely. "You wouldn't understand then. You see, if women get the vote, that means *all* women get the vote, including Black women."

"But *all men* already have the right to vote," Gideon pointed out.

"Which many Southerners consider an outrage," she said. "But as I said, that is only one of the reasons men oppose the amendment. I didn't even mention that they believe women are too emotional and sentimental to be allowed to choose our leaders, besides being irrational and not very smart."

"Yes, I've heard those arguments, but some of the smartest people I know are women," Gideon said, thinking of his wife and his mother.

"I'm glad to hear you say that, Mister . . ."

"Bates. Gideon Bates. You'll meet my wife, Elizabeth, I'm sure. Are you with the Woman's Party or the NAWSA?"

"The NAWSA," she said proudly.

Then she might not meet Elizabeth. "I'm afraid my wife is with the Woman's Party."

This time her expression was definitely pitying. "I'm sure we'll be working together this week to get the amendment passed. That's what we all want, no matter which group we belong to."

"I'm glad to hear it. Now don't waste any more of your time on me. Go find a wavering legislator," Gideon advised with a smile.

She smiled back and moved on to another gentleman sitting nearby. He had been reading a newspaper, but when he lowered it to reply to the suffragist, Gideon saw it was the Old Man. How long had he been sitting there and how had he come in without Gideon seeing him? Well, no matter, Gideon needed to speak to him, so he waited until the young lady had moved on, obviously satisfied with whatever Mr. Miles had said.

Gideon carried his newspaper with him and sat down on a chair next to Mr. Miles. The Old Man looked as dapper as ever with his neatly styled silver hair and his custom-made suit. "Nice weather we're having, isn't it?"

"It's a bit warm for my taste," Mr. Miles replied without really even looking at Gideon. This was easy since their chairs were at right angles, placed to encircle one of the marble columns holding up the massive stained glass ceiling.

"What are you doing here?" Gideon couldn't resist asking.

"Trying to make a living."

"Then you didn't come here because of the Woman Suffrage business?"

"Of course, I did. Lots of highfliers will be gathering here this week."

Then Elizabeth had been right. "I suppose you want us to act like we don't know you."

"That is correct. And I suppose you're here because of Elizabeth and Hazel's suffrage work."

"Yes, and don't worry, we'll leave you to it."

"I hope Elizabeth won't be, uh, playing any tricks while she's here."

"If you mean engaging in your trade, no, she won't."

To Gideon's surprise, the Old Man chuckled. "Are you sure?"

Gideon thought he was. "That wouldn't work in this situation," he tried.

"You never know. It might come in handy."

Gideon didn't know what to say to him, but he was sure whatever he said would amuse his father-in-law even more.

"Politics is really just one big con, my boy," Mr. Miles said after a moment. He was still looking at his newspaper, as if they were two strangers.

He was right about politics, of course. Gideon had just never thought of it that way. He should probably encourage Elizabeth to run for office when the amendment was finally ratified. With her skills, she would go far. "Are you conning the legislators?"

Mr. Miles did finally look at him, his eyes wide with shock. Whether it was real or feigned, Gideon couldn't guess. "I don't know where you get these ideas, my boy." He apparently caught sight of someone then because he said, "You don't know me."

Gideon raised his newspaper and pretended to peruse it, but he was listening to see what he could learn.

Two men had approached the Old Man.

"Excuse me, Mr. Smith," one of them said.

The Old Man lowered his newspaper and looked up. "Coleman, good to see you." He rose to his feet. Coleman was a short, nondescript man. His suit was expensive but rumpled, as if he didn't care much about his appearance.

"I wanted to introduce you to a friend of mine," Coleman said. "This is Homer Billingsley."

The men shook hands and murmured the usual polite things.

"Coleman here has been telling me you have a good business proposition," Billingsley said. He was in his middle years with a thickening waist and a receding hairline, but his suit marked him as a man of means.

"Yes, well, it isn't something I want to talk about in such a public place," the Old Man said, and Gideon smiled behind his newspaper.

"Perhaps we could go to the Grill Room," Billingsley said.

"We might still be overheard there, and as I explained to Mr. Coleman, I am only offering this opportunity to men who have been personally recommended to me," the Old Man said with a straight face.

But Gideon knew perfectly well he'd offer it to anyone with the cash.

"Perhaps we could go to your suite," Coleman said knowingly. "The Grill doesn't serve intoxicating beverages, but Mr. Smith does."

"By all means let's go up to my suite," Mr. Miles said. Then to Gideon's surprise, he turned to him. "Would you care to join us, Mr. Bates? I know we just met, but you strike me as a man who would enjoy a glass of good whiskey."

Gideon knew a moment of indecision. Hadn't Mr. Miles just warned him to pretend they were strangers? On the other hand, he was also the one who had issued the invitation. This could solve the problem of trying to pretend they didn't know each other, at least. And besides, he was dying of curiosity to know what kind of a con the Old Man was running. Elizabeth would certainly want to know, too, so he was almost honor bound to discover it. "Thank you, that does sound inviting."

Gideon laid his newspaper aside and introduced himself to the other two men. Then they all headed for the elevators.

W ILL THEY VOTE ON THE AMENDMENT TOMORROW?" Mother Bates asked Miss Sue and her cohorts.

"It's unlikely," Miss Sue said. "There are parliamentary things they must do first, and don't be surprised if the Anti legislators try to use some tricks to delay the vote or even avoid it altogether."

"Could they do that? Even after the governor called them into special session?" Mother Bates asked.

"Anything is possible. What we have to push for is a quick vote, before the Antis have time to win over some of our men. I believe we will win in the Senate, although the vote might be close. It's the House we need to worry about, but fortunately, we have Seth Walker in our corner."

"Betty Gram told us he's the Speaker of the House," Elizabeth remembered.

"Yes," Catherine said. "He's awfully young to have won that job, not even thirty yet, but he's an expert at parliamentary procedure, so anything the Antis try, he'll be ready for them."

"Because he's the Speaker, he can also put pressure on the individual legislators to influence their votes. His support is going to be invaluable," Miss Sue said.

"He wasn't always on our side, though," Anita said. "A year

ago, when the legislature was voting to give Tennessee women limited suffrage, he was against it at first, but then he changed his mind for some reason."

"It was like a revival meeting where the most evil man in town suddenly sees the light and is born again," Catherine said, smiling at the memory.

"A real hallelujah moment," Anita said, grinning gleefully. "He stepped down from the Speaker's chair and announced he had been converted to the cause of Woman Suffrage."

"It sounds like we can really count on him," Mother Bates said.

"Oh yes. He won't let us down," Miss Sue said.

"He better not," Catherine said with a smile, "because I don't think we can win without him."


THE OLD MAN HAD A SMALLER SUITE THAN GIDEON AND HIS ladies, but it was just as elegant. He invited all of them to take a seat. A sofa and two armchairs were arranged at one end of the room and a table and chairs at the other, to accommodate in-room dining. Gideon was not surprised to see several decanters holding amber liquid and a collection of glasses on the table.

"May I offer you gentlemen a drink?" Mr. Miles said, still standing. "I'm anxious to get your opinion of a new brand of whiskey I'm trying."

"Since we'll be doing you a favor, I don't see how we can refuse," Coleman said, smiling broadly at his own wit.

"No, indeed," Billingsley agreed.

All three men looked at Gideon, who said, "I'd enjoy a drink."

The Old Man nodded and proceeded to pour out four generous glasses of the liquid in the decanter. He carried two glasses over to Coleman and Billingsley, who were seated on the sofa, and returned to get one for himself and one for Gideon, who was in an easy chair. The Old Man sat in the other.

"Hmmm, this is very smooth," Billingsley said.

"Are you a native of Tennessee, Billingsley?" the Old Man asked.

"Born and bred."

"He represents a district west of here," Coleman offered.

"You're in the Tennessee House, then?" Gideon asked, more interested now.

"Yes, and proud to serve, although I can't believe the governor called us back into session in the summer just to vote on this amendment thing."

"I'm sure the governor appreciates your dedication," Gideon said.

"I see your yellow rose there, son, and I hope you don't intend to lecture me," Billingsley said.

Gideon glanced down at the flower, having forgotten he was a marked man. "You don't need to worry about me. My wife is the one you need to watch out for."

"A suffragette, is she?" the Old Man asked with just a hint of a smirk.

Gideon replied, "It's suffragist," as the Old Man knew perfectly well. "And yes, she is."

"This really is good sippin' whiskey," Coleman said, finishing his. "I don't suppose you have any more?"

The Old Man got up and refilled Coleman's glass. He also topped off Billingsley's and Gideon's. Coleman was right, it really was good.

"Did you say it was a new brand?" Billlingsley asked.

"Yes, I did. I was thinking of investing in it," the Old Man said.

"Why would you invest in the liquor business, Smith?" Coleman asked. "With Prohibition in effect now, the demand will dry up and you'll go bust."

"I have my doubts about the demand drying up," the Old Man said. "They can close the saloons and make selling liquor illegal, but that won't stop people from wanting to take a drink. I'm from Chicago, and do you know what's happening there?"

Gideon shook his head like the rest of them because he didn't know, either. He wondered if the Old Man really did, but he didn't say so.

"They're bringing liquor in from Canada by boat across the Great Lakes and trucking it into the cities. On the East Coast, they're also bringing it in by boat across the ocean. People who have access are drinking as much as they ever did. Maybe more."

"But a lot of states are a long way from the ocean or the Canadian border," Billingsley said. "The revenue agents would catch you for sure if you tried to drive a truck all the way from the coast to Tennessee."

"Which is why we need to keep making whiskey right here in the old United States."

"But that's illegal now," Coleman reminded him.

"Not the way I'm doing it."

The other three men stared at him, unable to believe what he'd said.

"And how are you doing it?" Gideon felt compelled to ask.

"It's simple, really, and also perfectly legal. You see, the Volstead Act allows the manufacture of alcohol for medicinal purposes. A doctor can prescribe whiskey and a person with a prescription can legally purchase it from a drugstore."

"Do you operate a drugstore?" Gideon asked, fully aware of how silly his question was.

The Old Man apparently agreed because he gave Gideon an

impatient glance. "No. I'm operating a distillery that supplies whiskey to the drugstores."

"How do you get around the laws, though?" Coleman asked.

"The distillery only makes liquor for medicinal purposes. I was able to buy it at a bargain after the new laws were passed because not everyone saw the opportunity that I did. In fact, I was able to buy several distilleries. Contrary to what you would think, the demand for liquor has not dried up, as you so quaintly put it. As I said, it has increased, since humans are prone to want something more when it is forbidden."

Billingsley suddenly sat up straighter and said with wonder, "Is this the business opportunity Coleman told me about?"

Coleman smiled. "Indeed, it is."

Billingsley looked at the empty glass he held. "And this is the whiskey you made?"

"Yes. I know all the states that are far from the entry points for smuggled liquor are relying on locally produced moonshine and bathtub gin, but I can offer a quality product distilled nearby and charge more for it. No one will get blinded or crippled or, God forbid, even die from drinking rotgut whiskey, either, so we'll be performing a public service."

"It sounds like you've got this covered, Mr. Smith. Why do you need partners?" Billingsley asked.

The Old Man leaned back in his chair and took a leisurely sip of his whiskey. Gideon allowed himself another sip as well. It really was very good.

"You see, Mr. Billingsley, although I'm making a lot of money with my current setup, I'd like to make even more, but I don't have enough ready cash at the moment to buy up all the distilleries in the country."

"What?" Coleman and Billingsley said in unison. Gideon just choked on his whiskey.

"If I own all the distilleries—and they are almost all completely shut down at the moment so they are very cheap, but there are still a lot of them—then I can charge whatever I want for my whiskey and people will pay it."

"How much would you want your partners to invest?" Billingsley asked.

"A minimum of ten thousand dollars, but of course, the more you invest, the greater your share of the profits."

Billingsley frowned. "I don't know, Smith. This sounds a little shady to me."

"It's not shady at all, Billingsley. It's all completely legal, as any lawyer will tell you. You might consult one. I'm sure they're thick on the ground in Nashville with the legislature in session. And don't worry, I won't be hounding you. I have arranged to speak with several other gentlemen while I'm in town. I only need a few partners, so if you turn down the offer, I can easily replace you. In fact, I only agreed to see you because Coleman spoke so highly of you."

"I didn't say no," Billingsley said, a little nonplussed at being dismissed as unimportant. "It's just . . . my wife is the treasurer of our local Women's Christian Temperance Union. She wouldn't approve of this at all."

"Does she have to know your business?" the Old Man asked.

Billingsley perked up at that. "No. No, she doesn't."

"As I said, I won't hound you. Take some time to think about it. Not too long, though, since this vote or whatever it is that the governor has called you back for will be over soon and everyone will go back home, so I'll be interviewing potential investors quickly."

Billingsley wasn't happy. He glanced at Gideon. "What about him? Is he an investor, too?"

Gideon managed a smile and held up his glass. "I just came for a drink."

The Old Man gave him a patronizing smile. "I invited Mr. Bates to join us because I thought he might also be interested in this opportunity and however brief our acquaintance, I enjoy his company."

It was Gideon's turn to return a patronizing smile. "I'm learning to enjoy yours, too, Mr. Smith."

# CHAPTER THREE

A ND WHAT AM I SUPPOSED TO DO THIS EVENING WHILE MY wife is downstairs flirting with a bunch of old men?" Gideon asked with mock despair after Elizabeth and his mother had explained the plan to him. Elizabeth and Mother Bates had found him relaxing in their suite.

"I'm afraid you'll have to go down to the Grill Room and figure out the secret way to order whiskey in these difficult times, darling," Elizabeth said, thinking he probably had just as much chance of success as they did. "Then you can chat with the legislators who are hiding down there to avoid the women and convince them to support ratification."

"Or you can stay here in the suite with me, since I'm not going to be participating in the charm offensive," his mother said.

"I don't know why not, Mother. You're every bit as pretty as any woman I've seen in this hotel," Gideon said.

His mother turned to Elizabeth with a look of wonder. "Your influence is beginning to show, Elizabeth. Gideon just told a lie, and he did it beautifully."

Gideon's reluctance to lie and inability to do so convincingly had been a long running joke among them. "But I wasn't lying," he protested.

"And another lie," she laughed. "Then thank you, son. You have brightened my day."

"And mine," Elizabeth said, jumping up to give her husband a kiss as his reward for being so lovely to his mother.

"I'm still not happy about you flirting with all those men downstairs, though," Gideon said.

"Who said anything about flirting?" Elizabeth said, schooling her expression to innocence. "Men just like talking to attractive females, and we're anxious to talk to them in return. I assure you, flirting is the furthest thing from our minds."

"But not theirs, I'll wager," Gideon said. "Just don't let one of those slick Southern gentlemen lure you away."

Elizabeth and Mother Bates both laughed at that possibility.

"But what are you going to say to them to win them over to the Cause?" Gideon asked. "I need to know in case I run into some wavering politician."

Mother Bates nodded to indicate Elizabeth should explain.

"First, I ask him if he supports Woman Suffrage. If he says yes, then I thank him and ask him to sign a pledge, if he hasn't already."

"Or even ask him to sign another one," Mother Bates said. "You can't get them to commit too many times."

"And what if he says he's an Anti?" Gideon asked.

"Then I ask him his objections, although they almost always volunteer that information without being asked," Elizabeth said with a grin. "Then I answer whatever objection it is with the facts."

Gideon nodded. "What if he says women are meant to be protected. We can't let them be corrupted by politics."

"Women can help purify politics and end corruption. Don't we all want honest government?" Elizabeth replied.

"I'm sure there are some people who don't want honest government," Mother Bates said, "but no one is going to admit that."

"Who will care for the children and the home if women take up politics?" Gideon tried.

"Men have been taking up politics for centuries without it interfering with their work. Why should women be any different?"

"Women are too emotional to make good decisions," Gideon tried, earning a mock glare from his mother.

"And yet you allow your wife to raise your children, the most precious people in the world to you. If women can't make good decisions, how can you trust her to do that?"

"And before you say it," his mother said, "women aren't smart enough to choose between candidates."

"That's not what I was going to say," Gideon protested, earning a grateful smile from his wife.

"But other men will," Elizabeth said. "The answer is that we allow illiterate men to vote while denying educated women who are much better able to judge a candidate's worthiness."

"I'm afraid to say anything else," Gideon said, raising his hands in surrender. "I think I know enough now to answer any objections."

"You should," his mother said. "You've been listening to me talk about this for years."

"But you're right, we have an answer for all their objections if they'll just listen to us," Elizabeth said.

"You're obviously ready to win the votes. But aren't you going to ask me how I spent my afternoon?"

Elizabeth recognized his tone. He had news. "What did you find out?"

"I had a drink with your father in his suite, and I know what he's doing here."

"I thought we were supposed to pretend we didn't know him," Mother Bates said.

"He invited me, so I figured it was safe to do it, and besides, now that we've officially met, I don't have to worry about pretending I don't know him."

"Why did he invite you?" Elizabeth asked. Her father never did anything on impulse, so he must have had a very good reason for "befriending" Gideon.

"So I would know what he's doing here."

"He told you about his con?" Elizabeth asked in amazement.

"He explained it to me and even offered me an opportunity to invest." Gideon grinned at her shocked expression.

"Surely, he didn't think you'd—"

"No, no," Gideon hastily explained. "I had sat down beside him in the lobby, hoping to find out why he's here, and two other men approached him. Apparently, he had already told one of them the tale—"

"Listen to him, using grifter slang," Elizabeth said to Mother Bates. Gideon ignored her.

"—and that fellow had brought a friend he thought would also be interested in his scheme. Your father asked them up to his room to taste some very good whiskey and invited me to join them."

"Then he wanted you to know what he's doing," Elizabeth said with a sigh.

"Or he decided to answer me because I had just asked him why he was here when the other two men came up."

"These other two men, what were their names?" Elizabeth asked.

"Billingsley was the new one. He's a legislator. Coleman said he represents a district west of here and—"

"Coleman? That was the other man?" Elizabeth asked.

"That's right."

"Texas John," Elizabeth said, sure she was right. That's how these things worked. "He's the roper." She turned to Mother Bates. "The roper is the outside man who brings the mark to the inside man to con. The roper tells the tale and vouches for the inside man."

"Yes, I can see why it would be handy to have someone else tell the mark how important you are if you want to con someone," Mother Bates said.

"*Mother*," Gideon said in frustration.

"It's just very interesting, dear. Don't worry, I'm not going to start conning people in my old age."

"Or any other age for that matter," Elizabeth said. "Anyway, this Coleman is the Old Man's partner."

"That's good to know," Gideon said. "He did seem to be asking all the right questions."

"And you said the other man is a legislator," Elizabeth remembered. "Did you find out if he's voting for the amendment?"

"It didn't seem like the appropriate time to discuss it," Gideon hedged.

"I believe the next time you see him, whenever that is, will be the appropriate time, then, and don't let another opportunity slip by," Elizabeth said.

"Yes, ma'am," Gideon said with a smirk. "Don't you want to know what the con is?"

"Oh yes, I almost forgot. What is he doing?"

Gideon described the plan to them.

"Is it really true that doctors prescribe liquor to sick people?" Mother Bates asked.

"Yes, it is," Gideon said.

"My doctor never prescribed any for me." She sounded a little put out.

"I'm sure they only prescribe it in extreme cases," Elizabeth said.

"But now that it's illegal to sell liquor for other reasons, I'm afraid there will be a lot of extreme cases," Gideon said.

"And drugstores will buy alcohol to fill the prescriptions," Elizabeth mused. "Am I missing something, or does this actually sound like a feasible plan?"

"I've been thinking about it ever since he explained it, and it actually sounds very workable and even legal," Gideon said.

"Do you think your father is going into a legitimate business?" Mother Bates asked a bit hopefully.

"Not for a moment," Elizabeth said with certainty. "I'm sure he has no intention of buying a single distillery or of manufacturing whiskey. He just wants to collect money from his so-called investors and then leave town."

"After someone stabs him to death," Mother Bates said with just a little too much enthusiasm.

"Don't get any ideas, Mother," Gideon said. "If Mr. Miles fakes his own death, we will not be involved."

"Of course not, dear," his mother said with an insincere little smile.

"We should get some supper while we can, so we can get to work this evening," Elizabeth said in a transparent effort to change the subject.

"Yes, you'll need your energy for charming those old men," Gideon said with resignation.

"They aren't *all* old, darling," Elizabeth said.

GIDEON HAD DOZED OFF BY THE TIME ELIZABETH MADE HER way back to their suite after spending her evening lobbying the legislators who had been brave enough to show themselves in the Hermitage lobby. He sat up in bed and rubbed the sleep from his eyes.

"You couldn't even wait up for me?" she teased.

"I figured out how to order whiskey in the Grill Room and drank too much of it."

"You figured it out?" Elizabeth asked skeptically.

"Well, someone told me how. These Southerners are very hospitable." Elizabeth had started to undress, which made Gideon forget all about how much he had drunk tonight.

"Did you win any converts?" she asked.

"It's hard to tell. These Southerners are also masterful at being indirect."

"That might be politicians in general," she said wisely. She was down to her slip when they were both startled by an unearthly sound coming from the hallway.

"What is that noise?" Gideon asked.

"Oh dear, is that *singing*?"

"Caterwauling is more like it." Indeed, it was.

"I think . . . It must be the men coming back from the Jack Daniel's Suite," she said with some amusement.

Now that he thought of it, he realized she was right. The legislators who had imbibed too freely and were now roaring drunk had decided to express themselves by singing. "Is that 'Daisy Bell'?"

"I think so, although it's hard to tell. I think we may have a difficult time sleeping tonight, darling."

"Then come over here and we'll figure out something else to do until those drunks pass out."

MONDAY MORNING DAWNED CLOUDY AND THREATENING. "Maybe the rain will cool things off," Mother Bates remarked over the breakfast they had had delivered to the room.

"Maybe," Elizabeth said. "I just hope the rain holds off until we get our supplies over to the Capitol. We're going to decorate the place."

"Are the Antis going to decorate, too?" Gideon asked.

"We'll see," his mother said.

As soon as they had finished eating, they made their way to Miss Sue's hotel room where the supplies were waiting. Miss Sue had moved the Woman's Party headquarters to the Hermitage because they wanted to be in the center of the action with the vote coming in just a matter of days. Gideon went along to help, and they joined a long line of Suffs making their way one block across to the Capitol building. Everyone was complaining about not being able to sleep the night before because of the drunken legislators singing in the hallways. Gideon gave Elizabeth a sly grin.

Gideon was recruited to climb a ladder the instant they walked into the Capitol. The stately building was already awash in suffrage yellow, and women wearing yellow roses seemed to be everywhere. Elizabeth was surprised to see that vendors had also set up booths in the corridors, selling political wares.

Mother Bates was recruited to help unpack the fresh supply of yellow roses that would be offered to each legislator and every other possible supporter while Elizabeth followed Betty Gram to the second floor and then to the Senate gallery to help drape yellow bunting across the front of it.

"This is so exciting," Elizabeth said.

Betty didn't seem quite as enthusiastic. "It's exciting all right. I just wish the numbers were better."

"Didn't Mrs. Catt already guarantee victory?" Elizabeth asked a little snidely.

"She was exaggerating. There are far too many men claiming

to be undecided for anyone to really know what the outcome will be."

"I suppose we can count the roses when all the lawmakers arrive," Elizabeth said.

"If they choose to wear them, but even still, some of the men aren't even in town yet. The governor didn't give them much notice, so some won't be arriving until this afternoon or evening."

"Which means they wouldn't be able to vote even if they could," Elizabeth realized. "Did you find out what Mrs. Catt and her people talked about at the meeting last night?"

Betty finally smiled at that. "Rumors are flying, of course, but it seems she decreed that only the Tennessee women could go to the Capitol and talk to the legislators. Everyone else will stay back at the hotel. She doesn't want anyone to claim they are sending outsiders to influence the vote."

"She isn't from Tennessee, is she?"

"No, which means she won't be showing her face here."

Elizabeth frowned. "But she's been the face of the NAWSA for years."

"And she's afraid she's stirred up too much bad will during those years, so she's going to let her Tennessee volunteers plead the case with their sweet Southern accents and ladylike graces."

"Is the Party going to do the same thing?"

Betty shrugged. "We can't. We don't have enough Tennessee volunteers, and those of us who personally contacted the legislators at home over the past few weeks need to keep an eye on them, so they don't stray. One thing is sure, though, we won't be using our ladylike graces."

"I wish Miss Paul was here," Elizabeth said.

"I do, too, but Miss Sue is a great leader, and she knows Tennessee. She was the one who got Seth Walker to pledge, after all.

I've also been thinking that maybe Mrs. Catt is right about using Tennessee women to appeal to Tennessee men. If she is, then Miss Sue is the best one to lead the fight."

Yes, Tennessee women would probably make the best ropers in this political confidence game. People were more inclined to listen to someone they perceived as being like them. Elizabeth's Yankee accent marked her and the others like her as interlopers. She had noticed last night that the Southern women were getting more men to listen to them when they spoke about the advantages of Woman Suffrage. But the Woman's Party didn't have the luxury of limiting who came to the Capitol because they didn't have that many volunteers. They would just have to make do.

"The Republicans are meeting this morning at the Hermitage," Betty said after they had successfully hung a swath of bunting. "Unfortunately, Herschel Candler is the Senate caucus leader."

"Who is he?"

"He's impossible, that's who he is. He claims his conscience won't allow him to support ratification."

"So, he's an Anti?"

"Yes, and unlikely to change. The real problem is that he is so influential that he can convince others to vote against the ratification, too."

"We saw that happen in Delaware, and it caused us to lose a state we were sure we'd win," Elizabeth said. "But what about the Democrats? Surely, Governor Roberts has them securely lined up."

"The governor isn't what you would call a forceful leader. He'll do what he can because the powers that be in the Democratic Party demand it, but I'm afraid he won't be as effective as Herschel Candler."

"Are the Democrats meeting at all this morning?"

Betty pulled another piece of bunting out of the box. "The governor summoned the leaders of the various suffrage organizations to his office this morning. Miss Sue thinks he is going to demand that we put aside our differences and work together, at least for the next few days until we get the amendment safely ratified."

"Is that possible?" Elizabeth asked in amazement.

"Probably not, but we can at least try to work together. Of all the things we've done, this is the most important effort. We need to succeed, and it really doesn't matter who gets the credit."

"No, it doesn't," Elizabeth agreed, even though she didn't really believe it. People usually only did the right thing so they could get credit for it. She wouldn't shatter Betty's illusions, though.

MISS SUE HAD RETURNED FROM THE MEETING WITH THE governor a little skeptical that even his admonitions would be enough to keep the different suffrage factions from disagreeing, but she was at least glad he had made the effort. Since both the House and the Senate would be convening at the same time that day, Miss Sue divided her troops between them. She asked Elizabeth and her family to attend the House's session.

The House chamber was the larger one since the House was the bigger body. The gallery was larger, too, boasting four rows of seats and stretching down the length of the large chamber on both sides. Impressive marble pillars held up the ornate ceiling, but Elizabeth noted they also blocked the view in some places, so she was careful to choose seats that were unobstructed.

"We'll be able to see everything that happens," Mother Bates observed.

They had come early to be assured of seats, but soon the

gallery was flooded with Suffs and Antis, all anxious to see everything that happened. Gideon felt honor bound to give up his seat to a lady, and he took his place in the back, behind the chairs, where other men were already standing. Elizabeth was pleased to see so many men had come to support their wives and sisters and daughters. When the chairs were filled and the standing room was shoulder to shoulder, people clustered in the doorways in hopes of hearing what was happening.

The floor of the chamber was no less crowded. This was undoubtedly one of the few times that females—especially in such numbers—were lobbying the representatives right on the floor of the chamber, defying all rules of lobbying decorum. The legislators could hardly get to their desks for the press. Men, too, were lobbying, and there were as many red roses in evidence as yellow ones. Elizabeth only hoped Betty's information about the vote count was wrong.

The session itself was rather dry when it finally started. At a little past noon, Speaker Seth Walker pounded his gavel to call the session to order. He really was remarkably young for such a position. Handsome, too, Elizabeth had to admit. How fortunate he was on their side. The chaplain said his prayer and the clerk called the roll. As Betty had predicted, quite a few desks were empty, and many names received no response of "present." Still, the clerk said they had a quorum and could conduct business.

An invisible wave of anticipation swept the gallery and Elizabeth found herself leaning forward in her chair. But the Speaker simply called the newly elected representatives to come forward and take their oaths of office.

Only when that was done were they able to address the issue on everyone's mind. The Speaker called for the formal transmission of the amendment to the legislature and asked the clerk to read aloud the governor's accompanying message.

Betty Gram was in the row behind Elizabeth and Mother Bates, and she leaned forward to whisper, "We're a little worried about this part. Nobody knows what Roberts will say or how enthusiastically he will encourage them to ratify."

Elizabeth and many other Suffs held their breath as the reading began. But Governor Roberts surprised them all. His message was an impassioned plea for the legislature to ratify the amendment. He summarized all the reasons why he felt this was necessary, ending with the challenge, "I submit this issue to you as perhaps the most far-reaching and momentous one on which any body of men has been called to pass since the establishment of our government."

Everyone wearing a yellow rose sighed in relief while those wearing red roses frowned. But these were only words, and the governor's opinion counted for little since he wouldn't even have a vote. They could only hope he had swayed some of the lawmakers.

The Speaker announced that according to the rules, the joint resolution to ratify the amendment would normally "lay over" for a day and then be referred to an appropriate committee for a recommendation. However, the governor had not attached the actual resolution document to his message, so there was nothing to consider. This meant it would be at least two more days until the vote could be taken instead of just one.

The Suffs all sighed in dismay. They needed a quick vote before they lost any more supporters. The Antis grinned in delight. This error gave them an extra day to sway undecided or even pledged delegates to their side.

W HEN THE SESSION ADJOURNED, THEY LEARNED THAT THE Senate, in order to keep pace with the House, had not presented the amendment, either, so it would be at least another two days until it could be referred to a committee and after that, who knew when it would actually come to a vote? As an attorney, Gideon was used to delays for reasons that seemed trivial, but he could see Elizabeth was fuming.

"It's just one more day," he said reasonably.

"And one more night with the lawmakers drinking free whiskey in the Jack Daniel's Suite and promising who knows what," she said in disgust.

"I doubt these men can be swayed by a free drink or even many free drinks," Gideon argued.

"Maybe not," Betty Gram said. She'd been walking with Elizabeth and his mother as they made their way down the crowded Capitol corridors. "But they can certainly be swayed by bribery."

"Have you heard anything definite about that?" Elizabeth asked with great interest.

"We've been hearing about it ever since the states have been holding ratification votes," Betty said. "The problem is no one can prove anything because these things are done so secretly."

"The ladies I was working with this morning mentioned that Mrs. Catt is very worried about some suspicious-looking men who were in the lobby last night," Mother Bates said. "The men give different answers when asked who they are and why they are here. She thinks they're here to influence the lawmakers."

"Does Mrs. Catt really think the legislators will take bribes?" Gideon asked.

"Most honest men would probably balk at accepting money to change their vote, but there are different kinds of bribes, Mr. Bates," Betty said. "Not all elected legislators are wealthy. The legislature only meets a few weeks a year, so they have jobs or farms back home and must earn their livings. If someone offers them a better job that pays more money, a job that could mean a lot to his family and the future of his children, how can he refuse when all they ask of him is that he cast one vote a certain way?"

"When it comes to making decisions, people usually do what is in their own best interest," Elizabeth said.

She was right, of course. "I suppose Mrs. Catt thinks these suspicious men are offering the legislators jobs," Gideon said.

"Yes, jobs with the railroad or with a very successful business that relies on child labor to maximize their profits," Betty said. "I'd also say jobs with the liquor industry, but I'm not sure there is one anymore."

Gideon glanced at Elizabeth and from her expression, she was thinking about the Old Man and his latest con. Could he be involved in influencing the legislators, too? That hardly seemed possible, but if he was, Elizabeth would have something to say about it.

"I'm sure there will always be a liquor industry somewhere," Elizabeth was saying, "although you're right, offering jobs in it doesn't seem like a good plan at the moment."

"They're probably just supplying money," Gideon said.

"For cash bribes?" his mother asked.

"Quite possibly, although I'm sure they call them campaign contributions or something like that."

"But what can we do about it?" his mother asked with a frown.

"We keep working," Betty said. They had reached the outside doors and saw the rain was falling. People were opening umbrellas and setting out to various destinations.

Elizabeth turned to his mother. "You shouldn't be out in this all afternoon, so go back to the hotel with Gideon." She and Betty were going to join the other Suffs in visiting various restaurants, cafés, and boarding houses where a lot of the legislators could be found because they couldn't afford the Hermitage Hotel's rates.

"But I want to help," his mother protested.

"Then sit in the lobby and see what you can find out about those suspicious men, especially the Old Man. Darling," she added to Gideon, "get her to go back to the hotel and keep her there. I'll see you at supper."

He unfurled his umbrella, wrapped his arm around his mother, and hurried her along while Elizabeth and Betty went in the opposite direction.

ELIZABETH AND BETTY ARRIVED BACK AT THE HOTEL THAT evening, weary and damp, but they'd found some lawmakers who had just arrived in the city and who had missed the opening sessions in the House and Senate. They confirmed some pledges and got a few more men to promise to at least consider supporting the amendment.

"We're going to meet with Seth Walker to discuss strategy in just a few minutes," Betty said as they entered the hotel lobby through the ladies' entrance on the side of the building since they did not have a gentleman escorting them. "Would you like to come along?"

"I'd be happy to meet the Speaker of the House and thank him personally for his support," Elizabeth said, "but I probably won't stay for your strategy meeting."

"Miss Sue thinks very highly of you after your suggestion to send our younger members to lobby yesterday," Betty said with a grin.

"Someone else probably would have thought of it if I hadn't," Elizabeth said, knowing modesty was the best way to handle compliments. "But maybe I'll stay for a few minutes to hear what he suggests."

Elizabeth stopped by her suite to let Gideon and his mother

know what she was doing and to change into a dry dress. Then she found Miss Sue's room. Betty was already there, along with Catherine and Anita and a few others she had met. Miss Sue introduced her to someone she had not met, Miss Charl Williams, who was the first female superintendent of schools in Nashville and who had recently been appointed vice chair of the Democratic National Committee, a good sign the Democrats were serious about supporting women's rights.

"This morning the governor appointed Charl as director of the Democratic Women's Steering Committee, which he just created to help unify the ratification effort," Miss Sue said.

"Should I congratulate you or commiserate?" Elizabeth asked with a smile.

"I'll let you know later," Charl replied.

Elizabeth was still chatting with Charl when Walker arrived. All conversation ceased.

Walker was even more handsome up close, Elizabeth noted, which was always an advantage for a politician. Miss Sue came forward to greet him, but before she could even begin to make introductions, he said, "I'm afraid I have to tell you that I have had a change of conviction, and I will not be introducing or sponsoring the ratification resolution. I also can no longer support or vote for ratification."

From the gasps in the room, everyone was as shocked as Elizabeth. She felt as if someone had knocked the wind out of her. Walker, however, seemed unmoved. He'd made the announcement with as much emotion as he might have used to mention the rainy weather.

"But Mr. Speaker," Miss Sue said a little breathlessly, "you gave me your word."

"I wish you all a pleasant evening," he said, turned on his heel and left the room.

For a long moment no one spoke or even seemed to breathe. Finally, Betty said, "He *betrayed* us."

Miss Sue seemed to shake herself and drew herself up to her full height. "Yes, he did, and we will most likely see more betrayals before this is over, but remember, we've suffered betrayals before in other states and still prevailed."

"Do you think the governor knows?" someone asked.

"I will send him word, just in case," Miss Sue said, "but first we should notify Mrs. Catt and her people. Charl, will you go with me?" Charl's position made her the ideal go-between for the two suffrage groups.

"Of course." The two women left the room.

Normally, a group of women would instantly start talking about what had just happened, but those remaining in Miss Sue's room were still too shocked. Elizabeth sank down into an empty chair. What a blow this would be. They'd been counting on Walker to use his position and skills to usher the ratification through successfully. Now he would use that same influence against it.

"I wonder what they offered him to get him to change his mind," Betty said, anger thick in her voice.

"He already does work for one of the railroads, the L&N," Anita said. "Maybe they offered him a more lucrative contract."

"I can't believe he lied to Miss Sue's face and pledged to support us," Catherine said.

"The Antis are right about one thing," Elizabeth said to shock them out of their self-pity. "Politics is a sordid business."

Catherine sat up straighter in her chair. "Yes, it is, which is why women need to be a part of it. We can bring order and honesty back to the political process."

"And end this disgraceful bribery that leads to laws favoring the lawless," another woman said.

Everyone murmured their agreement.

Elizabeth smiled. Her ploy had worked. The women were re-membering why they were here and what had brought them to this place. She didn't believe any of the things they were saying, of course. Women hadn't been able to influence men to be honest and upright in the many centuries since Adam and Eve, and she didn't think they would suddenly be successful at it if the amend-ment gave them the vote. Still, everyone needed a goal.

"What can we do while we're waiting for Miss Sue to get back?" Elizabeth asked.

"We can look at the current vote counts. That's what we were going to go over with Walker," Catherine said, letting them hear her disdain for the Speaker. "He was supposed to help us with some of those who are wavering."

"Maybe someone can help us with *him*," Anita said snidely, earning some reluctant chuckles.

"Since we're sure his betrayal isn't a matter of conscience, we'll have to find someone very rich," Elizabeth said.

Insulting Walker did the trick. All the tension seemed to drain out of the room. The women began to chatter, discussing each of the men they had personally contacted and debating the likelihood of changing a vote or confirming one. By the time Miss Sue and Charl Williams returned, they were making plans.

WHAT DID MRS. CATT HAVE TO SAY ABOUT WALKER'S BE-trayal?" Gideon's mother asked when Elizabeth had fin-ished telling them the story much later that night. They had ordered dinner sent up for her, and between bites she had re-counted what Walker had done.

"The same thing Miss Sue did," Elizabeth said. "We've been betrayed before, and she had already warned her people that it would probably happen again. This was especially bad, though, because Walker is such an important figure and has so much influence over what happens in that chamber. Miss Sue and Betty were really taking it hard because he had pledged to them personally. They feel like fools."

"They aren't fools," Gideon said. He was shocked by Walker's sudden change of heart, but he probably should have expected something like this. Politicians were known for being easily influenced. "They just can't compete on the same level as the other side."

"What do you mean, dear?" his mother asked.

"I've learned a lot from the hours I spent down in the Grill Room and now I have a better idea of how these things work. For example, Tennessee has been a dry state for a long time, but the liquor interests have invested a lot of money in the legislators here to ensure that the laws are not enforced. Now that we have Prohibition, they are doing that in all the states. They aren't about to let a bunch of temperance females use their votes on a national level to change things."

"Because the Suffs are so closely aligned with the temperance movement," Elizabeth mused, "they think women will use their votes against them."

"And we probably will," his mother said.

"Shhh, not so loud!" Elizabeth teased.

Gideon smiled, so very grateful that his wife and his mother got along so well. "I wonder if the governor knows about Walker's defection."

"Mrs. Catt telephoned him at his home. He already knew, but he couldn't bear to tell us himself."

"Coward," Mother Bates murmured.

"I think he wanted Walker to have to tell us himself and bear the brunt of our anger, although we were too shocked to display it until after he'd gone." Elizabeth turned to Gideon. "Have you seen the Old Man today?"

"No, but . . ."

"But what?"

"Do you think he's one of the suspicious men Mother told me about who are haunting the lobby trying to bribe the legislators?"

"The Old Man?" she asked with frank amazement. "He isn't the type to go around giving money to other people. I'm sure he's here for himself alone."

"We need to be certain, though."

Elizabeth sighed with resignation. "I guess that means I need to go see him."

# CHAPTER FOUR

I T'S AWFULLY LATE FOR A VISIT, ISN'T IT?" MOTHER BATES asked.

"Not for the Old Man," Elizabeth said. "He'll probably be up all night looking for marks."

"I'll call down to the desk to see if he's in the hotel," Gideon said. They knew he would have left his room key at the desk if he'd gone somewhere else, but he would have it with him if he was still in the building.

Gideon obviously learned the Old Man's key was missing and asked to be connected to his room. After a few moments he said, "There's no answer."

"Which means he's down in the lobby or in the Grill Room," Elizabeth said as Gideon hung up the telephone.

"Which means I will have to seek him out," Gideon said.

"I know I can't go to the Grill Room with you, but I can certainly go to the lobby."

"At this time of night?" Mother Bates said in surprise. "And

Gideon would have to leave you alone if your father is in the Grill Room."

"The place is probably still full of Suffs lobbying," Elizabeth argued.

"I know you're tired after running around Nashville all day, so just stay put," Gideon said. "I'll bring him back here."

True to his word, Gideon returned shortly with the Old Man in tow.

"Hazel, how nice to see you," he said, going straight for Mother Bates. He would know she was the most sympathetic toward him.

"And how unexpected to see you here, Buster," she replied, calling him by his childhood nickname. Very few people had that privilege.

"Yes indeed," was his only response. He turned to Elizabeth. "And it's nice to see you, too, Lizzie, although I hope you won't make a habit of sending for me at odd hours. I might be working."

"We have some questions for you," she said, ignoring his complaint.

"I suppose I need to sit down, then," he said with a theatrical sigh. He chose the empty side of the sofa next to Mother Bates.

Elizabeth claimed a chair and Gideon took the remaining empty chair.

"Why are you really here?" Elizabeth asked without bothering with the social niceties.

"Here at the hotel or here in Nashville or in Tennessee in general?" he asked right back.

"Don't play dumb. Here where the suffrage amendment is being decided."

"Because, as I told you, I knew it would be a protracted battle and I also knew a lot of men with money would be gathering to spend some of it in hopes of influencing the vote. I thought they might give me some of it, too, if I asked."

"Are you working for any of those men with money?" Elizabeth asked, leaning forward in her chair to emphasize the importance of that question.

"Working for them? What are you talking about?" He seemed genuinely surprised, but he was a magnificent actor, so there was no telling.

"I mean, has someone hired you to influence the legislators into blocking the ratification?"

"Are they actually doing that?" he asked. Plainly, this was an opportunity he had not been aware of.

"Don't you dare," Elizabeth warned.

He smiled wanly. "You know I don't like working for other people. No, my dear girl, I am here working for myself alone, although now that you bring it up, I have seen several men in the lobby who were behaving like grifters but who didn't seem to have anything going on when I chatted with them."

"We think they're working for the railroads and the liquor industry," Mother Bates explained.

He gave her a fond look. "I'm sorry you have to be exposed to this ugly part of politics, Hazel."

Elizabeth was not surprised to see Gideon wincing, but he managed to overcome his personal feelings for the good of the Cause. "If you aren't working for the Antis, maybe you could work for the Suffs," he said.

The Old Man gave him a shrewd frown. "What do you mean?"

Gideon smiled. "I mean you could help us lobby the legislators."

Elizabeth had thought she couldn't love Gideon any more

than she already did, but she had been wrong. "What a wonderful idea, darling."

"It's not a wonderful idea at all," the Old Man said. "First of all, I'd have no idea what to say to them."

"Don't worry," Mother Bates said sweetly. "We can tell you the tale. It's just common sense, really."

His surprise at hearing Mother Bates using grifter slang was the first of his expressions Elizabeth trusted as authentic. "Tell me the tale?" he repeated in wonder.

"But we wouldn't expect you to buttonhole legislators in the lobby or anything," Elizabeth said, her mind racing as she considered the possibilities.

"And I'm here on personal business, don't forget," he said, obviously very unhappy with the turn of the conversation. "I have to make expenses at least."

"And you can do both at the same time," Elizabeth said, earning surprised looks from all three of her companions. "When you explain your business, just make supporting the ratification a requirement for investing in it."

"How could I do that?" the Old Man protested. "The two things don't have anything in common."

"But they do," Elizabeth said, proud that she had thought of it. "Your business is a perfectly legal way to make quality alcohol available to people who use it for medicinal purposes. You are helping those in need."

He blinked in surprise. "Of course, I am."

Gideon, she noticed, had to cover a smile.

"But your liquor won't be sold to those who merely want to use it for pleasure, so the temperance folks can't possibly object. In fact, they will probably support you."

"That may be going a bit far, dear," Mother Bates said.

Gideon had to cough to stop himself from laughing.

"No, no," the Old Man said with a smile of his own. "This could work out."

"And you tell them some story about how your dear wife was a temperance worker or something, which is why you are doing this," Elizabeth said, having just thought of it. "You want to make sure no criminal elements get possession of your liquor."

"But the marks will realize I'm being hopelessly naïve. Doctors will begin to write prescriptions to everyone or people will simply forge them. The demand for this liquor will be enormous, and the marks will see the potential for huge profits."

"And you will tell them you can't allow them to invest unless they support ratification," Gideon concluded.

"We would appreciate it if you would concentrate on the legislators wearing red roses," Mother Bates said.

"Or no rose at all," Elizabeth added.

"If I do this, will you promise not to send for me at inconvenient times or interfere with my plans?" the Old Man asked.

"We promise," Elizabeth said, knowing her husband and mother-in-law would never have done those things in the first place.

"Then I'll expect you to return the favor by sending people to me whom you would like to influence."

This time Elizabeth winced. "We can't do that."

"You can't expect us to send people to you so you can steal from them, Buster," Mother Bates said in her kindest voice.

"*Steal* is such an ugly word, Hazel," he protested. "But perhaps you will encounter someone who is so venal that they might deserve a little comeuppance, and in such a case, I do hope you will think of me. Humbling arrogant men is rather a specialty of mine."

Which was, Elizabeth had to agree, one way of looking at it.

THE NEXT MORNING, AFTER ANOTHER RESTLESS NIGHT LIS-
tening to carousing lawmakers, they took breakfast in their
room. Then Elizabeth, Gideon and Mother Bates went down to
the lobby to see what was going on before heading over to the
Capitol for the day's session at ten o'clock. They found Anita Pollitzer, who looked as if she had been up all night.

"I just sent Miss Paul a telegram telling her about Seth Walker's betrayal and begging her to come," Anita said. "We're going
to need her very badly."

"Did you get any sleep at all?" Elizabeth asked.

"A little. We were up very late last night going over the votes,
but we were able to give the local Republicans a list of the legislators who are fighting ratification. They're going to send it to
Warren Harding and ask him to put some pressure on them to
change their minds. I'm not sure that's possible, but if anyone can
do it, it should be their presidential candidate."

"Who are the men you're targeting?" Gideon asked.

"In the Senate, there's Finney Carter and Herschel Candler. I
think I told you, I personally tried to get Candler to support, but
he absolutely refused. In the House, there's Boyer, Luther, and
Burn, although I'm afraid Harry Burn might be a lost cause, too.
He's studying to be a lawyer under Candler."

"I can see why that might be a problem," Gideon said.

Anita looked close to tears. "I was assigned those East Tennessee men, but I just couldn't convince them."

"We can't change everyone's mind," Elizabeth said, patting
her shoulder. "You did your best and that's what counts."

"What counts is the votes," Anita said sadly.

But now Elizabeth had a few names she might want to give
her father.

"That isn't the worst of it, though," Anita continued. "Seth Walker announced that he's actually going to lead the fight against ratification himself and use his power as Speaker to bring as many representatives with him as possible. He is also planning to refer the amendment to a hostile committee."

"A hostile committee could refuse to recommend the bill," Gideon said, as shocked as Elizabeth felt.

"Which would effectively kill it," Elizabeth said.

"Exactly," Anita said. "One reason we were so happy to have Walker on our side was his skill in using the system to get things done. Now he's using it against us, and we need to find someone who can thwart him."

Elizabeth was mentally adding Seth Walker to the list for her father.

"Shouldn't we head over to the Capitol if we want to get a seat?" Mother Bates asked.

"I have some things to do here first. I'll see you there," Anita said.

The three of them set out. They found the Capitol as busy as it had been the day before, but the sense of expectation was gone. Everyone knew nothing would really happen today. Elizabeth saw Catherine Flanagan and invited her to join them in the House gallery, where they managed to get front row seats.

"We've been worried about Senator Todd," Catherine told them. "He's the president of the Senate and he has never supported Woman Suffrage. He even voted against limited suffrage last year."

"Is he going to vote against it now?" Elizabeth asked in surprise.

"He promised us he would support ratification this time and even lead the fight, but so did Seth Walker," Catherine said with a sigh. "I guess we'll just have to see."

Elizabeth was starting to wish they'd chosen to watch the Senate's session instead. "Wasn't Walker supposed to present the amendment to the House?"

"Yes, but when he announced his change of heart, the governor recruited a group of representatives to present it instead."

"Thank heaven," Mother Bates said.

The wait seemed endless but finally Seth Walker called the House to order. He sat stone-faced as six men from the Shelby County delegation rose to sponsor House Joint Resolution #1. The Suffs all sighed with relief.

In accordance with procedure, the bill would have to "lay over" for a day before it could be assigned to a committee, so Walker adjourned the session.

"How can that man look at himself in the mirror?" Mother Bates asked, glaring down at Walker.

"I'm sure he has managed to justify his actions to himself," Gideon said. "Men like that usually do."

He was right, of course. Even her father could justify his grifting. If challenged, he would simply point out that you can't cheat an honest man. Everyone who fell for his schemes thought they would make a lot of money doing something illegal. It was hard to feel sorry for them, although—as Mother Bates would no doubt point out—stealing was always wrong, even if you were stealing from a rat.

They walked back to the hotel with the crowd, moving slowly because the day was already warm, and found Betty Gram in the crowd. She had attended the Senate's session, and they learned from her that Senator Todd had kept his word to introduce the resolution to the Senate, so at least that had happened without any drama.

The lobby was as full as it had been on Sunday, with legislators and Suffs and Antis and the people who supported one or the other of them. Everyone was talking about what had happened or not happened in the chambers this morning.

"There's Seth Walker," Betty Gram said through gritted teeth, her lovely face pink with anger.

Elizabeth spotted the Speaker across the lobby. Before she could reply, however, Betty had started in Walker's direction.

"What has brought about the change against the suffrage amendment in the house—the governor or the Louisville and Nashville Railroad?" Betty demanded of him in her magnificent voice that had been trained to project to the last row of the theater. "What kind of a crook are you anyway—a Roberts crook or an L&N crook?"

People in the lobby gasped. Many of them were probably wondering the same thing, but one simply didn't shout accusations like that in a very public place.

"How dare you charge me with such a thing!" Walker shouted back. "That is an insult!"

Betty smiled sweetly. "Why, I am just asking you for information," she replied with creditable innocence. Her theater training was serving her well.

Furious and obviously disturbed, Walker stormed off.

Before he even left the room, the crowd began to buzz with indignation or delight, depending upon the color of the rose displayed.

"Oh dear," Mother Bates said. "No wonder the press is calling this the War of the Roses."

"I'm not sure Betty intended to start an actual war," Elizabeth said with a small smile.

"No, but she wasn't very ladylike. Mrs. Catt won't like that one bit." Her smile said *she* did, though.

"Miss Paul will applaud her," Elizabeth said.

"We better rescue her," Gideon said.

Indeed, a cluster of men had closed in around Betty, and they were shouting at her.

"What on earth?" Elizabeth asked, following Gideon as he shouldered his way through the crowd.

"Reporters," Gideon said over his shoulder.

But Betty needed no rescuing. She was answering the reporters' questions with statements about why Woman Suffrage was necessary and ignoring any temptation to blacken Seth Walker's name any further. When she saw Gideon and Elizabeth waving to her from outside the circle of reporters, she excused herself and moved to meet them.

"Oh, Betty, what have you done?" Elizabeth asked with a weak smile.

"Brought us some attention," Betty said with satisfaction. "Miss Paul will be pleased."

I KNOW THE WOMAN'S PARTY IS PROUD OF BETTY'S OUTBURST this morning," Mother Bates told Elizabeth as they met in the lobby late that afternoon, "but not everyone is happy about it. That is all anyone is talking about now, too. The Tennessee Suffs are mortified, and Walker is demanding an apology."

Elizabeth had been out in the city since lunch, once again hunting for legislators in various restaurants, other hotels, and boarding houses, while Mother Bates had remained at the hotel to seek out anyone who happened into the lobby. "Yes, that's all the legislators wanted to talk to us about when we did manage to track them down. They asked if we had witnessed the scene and they wanted to know all the details. When we tried to change the subject, they lost interest and walked away. But Betty isn't going to apologize. I'm sure of that."

"I heard that Mrs. Catt told reporters that Walker's defection hasn't changed the vote count at all, and all those pledged are holding firm," Mother Bates said.

Elizabeth sighed. "We know that isn't true. She's just bluffing in hopes of keeping the pledged delegates we already have. No one wants to back a losing cause, so we can't show any signs of weakness."

"Word is that the Senate, at least, will pass the resolution," Mother Bates said. "About a hundred of Mrs. Catt's people met with the Democratic senators at the Capitol this afternoon." She glanced around for eavesdroppers and then lowered her voice. "Only about a dozen of them showed up, and Charl Williams promised they wouldn't try to influence them and would put their cause in the men's hands and trust them to do what is right."

"She didn't!" Elizabeth exclaimed, suddenly furious. "If we could trust men to do that, we would've had the vote seventy years ago."

"The NAWSA is worried that the Antis will use Betty's outburst this morning to convince the men that it is an example of the horrible 'sex wars' they predict if women are allowed into politics."

"What on earth is a 'sex war' and who would fight it?" Elizabeth asked.

"I have no idea, but it seems to strike terror into the hearts of Southern gentlemen. I also heard that Senator McKellar is summoning every Democratic senator who is uncommitted or wavering to his room this evening where he is privately urging them to support the amendment."

"You are rather well informed," Elizabeth said with approval. "McKellar is the junior U.S. senator from Tennessee, isn't he?"

"That's right, and he wants his state to be the one that seals ratification. I wonder how he hopes to influence them."

"That is probably one of the uglier parts of politics that they want to protect females from," Elizabeth guessed. "Where is Gideon?"

"I believe he is down in the Grill Room. He is wishing he could do more, I know."

"I'm sure there will be plenty for him to do before this is over."

"He'll certainly come up to our rooms soon to get ready for dinner. He'll tell us all about his adventures then."

Elizabeth smiled at the thought of Gideon having adventures in the staid Grill Room. "I was thinking I would stop by Miss Sue's room to see if she has heard from Miss Paul. We really need her help."

"If you don't mind, I'll go straight to my room. I'd like to rest a bit before dinner."

They parted when Elizabeth got off the elevator. Miss Sue's door was ajar, and she could hear voices from within. She slipped inside and found Miss Sue on the telephone and Betty, Anita, and Catherine hovering over her.

Miss Sue was holding out the earpiece of the candlestick phone so they could all hear the person speaking on the other end. Elizabeth moved closer.

"I'll issue a statement this evening castigating Governor Cox and Governor Roberts," the voice said, and Elizabeth realized it was Miss Paul in Washington. Thank heaven she was going straight to the top with a presidential candidate and the governor of Tennessee. "Our support is slipping away because neither of them has taken a strong enough stand in favor of ratification. If it fails, it will be because those two men refused to accept their responsibilities. I will make that clear and shame them into action."

Elizabeth knew they all agreed with her. She waited silently as Miss Sue asked a few more questions and took Miss Paul's instructions.

When Miss Sue ended the call, she looked over to where Elizabeth was waiting. "You heard?"

"The last part. I know the Democratic Party officially supports suffrage, so why won't Cox take a stronger stand?"

"Because he wants to be elected president," Anita said, her contempt obvious. "He's afraid of all those former slaves who have moved to Northern states and become Republicans. If women get the vote, that will double the number of them, and he could lose the election."

"Or perhaps he just isn't a very strong man," Miss Sue suggested. "I believe that is Governor Roberts's issue. For example, he gave a wonderful introductory speech but then forgot to attach the amendment. In any event, Miss Paul still can't come to Tennessee." Miss Sue turned to Elizabeth. "She told us that all the wealthy women who usually support the Woman's Party are on vacation and she hasn't been able to reach them yet. We may have to do this without her."

Elizabeth could easily see the disappointment on all their faces, but she couldn't let them dwell on that. Doubt could lead to failure, just like in a con. "Miss Sue, I know Miss Paul wouldn't have put you in charge if she didn't have every confidence in you. Even Mrs. Catt understands the importance of using Tennessee women to influence the Tennessee men, so no one is more qualified to do that than you are. We are behind you. Just tell us how we can help."

Miss Sue actually squared her shoulders, and the other women broke into smiles.

"Elizabeth is right," Betty said. "You know exactly what to say to those men."

"And Betty knows exactly how to cause a fuss," Catherine teased.

Betty's face reddened but her smile didn't fade. "I just hope Walker doesn't decide to sue me for defamation."

"I don't think he would dare," Elizabeth said. "Someone might find out the railroad did offer him a job if he changed his position."

"He's been working very hard all day trying to win over our supporters in the house," Catherine said.

Of course, he was. He needed to be distracted, and Elizabeth knew exactly what that distraction could be.

GIDEON THOUGHT THE GRILL ROOM WITH ITS ARCHED CEIL-ings and mahogany woodwork resembled Aladdin's cave more than anything. He wondered if a genie could predict the outcome of the upcoming votes and decided ratification would be one of his three wishes if such a genie did appear.

He stared down at his nearly empty cup—they served whiskey in teacups in case they were raided—and realized he was in danger of being one of the drunken men wandering the hallways at night if he wasn't careful. But Elizabeth had given him a mission, and it was his duty to accomplish it, if possible, which meant he'd been sitting at the bar in the Grill Room most of the evening with occasional trips to the lobby to see if he could spot the Old Man.

The best he had been able to do was find the Old Man's associate, Coleman, but he had come into the place with another man. They had taken a table and appeared to be in earnest conversation, so Gideon knew better than to interrupt. He also concluded there was a good chance the Old Man might appear because Coleman was probably going to do the point-out. This was the part of the con where the outside man, Coleman, "happens to see" the inside man, Mr. Miles, and points him out as a very successful businessman or whatever he was supposed to be for this particular con.

Gideon knew way too much about grifting.

Gideon could see the two men in the large mirror behind the bar, so for a while he just watched them. Sure enough, the Old Man finally came in. He took a seat at the bar, leaving an empty stool between himself and Gideon. He gave his coded order for a glass of whiskey to the barman and glanced at Gideon. "I thought you weren't going to bother me when I'm working."

Gideon didn't glance back. "I'm not bothering you. Elizabeth has some names for you." He reached into his suit-coat pocket, pulled out a folded piece of paper and laid it on the bar. He glanced in the mirror, but Coleman and his companion were deep in conversation and didn't seem to be paying them any attention.

"I'm sure they're all Antis," the Old Man said, disapproval obvious in his voice. "She's trying to make my life difficult."

"She's trying to get the amendment passed," Gideon corrected him.

"Then she should come up with her own plan and leave me out of it."

A prickle of unease raised the hairs on his arms. "Are you having difficulty?"

"I lost someone today with her little requirement," he said with disgust. "He said his honor wouldn't permit him to vote in favor of the amendment so he would have to pass on my proposition. Since when do politicians have honor?"

"Southerners like to talk about it, I've noticed."

The Old Man made a disparaging sound.

"Excuse me, is that you, Mr. Smith?" Coleman asked. He had brought his friend over while they had been talking.

The Old Man pretended to be surprised and Coleman had to remind him of who he was, and then he introduced his companion, and the Old Man invited them to his room for a drink. Only after they left did Gideon realize the piece of paper he had laid on the bar was gone. At least he could tell Elizabeth that he had successfully delivered her message.

A FTER GIVING THE OLD MAN AND HIS COMPANIONS TIME TO get to the elevators, Gideon made his way to the lobby and was glad to see it rather quiet for a change. He did notice Seth Walker speaking with a man Gideon recognized as one of the reporters who had surrounded Betty Gram this morning. This should be interesting. He sauntered over and took a seat near enough that he could eavesdrop.

"I have become convinced that it is my duty to my state and to my constituents to oppose this thing," Walker explained to the reporter. "There is no question in my mind that a large majority of the people, both men and women in Tennessee, are against universal suffrage from principles, or are violently opposed to action through a federal amendment." This was, Gideon knew, a strong argument in the South, which had been forced to accept many things they had hated during Reconstruction, such as seeing freed slaves get the vote through a federal amendment.

"The cities, no doubt, would vote for suffrage, but by no great majority," Walker continued, "while the rural sections, which predominate in Tennessee, I know are strong against this ratification. The method is wrong from every angle as I view it, especially from the standpoint of the South. Tennessee has it in its power now to thrust upon every other state, whether agreeable to the people thereof or not, equal suffrage, and to enfranchise all elements of women. It is too much power to be wielded by a single state, especially since the present representatives have not been instructed in any way regarding it."

Gideon marveled at how Walker had summarized every argument the Antis were using against ratification. He was indeed a formidable foe. Walker went on to acknowledge that Governor Roberts had thrown his support behind the amendment, but he claimed that was only because the leaders of the Democratic Party had insisted. Although he had broken with the governor on this issue, that did not indicate a break between them.

Gideon gritted his teeth. Walker was making it sound as if betraying the suffragists and causing the amendment to fail was a little thing between friends, politics as usual. He had also managed to make Governor Roberts sound like both a victim and a puppet. The governor would not be pleased.

Gideon wasn't pleased, either. The reporter, obviously delighted with his interview, shortly took his leave, and when Walker strode by Gideon, he stood up. "I noticed that reporter didn't ask you about your work with the railroads, Mr. Speaker, or ask you to answer the whispers about a lucrative contract that has been offered in exchange for your change of heart."

Walker's face grew red, and he looked around, probably checking to see if anyone had overheard. "Nor should he have. None of that is true, and I'll thank you not to make baseless allegations. Who are you, anyway?"

"Gideon Bates, late of New York."

"Ah, another Yankee come down here to tell us how to run our state," Walker scoffed.

"No, we're just reminding you how to respect your women, something Southerners usually pride themselves on doing."

"We just want to protect our women from the taint of politics," Walker said piously.

"The kind of taint you're guilty of, Mr. Speaker? Breaking your word and then pretending it was a matter of conscience?"

"Mr. Speaker?" a man called and waved to get Walker's attention.

Walker smiled with obvious relief. "Excuse me. I have important business."

Gideon watched him stride away, knowing he was really running away from Gideon because he had no satisfactory explanation for his behavior. For a moment he let himself feel the full weight of frustration at dealing with a man who had promised to help and then betrayed that promise. For that moment, he knew just a taste of the frustration thousands of women had felt for over seventy years as one man after another betrayed them in their quest for equality. Please God, let this be the last time.

O H, GIDEON, I'M SO PROUD OF YOU," ELIZABETH EXCLAIMED when he arrived at their suite and told them about his encounter with Seth Walker. She was so very glad she'd married him.

"And so am I," his mother said, beaming at him.

He seemed a bit abashed. "It's not like I changed his mind or anything. He's still going to be a formidable adversary, and that interview will be in the newspaper, probably tomorrow, and it won't help the Cause at all."

"Still, you can't tell me you didn't make him feel ashamed, just like Betty did this morning," Elizabeth said.

"I certainly hope so, but do men like that really feel shame? I doubt it."

"I hope he did," Mother Bates said. "We also have some interesting news to share."

"Good news, I hope," Gideon said.

"Very good news. This evening Senator McKellar—he's the junior senator from Tennessee—was meeting with all the state Senate Democrats who were uncommitted or wavering. He reported that fifteen Democratic senators have pledged to vote in favor."

"That's not quite a majority," Elizabeth had to admit. "There are thirty-three state senators, so we need at least two more votes to win, but we already know some of the Republicans will vote in favor, although we don't know exactly how many."

"That sounds very close to victory to me," Gideon said, making Elizabeth want to kiss him.

"In the Senate, at least," she said. "The House is a different story, and it sounds like Seth Walker is determined they won't pass it."

"I spoke with two legislators today who had been pressured to change their vote," Mother Bates said. "They promised to hold firm, but who knows what will happen in the next few days."

"Yes, we need to bring this to a vote as quickly as possible, so more legislators aren't tempted to change," Elizabeth said.

"Things have to move along now," Gideon said. "Today was the lay-over day so tomorrow they'll assign the resolution to a committee, and they'll probably vote on Thursday. Surely, we can hold on to our votes that long."

THE NEXT MORNING, EVERYONE WAS TALKING ABOUT THE interview Gideon had overheard Seth Walker give the previous night. The Antis were crowing. They could now officially count the Speaker as their ally and champion, which was a bitter pill for the Suffs. They also had received word that North Carolina, one of the only remaining states that hadn't considered the amendment yet, would probably not ratify. They were now sure that if it didn't pass in Tennessee, it would fail.

Elizabeth decided they should observe the proceedings in the House again today. She wanted Walker to see Gideon in the gallery so maybe he would feel at least a twinge of shame as he went about his machinations. They didn't have to wait long to find out what those were, either.

As soon as Walker pounded his gavel and all the preliminaries were over, House Majority Leader William Bond stood up and was recognized. He presented House Joint Resolution #4 and proceeded to read it. The first several clauses were a history lesson, reminding everyone of all the ways the federal government had forced the South to conform after the War Between the States. This was why the Tennessee Constitution contained the provision of holding an election before voting to ratify an amendment to the federal Constitution. Although the Supreme Court had ruled they didn't need an election before they voted, Bond's resolution insisted they still needed to know the will of the people.

His resolution called for mass meetings to be held in every Tennessee county on Saturday, August 21—a delay of almost two weeks—and a chairman from each county would report to the representatives the prevailing view of their constituents. Only then would the representatives know how to vote.

Except that two weeks would give the Antis time to bribe or influence every legislator.

Seth Walker had figured out a way to defeat the amendment.

# CHAPTER FIVE

L IKE A STORM THAT HAD BEEN GATHERING FOR WEEKS, building strength, the chamber erupted into a thunderous cacophony of shouts and jeers, cheers and protests as everyone rose to their feet to voice their individual opinions. Elizabeth found herself booing along with most of the other Suffs while the Antis were cheering with wild abandon. Seth Walker was furiously pounding his gavel for order, but it took him several minutes to get everyone quieted down and back in their seats. Only then could the orderly business of the chamber be conducted.

Dozens of hands went up from legislators wishing to speak for or against William Bond's outrageous resolution. By rights, it should have been held over for a day for a second reading, but Walker quickly entertained a motion to suspend the rules so they could consider the resolution immediately. With that taken care of, pandemonium reigned again as legislators clamored to be recognized.

"They can't pass this," Mother Bates said to no one in particular. "They just can't."

Elizabeth agreed, and fortunately, so did many legislators, even some of those wearing red roses. Seth Walker left his Speaker's chair to circulate on the floor and try to sway lawmakers to support Bond's outrageous resolution.

But he wasn't the only one circulating.

"Who is that woman?" someone sitting behind Elizabeth asked.

"That's Anne Dallas Dudley," Elizabeth said. Even though Anne was a member of the NAWSA, she was respected by the Woman's Party members, too. A photograph of her reading to her two angelic children had been widely circulated for years to prove that suffragists were just as womanly as any other female. She was also a smart and savvy advocate for suffrage and a Tennessean to boot.

They watched Anne Dudley moving from one legislator to the next, no doubt reminding them they had pledged their support and warning them not to waver.

"Some of those men she's talking to now made fun of her several years ago when she led a suffrage parade down the streets of Nashville," another woman sitting nearby said.

"But she didn't let that stop her," Betty Gram said. "Who can forget her famous retort when she was informed women shouldn't be allowed to vote because they can't bear arms in wartime?"

"Yes," Mother Bates said with a trace of pride. "She said women bear armies."

"Anne could probably bear arms as well," Betty added with a grin. "When someone threw a bomb into the room when she was making a speech, she never even blinked. When it didn't explode, she just went on with her talk."

"Elizabeth, you should get down there and help her," Mother Bates said.

"I'll go with you," Betty said. "We can't let the NAWSA do all the work."

Elizabeth followed Betty out and down the stairs to the chamber. The atmosphere on the floor was even more intense than it had been in the gallery. They saw Miss Sue and Anita Pollitzer and other suffragists also moving around the floor, talking to their legislators.

"What is that?" Elizabeth asked when she noticed the printed materials that seemed to be on every legislator's desk. The headline read, "CAN ANYONE TERRORIZE TENNESSEE MANHOOD?"

"It's Anti propaganda," Betty whispered. "Awful stuff, hinting about all the horrible things that will happen if women get the vote."

"Oh yes, the infamous sex wars," Elizabeth said.

"That's not the worst. They also warn about race wars and the North forcing the South to accept Black supremacy."

"But effective, I'm sure," Elizabeth said. "Isn't that Harry Burn?"

"Yes," Betty said with a weary sigh. She hurried over to him, even though he was trying very hard not to meet her eye.

Betty started to give him her arguments, but he stopped her with a raised hand. "Miss Gram, I will never do anything to hurt you," he said and then ducked away as if he had been summoned elsewhere.

"What did he mean by that?" Elizabeth asked with a mystified frown.

"I don't know, and he won't explain himself. I know his mother is a suffragist, so he should support the amendment, but he just won't commit."

The noise in the chamber suddenly ceased as Joe Hanover was recognized to speak against Bond's resolution. He spoke not as a Southern gentleman but as an immigrant whose parents had brought him to America to escape pogroms against Jews in their native Poland. He was a living example of the American dream. He had educated himself in night school and now had a promising legal career and a seat in the legislature. Even still, the American dream wasn't the same for all because women—his own mother included—couldn't share in the equality.

As they listened to his moving speech a ripple of awareness went through the crowd and when they turned, they saw that Governor Roberts had come into the chamber. He was sweating through his shirt and jacket, but he was conferring with the leaders who supported the amendment and sending notes that were being carried to various lawmakers, obviously trying to influence them.

"Finally, Roberts is working for us," Betty said.

Man after man spoke, either for or against the resolution to delay the vote to hold countywide meetings across the state to determine public opinion. Many pointed out the difficulty in determining any consensus from a public meeting. How would one determine which side prevailed? By how many showed up? By how loud they were? There was too much room for manipulation and even fraud.

Finally, someone moved to table Bond's resolution, which would effectively kill it if they could get the votes. A hush fell over the chamber as the clerk called the role.

Elizabeth and Betty found Anita Pollitzer in the rear of the chamber. She was keeping a running tally of the votes. They winced each time one of their pledged delegates voted against tabling this damaging bill. Harry Burn was among them. So much for not hurting them. Elizabeth shot him a murderous

glare, which was wasted because he wasn't looking in her direction.

But in the end, the measure failed. The Suffs in the gallery
and on the floor all cheered while the Antis sat in grim silence.
Seth Walker had returned to his Speaker's chair. He now had no
choice but to send the amendment to committee for approval.
They all knew he had intended to send it to the House Judiciary
Committee, chaired by his pal Bond who had just tried to sabo-
tage the whole thing with his resolution. Now Walker realized
such an act would be foolish, so he referred it to the House Committee on Constitutional Affairs and Amendments, and he named
Thomas Riddick as chair.

"Riddick?" Elizabeth exclaimed. "He just gave a speech
against that resolution. He's one of ours."

"Yes, but he's brand new to the House," Anita said with a
frown. "He was just sworn in on Monday. Walker didn't appoint
Riddick as a favor to us. He thinks giving Riddick so much power
will make others jealous of him and less cooperative, plus he has
no experience in rounding up votes. He'll have a hard time."

Politics, Elizabeth was learning, made grifting look honest.

Elizabeth and Betty found Gideon and Mother Bates after
Walker adjourned the session. They all walked back to the Hermitage Hotel with the rest of the crowd. They learned from those
who had attended that the Senate's session had been much tamer
than the House's and had resulted in the same end. The amendment had been referred to the same committee in the Senate,
which was also known to be friendly. The committees would
meet and decide whether to recommend the bill or not. Then the
House and the Senate would hold a joint public meeting to hear
arguments on both sides before voting.

The hotel lobby was buzzing as people found their cohorts and gathered in small groups to discuss what they should do next. Some adjourned to suites or meeting rooms to strategize. Elizabeth was trying to decide what to do when she heard someone calling her name.

"Good heavens," she cried when she saw who it was.

"Is that Anna?" Gideon asked. Being taller, he had the advantage in this crowd.

"I believe it is."

"And she's got Freddie with her," Gideon reported with a grin.

Anna and her friend, Frederica Quincy, had both been more helpful in some of Elizabeth's cons than she liked to admit, and she could certainly use their help now. After everyone had embraced and exclaimed how happy they were to see one another, Elizabeth tried a disapproving scowl.

"I thought you had to stay home and take care of your mother, Anna."

"Freddie's mother is staying with her," Anna said a little gleefully.

"Mother knew how much I wanted to be here," Freddie said. "We've been following everything in the newspapers, and now that it's dragging out so long, we thought we might be able to help."

"So, Mrs. Quincy offered to come to the city and stay with Mother for a few days," Anna said. "Oh, Elizabeth, this is so exciting."

"Not as exciting as you obviously think," Gideon said.

"But to actually be present when the amendment finally passes," Anna argued.

"If that happens," Elizabeth said.

"But we had the votes to table that awful resolution today," Mother Bates reminded her.

"Not all of those who voted to table it will support the amendment, though," Elizabeth said. "Anita told me that we need fifty votes in the House for it to pass and that is exactly how many we have at the moment. We can't afford to lose a single one."

"That is worrisome," Anna said.

"But we mustn't be discouraged," Elizabeth said. "There is still hope. Oh, Anna, Betty Gram is here. I know she'll be happy to see you've come to help."

"And I'll be happy to see her, too," Anna said, smiling. She turned to Freddie. "Betty was in the Occoquan Workhouse with us." Anna reverently touched the prison pin she proudly wore.

Freddie nodded her understanding. She knew Anna had almost died on hunger strike in that horrible place.

"Are you girls staying here at the hotel?" Mother Bates asked.

"We couldn't possibly afford that," Anna said. "We were very lucky, though. The cabdriver who picked us up at the station has a sister with a room to let. He told us the hotels and rooming houses are full because so many people have come to the city because of the special session of the legislature. He said it was over a thousand."

"From this crowd, it looks like he was right, too," Freddie added, glancing around the mobbed lobby.

"We know there was a session today," Anna said. "Did anything important happen?"

"Not yet. Both the House and Senate referred the amendment to committees, and tomorrow evening they will hold a public debate," Gideon said. "They may vote as soon as Friday, though."

"Then we haven't missed all the fun," Freddie said to Anna.

Elizabeth managed not to roll her eyes. None of this was fun.

"Why don't you girls join us for lunch in our suite," Mother

Bates said. "We have some other things to tell you that we shouldn't discuss in public." She gave Elizabeth a meaningful glance to remind her about the Old Man and his shenanigans.

"Oh dear," Anna said in mock dismay. "Does this involve your family, Elizabeth?"

"Of course, it does," Elizabeth replied. "There's nothing else we can't discuss in public."

GIDEON WAS NEVER CERTAIN EXACTLY HOW IT HAPPENED that the Old Man was invited to join them for lunch. Elizabeth had explained what he was doing in Nashville, and Anna and Freddie had seemed to understand, but somehow, they had questions no one else could answer so his mother—Gideon was fairly sure it had been his mother—had suggested they telephone Mr. Miles to see if he might be free. The next thing he knew, Elizabeth's father was in their suite, greeting the two newcomers warmly, as well he might since both of them had proven themselves to be expert amateur con artists.

"It's a shame you girls didn't arrive sooner," the Old Man said after explaining the con again and answering Anna and Freddie's questions. By then they were enjoying the lunch that had been delivered to the suite. "I don't have much time left, since I understand they'll be voting on ratification as soon as possible after the public hearing tomorrow night. After the vote, the legislators and all the people trying to influence them will leave town."

"Perhaps there is still a way for us to help," Anna said. "After all, we don't actually have any official duties with the Woman's Party, so if we could steer a few wavering legislators to you in the next day or two . . ."

"Now Anna," Elizabeth said quickly, "my father isn't running his con to help anyone. All the money is going to him and his cohorts."

Gideon reached over and patted her hand in silent thanks.

"That's right," his mother said, giving the Old Man an apologetic smile at this slight betrayal. "But the Woman's Party is in serious need of funds at the moment. Miss Paul has been unable to join us here to lead this fight because of it, so I can't help thinking that if there was a way to use Buster's business venture to benefit the Party . . ."

Did she actually bat her eyes at Mr. Miles? Gideon tried not to look horrified.

For his part, the Old Man just looked thoughtful. After a long moment, he said, "That might be arranged."

"What might be arranged?" Gideon asked suspiciously.

Mr. Miles smiled as he obviously finished thinking the matter through. "I could give Anna and Freddie the steerer's fee for any investors they bring into the scheme. They, in turn, could donate it however they wish."

"I already sent you some prospects, so you can give me the steerer's fee, too," Elizabeth said a little huffily. She was probably annoyed that she hadn't thought of this herself.

He gave her a disappointed frown. "I could, but all the prospects you gave me were either penniless or too busy with political business to meet with me. Your Harry Burn, for instance, is the sole support of his widowed mother. He doesn't have two nickels to rub together. And Seth Walker might have some money, but he is in meetings from morning till night. It was the same story for all of them."

"I'm sorry about that, but you can't expect Anna and Freddie to go around the hotel shilling for you," Elizabeth said. Gideon wanted to pat her hand again but refrained.

"Women have been shilling for the amendment every hour of

every day I have been in Nashville," the Old Man reminded her. "This would be no different."

"Except that money would be changing hands," Elizabeth said, frowning.

"My darling daughter," the Old Man said with a condescending grin, "money is changing hands to influence votes every day. The only difference is that our money would benefit me and the Woman's Party while their money benefits only the legislators."

When he put it like that, even Gideon could see the logic, if not the morality, of it. "But how could Freddie and Anna explain sending legislators to you for some sort of business deal?" he asked. "None of the other suffragists are doing anything like that."

"Although the Antis probably are," his mother said slyly.

"Oh, Mother Bates, you are certainly right," Elizabeth said. "Why wouldn't they send the legislators to the railroad men or the liquor men?"

"Are you talking about bribing the legislators?" Freddie asked with more glee than Gideon liked to see when discussing cons.

"Yes, she is," Gideon said. "They keep things very private, so no one has been able to prove anything, but we know it goes on."

"And how can the Woman's Party compete with that?" Anna said bitterly. "We can't even afford to bring Alice Paul to Tennessee."

"Well," Freddie said, still a bit too gleefully, "we could send men to Mr. Miles for the opportunity to become very rich."

"And he wouldn't even care if people found out since he's planning to disappear when this is all over," Elizabeth said.

"But you still haven't figured out a reason why Anna and Freddie would even know about such a business," his mother reminded them.

"That's easily explained," Mr. Miles said. "They could be my daughters."

His real daughter scowled at that, but Freddie and Anna seemed inordinately pleased by the prospect.

"Of course," Anna exclaimed. "That would explain everything. Naturally, we would be supporting our father."

"Would people believe we're sisters?" Freddie asked. "We don't look much alike."

"Jake and I don't look much alike," Elizabeth said, mentioning her brother. At least Jake wasn't in Nashville. Heaven knew what he might be up to.

"You and Jake had different mothers, dear," Mother Bates said. "But siblings often don't look alike. If you say you're sisters, no one will challenge you."

"And if I say they are my daughters, no one will challenge me," Mr. Miles said.

"You don't have to get involved in this," Gideon said to Anna and Freddie.

"But we want to help," Anna argued. "And this sounds like more fun that just buttonholing legislators and giving them a lecture."

"She's right," his mother told Gideon. "It does sound like more fun. Could I be one of your daughters, too, Buster?"

Even Gideon laughed at that.

When they had settled down again, Elizabeth said, "As I was just explaining to Anna and Freddie, we only have fifty votes pledged, which is the bare minimum we safely need to ratify the amendment. If we lose even one, it won't pass."

"Then we need to find a few more just in case," Freddie said.

"And I am more than happy to help you," Mr. Miles said as if he were conferring a great favor. "Are you girls staying here at the hotel?"

"No, we found a rooming house," Anna said.

"Nonsense, I need you nearby. I'll arrange to pay for your room here. Would you like a suite?"

"That's very generous, Mr. Miles," Freddie said, obviously impressed.

Gideon didn't mention that Mr. Miles typically skipped out without paying his hotel bill after a con. If he did mention it, his mother would probably chide him for spoiling the mood.

T HE LEGISLATURE RECONVENED BRIEFLY AT THE CAPITOL after lunch. Representative Story presented a resolution that would have prohibited them from taking any action on ratification until the following year, another worry for the Suffs. It had to lay over for a day before it could be considered, so no vote was taken.

Elizabeth found Anna and Freddie in the lobby late that afternoon. They had moved over to the hotel into a double room, which was all that was available. She had to admit they looked a bit less enthusiastic about their plan than they had at lunch.

"Are you having any success?" Elizabeth asked them.

"We sent one fellow up," Freddie said. "He seemed disappointed when he found out we weren't going with him into the hotel room, though."

"He may have gotten the wrong idea," Anna said with a sly grin, "although we certainly didn't give it to him."

"Did he invest?" Elizabeth asked.

"We have no idea, but he didn't seem very enthusiastic about the amendment. We heard that the majority of the North Carolina legislature sent word to the Antis that they will not inflict the Nineteenth Amendment on the rest of the country by ratifying it and they are asking Tennessee legislators to make the same pledge."

Elizabeth shook her head. "It's discouraging, all right."

"And we can't seem to find many legislators to talk to," Freddie said. "They have all disappeared."

"Not completely," Elizabeth assured them. "I think you'd find a lot of them up in the Jack Daniel's Suite."

"We'd happily go there to find them, but they won't let us in," Anna reported with a grin.

"I don't suppose they will," Elizabeth said. "I did see a lot of delegates going into Mrs. Catt's room for meetings, and they all smelled of whiskey."

"Which would have upset her," Anna said. "She's strictly temperance."

"She'll have to overlook it, then," Freddie said, "since it seems like all the legislators are drunk."

"I wouldn't be surprised," Elizabeth said.

After dinner, Elizabeth visited Miss Sue's suite to see what the news was. Anita Pollitzer and Betty Gram were with her.

"Everyone in the lobby is talking about the public meeting tomorrow night. They're speculating on who will be speaking," Elizabeth reported.

"I wish I could tell you," Miss Sue said, her frustration obvious.

"At first they insisted only men be allowed to speak," Betty said. "They didn't want to offend the more conservative legislators."

"We should have expected it," Elizabeth said.

"Yes, we should have," Anita said. "But this is clearly an issue women should address."

"Not if the men won't listen to them," Miss Sue said, "and

that's what they're afraid of. In any event, the Antis wouldn't hear of it. They insisted that Charlotte Rowe be one of their speakers."

"She is the best public speaker they have," Elizabeth allowed.

"So, the NAWSA people insisted on allowing Anne Dudley to speak for the Suffs," Miss Sue continued.

"And of course, the Woman's Party should be represented, too," Anita said. "We suggested Miss Sue."

"Then you'll be speaking, too?" Elizabeth asked with a smile.

"We aren't sure. The men planning the event aren't keen on having women at all, and three might well be too many for them," Miss Sue said, still showing her frustration.

"At least we have some good men to speak for us," Betty said. "Edward Stahlman, for one."

"Who is he?" Elizabeth asked.

"He's the publisher of the *Nashville Banner*, and he and his paper have always supported Woman Suffrage," Miss Sue said. "He came to this country from Germany as a boy and worked his way up until he was vice president of the Louisville and Nashville Railroad and then finally commissioner of the Southern Railway and Steamship Corporation."

"When some legislation was proposed that threatened the L&N Railroad," Anita continued, "he bought a newspaper to help influence public opinion. He liked being a publisher so much that he left the railroad to do it full-time. He'll do a good job for us."

"So will Miss Sue," Elizabeth said.

"If they let me speak," Miss Sue said sadly.

"If the Antis can have a female speaker, then the Suffs can, too," Betty insisted.

"We'll see," was all Miss Sue said.

Catherine Flanagan burst into the suite without knocking.

"What is it?" Miss Sue asked, seeing her excitement.

"Senator Todd and Representative Riddick just announced that both the Senate and the House will vote on ratification on Friday," Catherine said.

"But they won't have time. The public hearing is tomorrow night and that's Thursday," Miss Sue said. "The committees won't even have a chance to consider the bills before Friday."

"They'll meet right after the hearing tomorrow, even if it takes all night," Catherine reported.

"And what about that bill that Representative Story presented this afternoon? If that were to pass, there will be no vote at all," Elizabeth reminded them.

"They must be confident they have the votes to defeat it," Catherine said. "They were adamant the vote will be held on Friday."

"Then let's hope the public meeting will persuade enough legislators to pass ratification in both houses," Miss Sue said, "because we don't have much time left for doing it ourselves."

THE SESSION THE NEXT MORNING WAS HARDLY WORTH THE walk over from the hotel. Gideon marveled at how many people could squeeze into the House chamber. Ninety-four representatives were in their seats and the gallery was packed, as usual. Those who couldn't find a seat there had crowded into the aisles on the floor and overflowed into the corridors outside the doorways. The crowd was just as great in the Senate chamber. Governor Roberts was back and working the House floor as he had done the previous day. Someone had obviously lit a fire under him.

Speaker Seth Walker called the session to order at ten o'clock, and after the usual formalities of prayer and roll call, the ratifica-

tionists moved to table Representative Story's resolution to pro-
hibit the legislature from acting on ratification. To the Suffs'
relief, the resolution went down in a voice vote. Then Walker
adjourned the session so the legislators could prepare for the public hearing that evening.

Gideon ushered his ladies out of the chamber and down the
stairs as the mass of observers exited.

"There's Anne Dudley," Elizabeth said when they reached the
ground floor. "Let's ask her if she's speaking tonight. Miss Sue
will want to know."

Gideon grabbed Elizabeth's hand so he wouldn't lose her in
the press and used his broad shoulders to make way through the
throng over to Anne Dudley. For her part, Anne was heading for
a gentleman that Gideon recognized as Lon McFarland. Recog-
nizing him was easy since he wore his signature white linen suit
and string tie. A bit of a scoundrel, McFarland had taken great
pleasure in refusing to commit to either side in the ratification
fight. He even wore a two-toned rose boutonniere—yellow with
red edges—so no one could guess which side he favored. Obviously, the beautiful Anne Dudley hoped to use her considerable
charm on him.

"I'm not an outsider," she was saying as Gideon and Elizabeth
approached. "I was born and bred in Nashville. If you want to
honor Tennessee women, as you say you do, you'll vote for ratification." She had reached up and was straightening his tie, pulling
the ends even and tightening the knot. It was a gesture that
would charm any man.

Before anyone could guess what he intended, though, McFarland reached into his jacket, pulled out a pocketknife, and sliced
off his tie just below the knot, leaving Anne holding the two limp
strings.

"Just keep it," he called over his shoulder as he walked away.

Anne stared after him, open mouthed with shock.

"What a cad," Elizabeth said, rushing to Anne's side. "I'm so sorry. He didn't cut you, did he?"

"No," she said faintly, looking at the strings she still held as if wondering what to do with them.

Elizabeth snatched them from her fingers and tossed them on the floor. "I don't suppose we can count on his vote."

Anne smiled at that. "I don't suppose we can."

"Are you all right, Mrs. Dudley?" Gideon asked, still fuming over McFarland's outrageous gesture.

"Except for a little wounded pride, I'm fine," she said. "Everyone knows Lon McFarland is a bit of a rogue. I should have known better."

"But we can't refuse to speak to the rogues," Elizabeth said. "We'd have no one left to convince."

"I'm afraid you're right," Anne said, now obviously recovered from her shock.

"I hope you'll be speaking for us at the debate this evening," Elizabeth said.

Anne's smile disappeared. "I don't think so. Our gentlemen can't be exposed to too many female voices, it seems."

"But if the Antis can have a female speaker, the Suffs should have one, too," Gideon said.

"Yes, well, those in charge have chosen Charl Williams to represent the Suffs."

Plainly, this outraged Elizabeth. "But she's—"

"Yes," Anne quickly agreed, "She's not exactly the firebrand that we would have liked to represent us, but she is also the vice chair of the Democratic National Committee and the director of the Democratic Women's Steering Committee."

Elizabeth nodded. "In other words, she has the credentials, and she won't offend the Southern gentlemen."

"Exactly. But it should still be a lively debate. The men speaking for us aren't a bit ladylike," Anne said.

"Can we escort you back to the hotel?" Gideon asked, thinking she might be a little shaken by the encounter with McFarland.

"Thank you, but I have a meeting to attend here, and I don't expect anyone else will pull a knife on me."

Elizabeth told her how brave she was and thanked her for her work. Then they found his mother, Anna and Freddie waiting for them on the other side of the corridor.

"Did that man pull out a knife?" his mother demanded when Gideon and Elizabeth reached them.

"Yes, he did," Gideon said. "Fortunately, the only thing he cut with it was his own tie."

"Mrs. Dudley looked quite shocked," his mother said with a worried frown. They all glanced back to where Mrs. Dudley had been standing, but she had gone.

"She seems to have recovered," Gideon said. "I can't imagine a thing like that would disturb a suffragist too much after all the things they've been through."

"Yes," Elizabeth said with a smirk. "Being force-fed is far worse than watching a man destroy his own tie."

"I'll take your word for it, Elizabeth," Freddie said with a shudder. "I hope this won't frighten Mrs. Dudley out of speaking tonight, though."

"She said she isn't one of the speakers," Gideon reported.

"Don't tell me we won't have any female speakers for the Suff side," Anna said, outraged.

"They have chosen Charl Williams," Elizabeth said, her disapproval obvious.

"Who is she?" Freddie asked.

Elizabeth briefly explained Charl's role.

"Then she isn't a member of the Woman's Party," Anna said.

"Or of the NAWSA, either," Elizabeth said.

"Which is probably why she was chosen," Mother Bates said. "It's obvious. The Antis are relatively united in their strategy, so they only need one voice to speak for them. The two Suff camps do not agree at all on our strategy, so either each must have a voice—which would mean two Suff speakers to the Antis' one—or they choose one Suff speaker who is not a member of either camp."

"You're probably right, Mother Bates," Elizabeth said. "And Charl is a lovely woman, but she is not known for being forceful in her remarks."

"Then we must hope that is what will persuade these Southern gentlemen," Mother Bates said.

"Or we can convince them ourselves," Anna said. "We still have the better part of today to work on them. The hearing doesn't start until eight o'clock."

"Then we'd best get to it," Elizabeth said. "What will you be doing, darling?" she added to Gideon.

"The Men's Ratification Committee is meeting to discuss our own strategy. We want to be prepared if anything untoward happens during the hearing this evening."

"Let's hope it won't come to that, although after McFarland's knife play, who knows?" Elizabeth said.

THE PUBLIC HEARING WAS THE HOTTEST TICKET IN TOWN, so they left early to be sure of getting a seat in the gallery. By eight o'clock, the gallery was packed, and the floor was jammed. The legislators from both houses were seated down there, along with other officeholders, judges and dignitaries, including Governor Roberts. Observers who could not find a place in the gallery had squeezed in around the walls and in the aisles and some stood out in the hallways, as close to the doors as possible.

"This feels more like a baseball game than a government proceeding," Gideon remarked, shouting to be heard above the din.

"I was thinking it was like a horse race," Elizabeth replied, "but you're right, it's not very dignified. I just hope the legislators didn't spend too much time in the Jack Daniel's Suite today."

"And I'm sure they did. How else can they endure all these speeches?"

"How many speeches will there be?" Freddie called from where she and Anna were sitting on the other side of Elizabeth.

"Each side has five speakers and ninety minutes to make their case," Gideon said. He'd learned all about it at his committee meeting that afternoon.

"That's three hours of speeches," Freddie said, plainly horrified.

"Oh, at least," Gideon confirmed. "That doesn't even count the introductions."

"You'll learn a lot," his mother called from where she was sitting on the other side of him.

"And it will be exciting," Elizabeth said. "You were the ones who wanted to see all this happening."

Poor Freddie looked like she might be regretting her enthusiasm, but Senator Todd and Representative Riddick were calling the meeting to order, so they had no further opportunity for discussion.

Once the chamber had quieted, Senator Todd welcomed everyone and said a few words about the importance of tonight's meeting. "And I also want to make this perfectly clear. We will not tolerate any outbursts or demonstrations from the spectators. Anyone causing a disturbance will be removed by the sergeant at arms."

"So much for the excitement," Elizabeth whispered in Gideon's ear.

# CHAPTER SIX

ELIZABETH WAS PLEASED TO SEE CHARL WILLIAMS INTRO-
duced first on the agenda until she realized that Charl wasn't
really one of the speakers. She had been chosen only to introduce
the program. Still, she managed to mention the Cause and the
reasons to support it.

"The women of this country have been fighting for suffrage for
sixty years," she began, underestimating the real time by at least
a decade. Then she gave a brief history of the struggle in her home
state of Tennessee that had resulted in partial suffrage for women
here just last year. She closed not with a rousing call to action, as
a member of the Woman's Party would have done, but rather a
plea. "We have asked the men of Tennessee to take the matter of
ratification and solve it for us," she said, using language that made
Elizabeth wince. She could only imagine how annoyed the other
members of the Woman's Party were. "We feel perfectly safe to
place it in the hands of our own men. The eyes of the United
States are upon Tennessee in this fight, and the women of the
state and nation stretch out eager hands to our men in this fight."

Polite applause followed, but not the rousing cheer the Suffs had hoped to inspire.

Mother Bates reached past Gideon to take Elizabeth's hand. "She's trying to appeal to the old men in the legislature. They love the damsel in distress whom they can rescue."

Elizabeth was tired of being seen as a damsel in distress. The old men in the legislature should have supported suffrage because it is the right and fair thing to do for the one half of the population who happened to be born female. On the other hand, Mother Bates was right, and if the ploy worked, she would gladly admit she had been wrong.

The early speakers for both sides were attorneys and judges who argued the legal questions surrounding voting on ratification. Even though the Supreme Court had ruled that it was legal for the legislators to follow the national Constitution and ignore the Tennessee Constitution's requirement to hold an election before voting whether to ratify an amendment, many members still claimed they could not, in good conscience, violate their oaths to the Tennessee Constitution.

Senator McKellar, who had summoned all the Democratic state senators to his hotel room to compel them to pledge for ratification a few days ago, spoke eloquently about the need for the Democrats to follow their leaders—President Woodrow Wilson and presidential candidate Governor James Cox—in supporting the amendment.

Tennessee Representative Finis Garrett, speaking for the Antis, attempted to strike fear in their hearts by painting a picture of a contested election in November if the amendment was passed and was later found to be illegal. He reminded them of the presidential election of 1876 when the results were in dispute for months. He predicted that if the amendment passed, every election held in November would be challenged, throwing the country into chaos.

The Antis cheered, which the leaders apparently did not consider a demonstration, so it was allowed. The Suffs hadn't had much to cheer about yet.

After another legal argument from the Suffs, Charlotte Rowe had her turn for the Antis, and she painted an even uglier future than Finis Garrett had if the amendment was ratified. "Under the pretense of political expediency and the fond dream of woman's emancipation from the laws of nature, suffrage leaders are working to destroy the states and enslave the American people," Rowe said in her usual rabble-rousing style. "The federal suffrage amendment is a deliberate conspiracy to crush the will of the American public. If the present legislature ratifies, it will be due to the Bolshevik and socialist influences at work on them."

Once again, the Antis cheered, this time jumping to their feet at the mention of the two most feared ideologies in the country. This time Senator Todd banged his gavel in an attempt to quiet the crowd. But Rowe wasn't finished. She launched into a tirade against Mrs. Catt and the Tennessee women who supported suffrage, vilifying them in every possible way.

The Suffs wanted to boo, or at least Elizabeth did, but they had been instructed not to sink to that level. Instead, they made faces at Rowe or stuck their tongues out. If Rowe noticed, she gave no sign. She just continued to pour out her vitriol.

"We are living in perilous times," Rowe warned. "The destroyers are at work. The wreckers are at our homes. The Bolsheviks are at your door and seeking the centralization of power. Tennessee has the opportunity to immortalize itself as the savior of the republic and redeem the principle of true representation and our union of states, without which American democracy must perish from the earth."

"She's being a little melodramatic, I think," Gideon whispered to Elizabeth.

"But too many of these men believe her," Elizabeth said. "How can they honestly think that giving women the vote will lead to a revolution like they had in Russia?"

Gideon just shook his head. Of course, he wouldn't know how to answer that. He was a rational human being.

But the Antis' joy evaporated moments later when General Charles Cates got up to speak for the Suffs. He had been Tennessee's attorney general for more than a decade, and he put Charlotte Rowe firmly in her place.

"When the men of Tennessee want to take lessons in honor they will take them from the women of Tennessee," Cates began, earning a round of thunderous applause from the Suffs. "Let me say further to these distinguished ladies from outside the state who come here to preach against the women of Tennessee receiving the ballot—you can come here and preach to us for a thousand years before you could make us believe the women of Tennessee had lost their grip on womanhood! There is no socialism or bolshevism among Tennessee women," Cates shouted. "The men of Tennessee trust their honor to their women, and they should not hesitate to trust them with the ballot."

The Suffs roared until they were hoarse. This was what they were hoping for, a champion who would challenge all the lies the Antis told.

But the evening also held disappointments. Judge G. N. Tillman was to speak for the Antis, but no one expected the heinous betrayal he would expose. When he stood up to speak, he pulled a piece of paper from his pocket and began to read it aloud. It was a letter from the Republican candidate for president, Senator

Warren Harding, who was, publicly at least, a supporter of Woman Suffrage.

"I quite agree with you that members of the General Assembly cannot ignore the state constitution," Tillman read. "I should be very unfair to you, and should very much misrepresent my own convictions, if I urged you to vote for ratification when you hold to a very conscientious belief that there is a constitutional inhibition which prevents your doing so until after an election has been held."

The Suffs in the gallery could hardly believe it. Harding was giving his approval to those legislators who chose to hide behind the discredited constitutional objections.

Tillman continued reading the letter. "I do not want you to have any doubt about my belief in the desirability of completing the ratification, but I am just as earnest about expressing myself in favor of fidelity to conscience in the performance of a public service. Under these circumstances, please say to Republican members that I cannot ask them to vote for ratification."

The Antis were crowing with delight while the Suffs gasped in horror. Harding had not only given Republican lawmakers permission to vote against ratification, but he seemed to be encouraging them to do so. Elizabeth saw her own dismay mirrored on the face of every Suff in the gallery.

"At least we still have Mr. Stahlman to speak for us," Mother Bates said to cheer them when Tillman sat back down.

"I found out today that Stahlman is a charter member of the Men's Ratification Committee," Gideon said. "He should be a good advocate."

Elizabeth remembered Miss Sue had spoken so highly of him, and she drew a steadying breath, prepared to hear the newspaper publisher speak on their behalf.

Stahlman rapped his cane as he came up to speak, assuring

that everyone would be listening. "I am in favor of giving the women the ballot," he began, curiously echoing the Antis' familiar refrain that always ended with a qualification, "but I am not in favor of giving them this power through any doubtful action by the Tennessee legislature."

Once again, the Suffs gasped in unison. This man who had assured them over and over that he supported ratification was betraying them just as Harding had.

Stahlman evidently took issue with the amendment's centralization of power with the federal government. "We fought for democracy in Europe, but now we are apparently attempting to take it away from ourselves at home. The most sensible expression I heard this evening was from Senator Harding, who demonstrated good faith, good taste and justice. I hope Governor Cox will do the same thing Senator Harding did. The truth is neither one had any business meddling in our affairs."

Stahlman spoke for only ten minutes, but it seemed like hours to Elizabeth. How could he have turned on them like that? Did these so-called gentlemen have no honor at all?

It was almost midnight when the last speaker sat down, and Senator Todd and Representative Riddick adjourned the meeting.

"Nearly four hours of speeches, and I can't see that we've changed a single vote," Elizabeth said. Everyone had risen from their seats to stretch but few people were leaving the chamber. Both the House and the Senate committees were meeting immediately to vote on recommending the amendment for consideration by the whole body. If they could accomplish that, they could hold the vote tomorrow, although no one was quite sure yet what the outcome would be.

"We don't need to change any votes as long as we don't lose any," Mother Bates reminded them.

"Harding may have lost us some," Anna said bitterly. "I can't believe he sent a letter like that."

"He probably didn't know it would be read aloud at a public meeting," Mother Bates said.

"Mother Bates, you are so kind," Elizabeth marveled. "You can even excuse an idiot like Harding."

"Doesn't he realize this could cost him the women's vote in the election?" Anna said.

"I would hope it does," Freddie said. "The man has no honor at all."

"I believe that has already been established," Gideon said with a small smile.

The women smiled back. They had all heard the rumors about Harding's mistress and their love child. "But those stories don't seem to be hurting him," Elizabeth said. "Let's hope this will."

"How long do you think we'll have to wait before the committees announce their results?" Freddie asked.

"Not long, I hope. I'll go down to the floor and see if I can find out how things are going," Gideon said. "Mother, if you're tired, you should go back to the hotel. We can tell you what happens."

"Nonsense. I'm not going anywhere. I don't often get the chance to see history being made."

"All right, but this could go on for hours, so if you change your mind . . ."

"If it goes on for hours, we'll all go back to the hotel," Elizabeth said. "Now go see what you can find out."

The spectators who had remained in the gallery to await the committee reports were dividing up into small groups to discuss what had happened. Elizabeth found Miss Sue, who was surrounded by her closest cohorts.

"Miss Paul will not be coming to Nashville," Miss Sue was saying. "In view of the way the press is attacking Mrs. Catt for being an outsider, Miss Paul feels she would only be a distraction."

"And you are the logical person to take her place," Anita Pollitzer said. "They can't accuse you of being an outsider, at least."

"No, they can't, but many people still don't like our methods," Miss Sue said.

"And they're angry at me for confronting Seth Walker," Betty Gram said a little sheepishly. "Even a lot of the other Suffs."

"Which is ridiculous," Elizabeth said. "How could a big, strong man like Seth Walker take offense at anything you said? You're just a silly, little female," she added sarcastically.

Betty grinned, obviously not a bit ashamed of her behavior. "I can't figure it out, either, unless I hit a little too close to home for Mr. Walker's comfort."

Which was what they all thought.

"What should we be doing, Miss Sue?" a woman Elizabeth didn't know asked. "If they're going to take the vote tomorrow morning, we don't have much time."

"By my count, we need seventeen votes in the Senate and fifty votes in the House. We should have the Senate easily, but the House is still uncertain. We think we have the fifty votes pledged but if one man changes his vote, all is lost."

"Then we should each find our delegates in the morning and confirm their support before they go into session," Anita said.

"Exactly," Miss Sue said. "And if you pick up a straggler or two, good for you."

They all laughed at that, although the laughs sounded a bit forced. No one expected to pick up any stragglers. By this time, almost all the delegates were pledged one way or the other.

"I just wish we could make Miss Pearson angry," one of the

other women said, naming the woman who led the Antis. "If we could, we would win for sure."

"Miss Pearson? Why would you want to make her angry?" Elizabeth asked.

"I guess you haven't seen her lose her temper," the woman said a little smugly. "She has a horrible temper and when she is confronted with something she considers a moral outrage, she becomes almost childishly emotional. She would lose all respect."

"If anyone figures out how to morally outrage Miss Pearson, let me know," Miss Sue said with a weary smile. Indeed, she looked exhausted, and she probably was. They all were.

"Let's just hope no one else betrays us like Harding and Stahlman did tonight," Betty said with more than a trace of bitterness.

"I think we can expect to be disappointed at least a few more times before this is over," Miss Sue said. "But we must not let this discourage us. We have never been so close to victory before, and we can't let it slip away because we lost our resolve."

A disturbance down on the floor distracted them and everyone crowded down to the front of the gallery so they could see what was happening.

Senator Todd had come to the podium. "Senator Gwinn will now make his report on the actions of the Senate's Committee on Constitutional Affairs and Amendments."

Gwinn, who chaired the committee, took his place and announced that the committee would return a favorable report, recommending ratification, in the morning. Senator Todd promised the Senate would consider the amendment and vote on it within an hour of receiving it from the committee.

The Suffs cheered while the Antis remained stubbornly silent. They would know that the Senate vote was only half the battle and the outlook in the House was still far from good.

"Friday the thirteenth," one of the Antis standing nearby said.

"What?" Elizabeth asked, confused.

"Tomorrow is Friday the thirteenth. It will be a hoodoo for suffrage, you'll see," the woman said maliciously.

Elizabeth couldn't help smiling. "We don't believe in old-time superstitions or in old-time traditions that prevent women from being full-fledged citizens."

"Then you're doomed to be disappointed," the woman said, stalking away before Elizabeth could reply. She sighed. If only she felt as confident as she was trying to sound. She needed to look at Miss Sue's list to see if there was anyone on it who might possibly change their vote. She was even willing give the names to the Old Man for help if necessary.

Elizabeth went back to where Mother Bates, Anna and Freddie had found seats in the back row of the gallery to tell them what Miss Sue had said. Just as she reached them, Gideon came back into the gallery.

"Did you hear the report from the Senate's committee?" she asked him.

"Yes, but the news isn't so good from the House's committee," he said grimly.

"What's wrong?" his mother asked, alarmed.

"It's the chair, Riddick. He may be a brilliant lawyer, but he's a novice legislator and has no idea how to control a meeting."

"But Seth Walker is an expert at that," Elizabeth guessed.

"Yes, and as Speaker, he's an ex officio member of every committee, so he attended that meeting and used his clout to force the committee to postpone consideration of the amendment until next week."

"Next week!" Mother Bates exclaimed in outrage.

"The committee can hold the resolution for up to seven days, and they may do just that."

"How can we keep our pledges firm for another week?"

Elizabeth asked, furious at Seth Walker and wondering how she could convince the Old Man to take him for every penny he had.

No one had an answer for her.

"Does Miss Sue know?" Elizabeth asked, looking around. She saw a group had gathered around their leader and from the raised voices, she could tell they had heard the news as well. After a few moments, the group started moving toward the exit.

"Gideon, what about your work?" his mother asked. "You only asked for a week off."

"Then I'll have to ask for another week," Gideon said. "I'm sure Mr. Devoss will agree when I tell him you have especially requested that I stay on."

"Yes," Elizabeth agreed. "He would do just about anything for you, Mother Bates."

She made a face that made Elizabeth giggle.

Betty Gram stopped beside them on her way out of the gallery. "We're going to Miss Sue's suite for a strategy meeting."

"I'll be there," Elizabeth said.

"And I'll be meeting with the Men's Ratification Committee," Gideon said. "We've already discussed some ideas on how to handle a situation like this."

"Has there ever been a situation like this?" his mother asked with some amusement.

"Probably not," Gideon admitted ruefully, "but there must be a way to handle it, and if there is, we'll find it."

E LIZABETH WASN'T SURE WHEN GIDEON HAD FINALLY crawled into bed beside her, but she guessed he hadn't gotten much more sleep than she had. Both of them had been in meetings until the wee hours of the morning, but they couldn't sleep in today. They had to be present when the Senate voted on the amendment this morning.

Gideon was the last to join Elizabeth and his mother for the breakfast they had ordered in their room. "The House Democrats staged a rebellion last night," he said around a huge yawn. "Or should I say early this morning? At any rate, they decided they couldn't depend on Tom Riddick because he's just too inexperienced at all this, so they chose Joe Hanover to take the lead."

"Isn't he the one who made that wonderful speech the other day in favor of suffrage?" Mother Bates asked.

"Yes. He had resigned from the legislature to take a job as the Shelby County district attorney, but he ran for election again this time because he knew they would need him to help in the ratification fight. Now he's officially the Democrats' floor leader for ratification."

"And surely he won't betray us," Elizabeth said with more hope than certainty.

They set out early because the Senate chamber was much smaller and seats in the gallery would be at a premium. The room was bursting with observers by the time Senator Todd called the meeting to order. Everyone, it seemed, wore flowers of one color or another. The Antis wore their red roses and the NAWSA members their yellow. Miss Sue and the Woman's Party members had chosen nosegays of white, purple and gold asters, the colors of suffrage, and those who qualified wore their prison pins. Elizabeth touched hers, proud that she had played a role, however small.

Senator Todd recognized Senator Gwinn, who gave the committee's report to the full Senate. It was surprisingly eloquent.

"The committee is of the opinion that the present legislature has both a legal and moral right to ratify the proposed resolution," Gwinn began and then listed the legal arguments in favor of ratification. "National woman's suffrage by federal amendment is at hand," he concluded. "It may be delayed, but it cannot be defeated; and we covet for Tennessee the signal honor of being the thirty-sixth and last state necessary to consummate this great reform. Fully persuaded of its justice and confident of its passage, we earnestly recommend the adoption of the resolution."

The Suffs cheered, earning a big smile from Senator Gwinn, who nodded to acknowledge their approval.

Not everyone on the committee had agreed, however, and two of them had written a minority report, insisting the Senate should refuse to act on ratification.

Mother Bates was sitting beside Elizabeth this time, and she grasped Elizabeth's hand as a vote was taken to table the minority report. But it passed by a comfortable margin, and the majority report was approved by voice vote. The Suffs cheered again.

A palpable wave of expectation swept through the chamber as everyone realized the next order of business was to vote on ratification, but Lon McFarland, curse him and his pocketknife, stood up and called for a point of order. Some wrangling occurred. McFarland asserted that the Senate had no right to vote on ratification. Senator Todd overruled him, but McFarland appealed, forcing a floor vote. Happily, McFarland was defeated by a large margin, which boded well for the final vote.

Then Senator Herschel Candler took the floor.

Betty Gram had said he was impossible. He was also vehement in his opposition to Woman Suffrage, as he made clear in his speech.

"I know of the pressure that has been exerted here," Candler began, "and I am humiliated to confess that Southern Republicans are Republicans for revenue only." A murmur of discontent went through the crowd. "I know of men who a week ago were against this thing are for it today, and I know why: Many of them now have their names on the state payroll. I am here representing the mothers who are at home rocking the cradle, and not representing the low-neck and high-skirt variety," Candler said as he pointed at a group of suffragists, "who know not what it is to go down in the shade of the valley and bring forth children. Motherhood has no appeal to them."

Elizabeth winced. She would gladly have gone down into that valley. Women around her began to hiss at Candler, and a furious Suff in the gallery shouted down, "I have six children!" Elizabeth had to smile at that in spite of her pain.

Candler pretended not to hear. "If there is anything I despise, it is a man who is under petticoat government!" he continued and this time men joined in the hissing. "You are being dictated to by an old woman down here at the Hermitage Hotel whose name is Catt. I think her husband's name is Tom," Candler tried to joke. It fell flat. "Mrs. Catt is nothing more than an anarchist." The hissing grew louder. "Have you read the speech of hers before an audience in New York, when she said that she would be glad to see the day when Negro men could marry white women and it is none of society's concern? This is the kind of woman that is trying to dictate to us." Even some of his fellow senators were hissing Candler now. "They would drag the womanhood of Tennessee down to the level of the Negro woman!" Protests poured down on him. He seemed oblivious. "Within a very few years after this amendment has passed, you will find that Congress has legislated so as to compel we people of the South to give to the Negro men and women their full rights at the ballot box. Then you will find many of your counties, now dominated by the Democrats and white people, sending up Negro representatives to this House. I have telegraphed to Senator Harding my unwillingness to violate the constitution of my state. I warn the majority in this chamber now that the next thing we know Negroes will be here legislating in Tennessee as they did fifty years ago." The chamber erupted into a frenzy of hissing, shouting and jeering, and finally Candler sat down.

No one, it seemed, was pleased. Candler had embarrassed his colleagues by accusing them of graft, he had outraged the Suffs with offensive and racist claims and had even offended the Antis who felt he had damaged their cause. Candler had managed to insult everyone.

Elizabeth turned to Gideon. "I think he helped us."

"I think you're right," he replied.

Andrew Todd left the Speaker's chair to respond. He spoke calmly in an attempt to quiet the room. "That is the most unfortunate speech that has ever been made upon the floor of the Senate. These slurs do not meet approval of the good women of Tennessee. I am convinced that there yet remains enough virtue among the womanhood of Tennessee and enough courage among the manhood of the state to see that no condition such as the senator from McMinn has pictured would ever occur. There are no sinister influences here," Todd said in an attempt at humor. "Talk about petticoat government. If there is a man in this house or in the gallery who has not been under petticoat government ever since he was born, I want him to stand up. I am ready to go into petticoat government. I have always been under that kind, and I thank God for it!"

The Suffs clapped and cheered as Todd made his way back to the Speaker's chair.

To everyone's surprise, Governor Roberts entered the chamber and walked slowly up to the front where he sat down beside Todd.

"He's letting everyone know he's keeping score of how they all vote," Gideon whispered to Elizabeth.

But the vote couldn't happen right away, not until the senators had an opportunity to explain themselves. Three hours of speeches followed, some for and some against but all impassioned. Many of them referred to the legal arguments or urged party unity, but almost all of them condemned or even ridiculed Herschel Candler's outrageous remarks.

Republican National Committee member John Houk, who had had to deal with the blowback from Senator Harding's awful letter, said, "In all my life I have never heard a sound argument against giving women the right to vote: A woman is a human being and so is entitled to a vote in the making of laws affecting her and her children."

Erastus Patton of Knoxville said, "If I thought for one minute it would work to the detriment of my little girl at home, I would vote against it, but you can't tell me that these magnificent women are going to turn the government into anarchy." Patton then gave them a saucy grin. "We have been accused of having petticoat government, but the senator is mistaken there. He's behind the times, because they don't wear 'em anymore!" The chamber broke into laughter, a welcome relief. Patton finished with a rousing appeal: "Let's make Tennessee the Perfect Thirty-Sixth!"

More senators rose to speak, including Senator Collins, who had left his sick bed to attend the session and had to be helped to his seat. Lunchtime had long passed when the last speaker sat down, and Senator Todd was finally able to call for a vote on the ratification resolution.

Betty Gram had a tally sheet, as did many other members of the Party, and she was sitting behind them. Elizabeth kept looking back to see where they stood as the clerk called the roll. Seventeen was the magic number for a majority of the thirty-three-member Senate.

One senator walked out of the chamber so he wouldn't have

to vote. Lon McFarland, the coward, abstained, as did two other senators. The Antis in the gallery began to protest as one after another of their pledged delegates voted aye. Slowly, the votes piled up, fourteen, fifteen, sixteen, and when Senator Matthews voted aye, the gallery erupted in shouts and screams and tears at the winning vote. The cheers went on so long, they had to suspend voting until Todd was able to quiet them enough for the clerk to hear the responses. In the end the count was twenty-five in favor, four against, one absent and three abstaining. Everyone, Suffs and Antis alike, was shocked by the margin of victory. Several men who had long been pledged to the Antis had changed their vote, and the Republicans had not chosen to accept Harding's free pass to vote against ratification.

Elizabeth instantly hugged Gideon and then her mother-in-law, Anna and Freddie, and after that she must have hugged a hundred more women wearing the tricolor Woman's Party flowers or the yellow roses of the NAWSA.

As the senators filed out of the chamber, they were met by a group of smiling Suffs holding their skirts up just enough to show a scrap of white lace to prove they did, indeed, still wear petticoats.

The triumphant mood didn't last too long. No sooner did they arrive back at the Hermitage than legislators began checking out. Both the House and the Senate were in recess for the weekend and those who lived close enough were taking the opportunity to spend the time with their families.

"Will they come back on Monday?" Anna asked as they watched the line of men turning in their keys at the front desk.

"We don't care if the senators come back," Gideon said with a smile. "They have more business but none of it involves ratification. We do need the representatives to come back, though, at least for the final vote."

"I think the governor made it clear that he's noting who fulfills their duty," Elizabeth said. "Let's hope that's enough to bring them back to Nashville next week."

"In the meantime, we'll have to watch the men who stayed," Mother Bates said.

"I'm sure the NAWSA will be keeping a close eye on them, too," Freddie said.

"And what about you and Anna? Will you be sending them up to the Old Man?" Elizabeth asked with a grin.

Freddie and Anna exchanged a frustrated glance. "We still aren't having much success," Anna admitted.

"Maybe you will over the weekend when they don't have any business to distract them," Gideon said.

"I hope you'll set your sights on Lon McFarland," Elizabeth said. "Tell the Old Man it doesn't matter that he won't pledge since the Senate vote has already been held. I just want him to get taken."

"I think we can all agree on that. I couldn't believe he refused to vote," Anna said.

"I'm not sure how we could approach him, though," Freddie said. "Since he can't vote for or against ratification now, we don't have any reason to speak to him."

"Ask the Old Man," Elizabeth said. "I'm sure he can think of something."

"Let's get some lunch," Gideon said. "I've got a meeting of the Men's Ratification Committee later, and I'm sure Elizabeth wants to visit with Miss Sue."

"We're meeting in one of the assembly rooms in about an hour," Elizabeth confirmed.

"And I'm going to rest," Mother Bates said. "These late nights are taking a toll."

After they had eaten, Elizabeth found the room off the lobby where the Woman's Party members were meeting. Miss Sue presided, and Elizabeth was glad to see her looking better than she had the night before. The victory in the Senate seemed to have invigorated her.

"Mrs. Catt has assigned her Tennessee volunteers to keep a close watch on their legislators. Their job will be to keep the men busy and entertained so they won't fall under the influence of the outsiders skulking around the hotel lobby or end up in the Jack Daniel's Suite."

A few of the women chuckled at that, but Elizabeth was wondering if the Old Man was one they considered a skulking outsider. He might not be winning anyone to support ratification, but at least he wasn't working against them.

"Should we step in to keep a legislator occupied if we see someone on his own?" Betty Gram asked.

"Of course. So long as it's a Suff keeping him busy, I don't think anyone will mind except the Antis. Another thing Mrs. Catt has done is notify President Wilson about Seth Walker's betrayal and ask him to intervene."

"Do you think Wilson can bring Walker back into the fold?" someone asked.

"I'm not even sure he'll try, but we can hope. Even to have Walker stop working against us would be a help."

"Unless Wilson offers Walker a job, I don't know how he's going to sway him," someone else said.

"Now, we don't know why Walker switched his allegiance, so we shouldn't make claims we can't prove," Miss Sue said.

"Or you'll end up a pariah like me," Betty Gram said to much laughter.

"How are we supposed to keep the men occupied without being accused of immorality?" another woman asked quite reasonably.

"Yes," Elizabeth added, "after that remark from Candler about low necklines and high hemlines, it's plain they will discredit us in any way possible."

"I'm not sure what Mrs. Catt is going to suggest to her ladies, but if we approach the men in pairs, they can't misinterpret our intentions. A trip to the picture show or a game of cards would be appropriate."

"And meals," Anita suggested. "Everyone has to eat, so inviting a man to join you for lunch or dinner would be a good idea."

"And be agreeable," an older lady said. "I'm not suggesting you flirt with these men but be sweet. They're from the South, remember, and they are accustomed to their women making a fuss over them."

"Ah yes, make a fuss over them, if that is what it takes," Miss Sue said. "If we can't convince them with reason, we'll do it with charm."

# CHAPTER SEVEN

IN SPITE OF HAVING BEEN AT HIS COMMITTEE MEETING UNTIL
very late, Gideon rose quite early on Saturday morning and left
their suite without waking his wife. Elizabeth awoke later to the
sound of water running in the bathroom. When she peeked in,
she found Gideon vigorously washing his hands, which were
quite black.

"Have you been hauling coal or something?" she asked
sleepily.

"Coal?" he asked with amusement. "Oh yes, I've been helping
stoke the furnace here at the hotel."

Which was preposterous because the weather in Nashville
was still oppressively hot. "Did you just tell me a lie?" she asked
in amazement.

"I was making a joke," Gideon said. "I would never lie to you."

She was sure of that, at least. "Where did you go this
morning?"

He was finished scrubbing his hands and began to dry them
on a towel. "Out. For a walk."

Which was probably true as far as it went. "Where did you go on your walk?"

"Not far. I met some other members of the Men's Ratification Committee, and we took care of a little business."

"What kind of business?" she asked, wondering what he could have been doing to get his hands so dirty.

"Nothing you need to worry about. Since we're up anyway, we should go down to the dining room for breakfast. I'm sure we'll hear some news."

"I hope you didn't do anything to break the law," Elizabeth said, still a bit confused by Gideon's behavior. He was the most honest man she knew, so this deception was very unlike him.

"I'm an attorney," he said with feigned outrage. "I know better than to break the law."

"I know you do, darling, but you're behaving so strangely, I don't know what to think."

"Just think I'm doing what I can for ratification and I'm not likely to be arrested for it. Should we wake my mother up for breakfast or let her sleep?"

In the end, they let Mother Bates sleep. The dining room was already crowded, which meant that Gideon was probably right about the news. They found seats at a table with Betty Gram, who was fairly bursting to bring them up to date.

"President Wilson sent Seth Walker a telegram, asking him personally to ensure that the House votes for ratification."

"How do you know?" Gideon asked.

"The president sent Mrs. Catt a copy of the telegram so she would know what it said."

"That was so generous of him," Elizabeth said. "I just hope it works."

"Miss Paul thinks it will. She heard about it, even though the president obviously didn't copy her with the telegram since he has no love for the Woman's Party," Betty said with a wink. President Wilson had grown very impatient with the women who protested outside the White House for almost two years.

"I imagine he wasn't too happy at being burned in effigy, either," Elizabeth said.

"Yes, but Miss Sue needed to get herself arrested so she could wear a prison pin like the rest of us, and burning the president's likeness seemed like a good way to do that," Betty said, still grinning. "At any rate, Mrs. Catt was kind enough to let Miss Paul know about the president's telegram, and Miss Paul released a statement to the press claiming victory."

"Hasn't anyone explained to her that a victory in the House is far from certain?" Elizabeth asked with a worried frown.

"I'm sure she would say that we want to give the impression that we are confident we will win," Betty said.

"That is often an excellent strategy," Gideon said.

"Let's just hope it works," Elizabeth said.

Their breakfast had just been served when Catherine Flanagan walked into the dining room and came directly to their table. "Have you heard?" she asked breathlessly. "Seth Walker replied to President Wilson's telegram."

Elizabeth could tell from Catherine's expression that this was not good news. "What did he say?"

Catherine looked around as if checking for eavesdroppers, but then she shrugged, probably deciding it couldn't possibly matter since news like this would soon be all over Nashville.

Gideon was already appropriating an unused chair from another table and pulled it up for Catherine to sit.

"He was so arrogant," Catherine began after taking a deep breath, "we could hardly believe it. Not only did he refuse to support ratification, he actually told the president he was *too presumptuous to ask it of him*. Can you imagine?"

"How do you know what Walker's telegram to the president said?" Gideon asked, obviously impressed at this bit of espionage.

Catherine gave him a pitying look. "No one can send a telegram in this hotel without its contents being revealed to anyone who wants to know it. We discovered days ago that telegrams the Suffs send are immediately carried by the bellmen to the Anti headquarters for review. We had to start paying the bellmen to return the favor."

"That's criminal," Gideon said. "In fact, I think we could have some people arrested for it."

"That hardly seems worth it," Elizabeth said. She was actually quite impressed that the Antis had taken such a step. They were far more clever than anyone had given them credit for. "Even if we have people arrested, their replacements will soon be bribed. No, just knowing there is no privacy in this hotel will keep us vigilant."

"Mrs. Catt is also convinced that her telephone is tapped," Betty said.

"I doubt they would go to so much trouble," Gideon said. "All they would have to do is pay the hotel operators to listen in and report back."

"I suppose you're right," Catherine said. "I hadn't thought of that."

"Because you're an honest, upstanding citizen," Elizabeth said.

"Listening to telephone calls isn't the worst of it, though," Betty said. "We've noticed every time any of us open our hotel room doors, there is a man out in the hallway. He seems to be listening, trying to overhear what we are saying inside our rooms."

"Which isn't very difficult," Elizabeth realized, "because we all have our transoms open because of the heat."

"We've started closing them when we're discussing something

delicate," Catherine said, "but that makes the room so stuffy, we can hardly bear it."

"Maybe the Men's Ratification Committee can help with this," Gideon said. "If you let us know when you're having an important meeting, we can post someone outside the room to scare off eavesdroppers."

"That would be wonderful, Mr. Bates," Catherine said. "I'll let Miss Sue know."

"And I'll inform the committee members. They've been looking for something really useful to do."

"Something besides stoking the furnace?" Elizabeth asked for his ears alone.

To his credit, Gideon didn't even blink. "Yes."


W E SHOULD PICK UP A NEWSPAPER OR TWO SO WE CAN SEE what they say about the vote yesterday," Elizabeth said when they were crossing the lobby on the way to the elevators after leaving the dining room.

Gideon gave her an odd look, but he said, "That's a good idea." But when they reached the newsstand it was surprisingly bare. "What newspapers do you have available?" Gideon asked.

"Hardly any at all," the man behind the counter said with a disgruntled frown. "We didn't get our usual deliveries today. Everybody's been complaining, but it ain't my fault. I can't sell papers I don't have, can I?"

"No, you certainly can't," Elizabeth said sympathetically.

Gideon bought one of the out-of-town papers that the vendor did have. As they walked away, Elizabeth said, "Newsprint."

"What did you say, darling?" Gideon asked.

"You heard me. Newsprint, which rubs off on your hands and turns them black."

"As black as coal," Gideon agreed. "We should have servants who iron the papers so the black doesn't rub off."

"What were you doing this morning? Did you and your co-horts steal all the newspapers in the city?"

"We didn't steal anything," Gideon said, obviously offended by the accusation. "We bought them."

"You what?" Elizabeth nearly shouted.

Since they were still in the lobby, surrounded by people, Gideon said, "Shhh, not so loud."

"You bought them?" she echoed, still not sure she believed him.

"Of course, we did. Stealing is illegal. We didn't want to embarrass the Cause."

He looked so proud, Elizabeth wanted to kiss him right there in the lobby, but she didn't want to embarrass him, either. "And what did you do with all those newspapers?"

"We bought them right off the delivery trucks. Just the Anti papers, mind you, so they couldn't influence any of the legislators who are still here. Then several of our local members carried the bundles off in their motorcars and disposed of them."

"Do you really think that will help?" she asked in amazement.

"It can't hurt. But as I said, we've been looking for something really useful, and patrolling the hotel hallways for spies is proba-bly more helpful than burning newspapers. The other fellows will be happy for the suggestion."

MOTHER BATES WAS ENJOYING THE BREAKFAST SHE HAD ordered up to the suite when they got back. She held up a newspaper. "Have you seen this?" she demanded, not even both-ering with a greeting.

Elizabeth and Gideon exchanged a look. "There aren't many newspapers available in the lobby this morning," she said with a smirk.

"How odd. This was on my tray when it came up," Mother Bates said. "At any rate, Mrs. Catt has responded to some of the things Senator Candler said about her yesterday."

"Just some of them?" Gideon asked, removing his suit jacket and draping it over a chair back. The day was already growing warm.

"Yes. She apparently doesn't mind the usual accusations of being unwomanly or sexless or whatever else he said about her. The only thing she took exception to was when he claimed she condoned interracial marriage."

"Why does everything in the South always come back to race?" Elizabeth asked, taking a seat at the table with her mother-in-law.

"Because it does," Gideon said. "And Mrs. Catt would understand that a charge like that would tarnish her with many of the Tennessee legislators."

"And give them an excuse to vote against ratification," Elizabeth added, leaning over so she could read the article Mother Bates had pointed out. When she had finished, she looked up in disgust. "I can see she would deny saying she had advocated for interracial marriage if she hadn't, but did she have to call it a *crime against nature?*"

"I wonder what her Aunt Susan would say about such racism from the NAWSA," Mother Bates said, glaring at the newspaper as if it were to blame.

"Aunt Susan?" Gideon echoed.

"That's what those closest to her called Susan B. Anthony. Mrs. Catt was one of her protégés."

"And Susan Anthony was close friends with many Black people. Frederick Douglass kept a special room in his house for her to visit him and his wife," Elizabeth added.

"Who also happened to be a white woman," Mother Bates added. "Sometimes I'm ashamed of my fellow Suffs."

"And yet she probably felt she must refute Candler's claim or risk giving the conservative representatives an excuse to reject ratification," Gideon said. "Politics is a dirty business."

Neither woman replied to that since all they could do was agree. After a long moment, Mother Bates turned to Elizabeth. "Isn't there something you can do?"

"Me?" Elizabeth asked in surprise.

"Yes. We agree that politics is a dirty business, but you know a lot about that sort of thing. Isn't there some kind of con to turn things our way?"

"Are you asking Elizabeth to con the legislators?" Gideon asked with some amusement.

"If she can," Mother Bates replied without a hint of remorse. "Everyone around us is lying and cheating to get their way. How else do you fight against that?"

"I . . . I don't know, Mother Bates," Elizabeth said. "Plainly, we're losing ground if the president himself can't help us, but I can't think of anything I could do to change that."

"Then keep thinking, dear," Mother Bates advised.

"Mother, you can't expect Elizabeth to save the amendment all by herself," Gideon said.

"Of course not. We'll help her. Anna and Freddie and Buster will, too."

Gideon grinned. "I can't wait to tell Mr. Miles you volunteered his services."

Mother Bates waved away any concern on that matter. "It's

down to the wire now, Elizabeth. If you can think of anything at all, now is the time."

ELIZABETH WAS STILL WRACKING HER BRAIN FOR AN IDEA ON how to save the amendment when she made her way down to the lobby later for a meeting with some of the Woman's Party leaders. She had been lost in thought when the elevator doors opened and she stepped in but then realized that the half-dozen women already inside were all wearing red roses.

She couldn't escape without asking the elevator operator to pull the door and the gate open again. Not wanting to appear a coward, she turned her back on them to face the doors and clamped her mouth tightly shut.

"Suff," one woman said contemptuously.

"Bolshevik," another said.

Elizabeth had been called worse and by her own flesh and blood. She stood firm.

Then, to her surprise, someone jostled her hard enough that she had to catch herself on the elevator gate. It clattered and she glanced at the operator in alarm. He refused to meet her eye.

"You've got no business coming here and telling us what to do," someone said.

"Go back where you came from, Suff," said another.

A glance upward told her the elevator would soon reach the lobby level, thank heaven. As the car stopped, Elizabeth glanced over her shoulder. "Someday you'll thank me for getting you the vote."

She had timed it perfectly. The operator had just pulled the door open, and she stepped out and quickly to the side so no one would be able to knock her over. The women glared at her as they passed, obviously annoyed they hadn't intimidated her. Elizabeth was annoyed, too. She needed to do something.

When she had regained her composure, she started across the enormous lobby and encountered Catherine Flanagan, who was staring at something. Elizabeth saw it was a group of men in clerical collars who had gathered in the lobby.

"What's all this?" Elizabeth asked.

"I guess you didn't see the ad in the morning newspaper," Catherine said. "The Antis invited all the clergymen in the city to come and see that display they have upstairs."

"Oh no, not the one with the *Woman's Bible*," Elizabeth said.

"Of course. The ad claimed Mrs. Catt was the author of it and that she believes all the claims made in it."

"That's unfortunate" was the only thing Elizabeth could think to say that didn't involve profanity. "Did every clergyman in Nashville come? There must be two dozen of them." Some women sporting red roses were rounding them up and ushering them upstairs to the mezzanine level.

"Indeed," Catherine said. "Imagine the sermons that will be preached about the evils of Woman Suffrage tomorrow."

While she was speaking, another woman had come up beside them to stare at the group of clergymen. A glance told Elizabeth she was Charlotte Rowe, the Antis' favorite orator.

"Let's move away from that notorious woman," Catherine said to Elizabeth, who readily agreed.

But Rowe had heard the remark, and her face had grown bright red. "What did you say?" she demanded, following them.

Neither Catherine nor Elizabeth had any intention of engaging with her, but she didn't stop.

"Did you call me a notorious woman?" Rowe asked in her trained speaking voice so everyone in the lobby could hear her. "How dare you. I'll sue you for public defamation."

Elizabeth and Catherine exchanged a horrified glance as they picked up their pace, but Rowe just kept following and shouting at them. The assembly room where the meeting was being held was on the other side of the lobby. By the time they reached it, everyone in the lobby was staring at the two Suffs fleeing from the outraged Anti.

"I'll see you in court!" Rowe yelled as Elizabeth and Catherine disappeared into the meeting room and slammed the door.

"Good heavens," Elizabeth said.

"Do you think she will really sue me?" Catherine asked in amazement.

"I doubt it, but she'll certainly make sure everyone in Nashville knows what you said."

"I didn't mean she was notorious in *that* way," Catherine insisted.

"Don't worry, no one would ever mistake Charlotte Rowe for a prostitute," Elizabeth assured her, and they both burst out laughing at the ridiculous thought.

They were still laughing when Miss Sue, Anita and Betty came in.

"What's happened?" Miss Sue asked, a little alarmed to see the two of them laughing for no apparent reason.

Elizabeth and Catherine sobered at once and told them about Catherine's remark and Rowe's reaction to it.

"Oh dear," Miss Sue said.

"Elizabeth doesn't think she'll really sue me," Catherine said.

"Then I'll encourage her to do it," Betty said mischievously. "That will guarantee people will stop talking about how I insulted Seth Walker and start talking about how you insulted Charlotte Rowe."

"Oh no," Catherine moaned. "She's probably right."

By now more women had come in for the meeting, and they

had to be brought up to date. A few were scandalized but most were just mildly amused that Rowe had made such a scene in the lobby. Wasn't she a little embarrassed? Apparently not.

When the subject had finally been exhausted, Elizabeth had to recount her experience in the elevator. "I just think all our people should know so they don't put themselves in danger. I was afraid those women were going to knock me down, and we don't want anyone to get hurt."

"You were right to tell us," Miss Sue said. "I'll make sure Mrs. Catt's people know, too. Joe Hanover has also been jostled in the hotel lobby and called worse names than you were. I certainly hope this isn't going to continue all weekend. Things are getting very unpleasant."

"The Antis are always unpleasant," someone said.

"They seem to be getting even more so, though," Miss Sue said. "I know I've been a bit jealous that the NAWSA gets all the attention and all the credit for getting the amendment this far, but I just learned that as a result of this attention, Mrs. Catt is also receiving the most awful hate mail, accusing her of horrible things. Bellmen deliver the letters to her room day and night. It has been very distressing for her."

"Will the Antis stop at nothing?" Anita asked. Everyone agreed they probably would not.

"Another thing that has come to my attention is the fact that the Antis are complaining that all the anti-suffrage newspapers have disappeared from the hotel," Miss Sue said.

Elizabeth was glad she had been trained to hide her emotions. She wasn't sure she could have kept a straight face otherwise. Did Miss Sue glance in her direction? No, that was just her imagination. Should she tell them? Probably not.

"Maybe they just sold out," someone suggested.

"If so, the Antis didn't buy them," Miss Sue said with a small smile. "In any case, we have far more important things to worry about. I understand that Elizabeth's husband has offered to organize the Men's Ratification Committee to provide guards to prevent Anti spies from eavesdropping on our meetings."

The other ladies reacted with cheers and applause, making Elizabeth glad she hadn't told them about Gideon destroying the newspapers.

G IDEON WAS TAKING THE FIRST SHIFT OF GUARDING MRS. Catt's suite on the third floor. He had frightened off a sneaky-looking fellow who had been loitering there when he arrived, which probably proved his presence was needed.

A woman had just gotten off the elevator and was heading this way. She wore a yellow rose, which told him she was a Suff. She slowed her pace when she saw he was standing outside Mrs. Catt's suite and frowned suspiciously. He quickly introduced himself and told her why he was there.

The woman introduced herself as Harriet Upton. Gideon knew she was Mrs. Catt's right hand. "That is a wonderful idea, Mr. Bates. Things are getting a little out of control when we have to have guards outside our hotel rooms, though."

"You're right about that, but the men are glad to have something important to do. You ladies have been doing most of the difficult work."

"Does Mrs. Catt know you're out here?"

"Yes, I introduced myself to her and explained that we would be keeping a close watch on her until the vote."

Harriet thanked him and let herself into the suite. Gideon leaned up against the wall across from the door to watch and wait. He wasn't there long before he could hear the murmur of voices from within. They sounded oddly alarmed. Could something have happened in the suite while he was out here? He could hardly imagine what it might have been, but he knocked on the door just in case.

"Is everything all right, ladies?"

The door opened and a wide-eyed Harriet Upton was staring back at him. He glanced up to see Mrs. Catt standing in the middle of the suite's living room holding a bottle of whiskey.

*Whiskey?*

Realizing he had seen it, Mrs. Catt instantly concealed it behind her back and said, "Quick, come in and close the door, Mr. Bates."

He did as instructed. What on earth was going on? Everyone knew Mrs. Catt was an avid prohibitionist. What was she doing with a bottle of whiskey?

"I just found this in my bed, under my pillow," Mrs. Catt said in outrage, holding up the bottle again now that the door was safely closed. "I was settling in for a short nap when I found it."

What better way to discredit Mrs. Catt than to have someone "discover" illegal alcohol in her hotel room? "Someone must have planted it," Gideon said.

"That is what I feared," Mrs. Catt said. She looked a bit pale, and Gideon remembered the rumors about her bad heart.

"And I was just trying to explain to her that nobody planted it," Harriet was saying. "A friendly newspaper woman asked if she could hide it in our suite for safekeeping."

"A *friendly* newspaper woman?" Gideon repeated skeptically.

"That is what I said," Mrs. Catt said. "If anyone knows it's here, the Antis are bound to send a search party to find it. Can you imagine how the Antis would crow if they did? We must get rid of it."

"Oh dear. You're always telling me I'm too trusting, aren't you?" Harriet said in dismay. "But what can we do with it now?"

Gideon almost offered to take it off her hands, but he thought perhaps she would question his motives. Indeed, they would have been questionable. So, he took the high ground. "You can just pour it down the sink, and I'll be glad to carry the bottle away and dispose of it."

"That's a good idea, Mr. Bates," Harriet said.

"No, no," Mrs. Catt said. "The smell might linger and that would be almost as bad as finding the full bottle. They would accuse me of having consumed it!"

Plainly, Mrs. Catt wasn't quite reasonable when it came to liquor. "I would be glad to take it away for you myself," Gideon said, deciding that was the only option left.

"I wouldn't ask that of you, Mr. Bates," Mrs. Catt said. "I need to take care of this myself. I want to take this out to the country somewhere to dispose of it so I can make sure no one can trace it back to me."

"Carrie, that isn't really necessary," Harriet tried, but Mrs. Catt was not interested in seeing reason.

"Mr. Bates, do you have access to a motorcar?" Mrs. Catt asked.

"Several of the men on the committee are local and have them. I can ask one of them to take you."

Mrs. Catt shook her head. "No, the fewer people who know about this, the less likely word will get out. Could you, perhaps, borrow a motorcar without explaining our purpose in using it and drive us yourself?"

Gideon silently thanked Elizabeth for nagging him into finally purchasing a motorcar and learning to drive it. "I'm sure I can. Just give me a few minutes to find one."

He had no trouble locating one of the committee members who owned a motor. Naturally, the fellow offered to drive Mrs. Catt himself, but he gracefully agreed to let Gideon do it when he explained Mrs. Catt wanted someone she knew to take her out for a drive so she could escape the pressure for a while. This didn't really make much sense since Gideon had only known the woman for an hour himself, but his friend didn't question him.

By the time he got back to the suite, Mrs. Catt had smoothed her frizzy gray hair, which had been mussed from her aborted nap, and put on a hat and gloves. She had hidden the whiskey bottle in a small bag, which Gideon carried for her. Harriet had decided to go along, too, so he and the two women made their way downstairs and found where the motorcar was parked.

After a few minutes, they had escaped the heat of the city and were enjoying the cooler air that blew across the farmland.

"I thought I needed a nap to refresh me," Mrs. Catt said, "but all I needed was a drive in the country."

"Do you have any idea where you'd like to go?" Gideon asked her, nearly shouting to be heard over the engine.

She glanced over her shoulder. "A little farther, until we're sure no one is following."

Harriet shook her head as if such a thing were ridiculous, but Gideon could understand. She had spent most of her life being falsely accused of all sorts of things in her fight for suffrage.

The countryside shimmered under the summer sun, but the breeze from the moving car was pleasant. Gideon kept watch for possible hiding places for the whiskey. He was thinking he should have brought a shovel to bury it when Mrs. Catt said, "Pull up there, beside that wall."

Gideon slowed and coasted to a stop beside an old stone wall that had partially fallen down. It was nearly covered by lush vines. Gideon walked around the motorcar to help the ladies out.

"Carrie, I think that's poison ivy," Harriet said in warning.

"I believe you are right, Miss Upton," Gideon said.

But Mrs. Catt was looking for a stick. She finally found one that suited her. "I know it's poison ivy," she said. "I can't think of a better form of protection for the bottle than that."

Gideon fetched the bottle from the motor and waited while Mrs. Catt poked and prodded the stones beneath the vegetation until she found what she was looking for.

"There's a hole here that I think is big enough. Can you put the bottle in here, Mr. Bates?"

Taking great care, Gideon managed to slide the bottle into the opening while Mrs. Catt held the vines back with the stick. When he stepped back, having completed his task, she let the vines fall back into place. If Gideon had entertained any notion of returning to rescue the bottle, he abandoned them then and there. No one would ever find that bottle.

"Well done, Mrs. Catt," he said with genuine admiration.

"Yes, well, now I can go back and finish my nap in peace," she said. "Thank you for your assistance, Mr. Bates."

"My pleasure, ma'am."

ELIZABETH AND BETTY GRAM HAD BEEN OUT ROAMING THE city, trying to locate legislators who might be hiding. They only found a few. When they finally returned to the hotel late that afternoon, they saw Anna and Freddie sitting in a corner of the lobby looking discouraged.

"Where have all the legislators gone?" Freddie asked them when they had sat down.

"Some of the Suffs may have taken them out for a drive in the country or to the picture show," Elizabeth said. "I heard even Edward Stahlman's daughter-in-law was entertaining one at the country club. At least she hasn't betrayed us."

"That must have made him furious," Freddie said in delight.

"I just hope it helps," Betty said. "I've got such a bad feeling about these pledges."

"I do, too," Elizabeth said. "Even the men who promise to vote in favor won't look you in the eye. There's no telling what they'll do when the time comes to actually vote."

"We've heard all kinds of rumors," Anna said. "Some people are saying that they're even paying legislators a finder's fee to bring other legislators to be bribed."

"One fellow claimed he'd been offered a hundred dollars just to leave town so he couldn't vote at all," Freddie reported.

"I heard that, too," Elizabeth said. "If they can get enough of them to leave town, they won't have a quorum, so they won't be able to hold a vote."

The four women sat silent for a long moment, contemplating what that would mean. Then Elizabeth caught sight of a legislator she had spoken with before. He had sworn to her then that he would support the amendment, but they weren't trusting anyone's word any longer. "I'll be right back," she told her companions and went to intercept him.

He wasn't difficult to catch. As she approached him, she could see he had probably spent most of his afternoon in the Jack Daniel's Suite and was none too steady on his feet. "Oh, Miz Bates, I can't talk to you now," he tried.

"Then I'll talk to you," she said cheerfully, pretending not to notice how drunk he was. "I just wanted to thank you again for pledging your vote for ratification. We're depending on you."

He groaned. He actually groaned, and Elizabeth's heart sank. "I wanted to help you, really I did, but I can't now."

"Why not?" she asked, trying not to sound panicked.

"Because . . ." He licked his chapped lips and glanced frantically around, as if looking for rescue. "Because the Antis paid me two hundred dollars to vote against it."

Elizabeth's panic instantly turned to fury. She wanted to punch him, but that was hardly likely to help matters. She needed to do something. Gideon expected her to. Mother Bates expected her to. *She* expected herself to. And she would.

"My goodness, I'm sorry to hear that. You sold out too cheaply. I heard they're giving everyone else five hundred."

His red-rimmed eyes grew wide, and his flushed cheeks grew scarlet. "Five hundred! Why, them crooked sons of . . . Oh, I'm sorry, Miz Bates. Those scoundrels!"

"Yes, they are indeed scoundrels. There is, as they say, no honor among thieves." Elizabeth knew that well.

"Thank you for telling me that, Miz Bates," he said, looking as sincere as a very drunk man could. "I'm gonna vote for you. You can count on it."

# CHAPTER EIGHT

HAD ELIZABETH DISCOVERED THE SECRET FOR CONVINCING legislators to support ratification? After the drunken legislator walked away, she stood there a little stunned, running the possibilities through her mind.

But no, that ploy couldn't be used often. First a man would have to admit he had been bribed and how much he had been paid. They might all be over-indulging in the Jack Daniel's Suite, but few of them would be foolish enough to confess to selling their votes, no matter how drunk they were.

She had, however, learned one important thing: She could lie to influence votes. She actually had no idea how much the Antis were paying men to change their votes, but she had always been a good liar. The Antis certainly didn't hesitate to lie to get votes, so why shouldn't the Suffs?

But what lies should she tell? What would work?

She wandered back over to where her friends were sitting.

"Did you lock him down?" Betty asked, only half seriously.

"Amazingly, I did." Elizabeth explained what had happened.

Freddie and Anna stared back at her, open mouthed at her cleverness.

"But will he remember his pledge when he sobers up?" Anna asked.

"We must have faith," Elizabeth said solemnly.

Betty's expression turned shrewd. "Can we use that on other legislators, too?"

"Only those who are willing to admit they've been bribed," Elizabeth said.

"Which they aren't likely to do," Freddie said.

"I wonder if the Antis keep a record on whom they bribed and how much they paid," Anna said. "If we could find it . . ."

They all knew no one had been able to find any concrete proof of the bribery that had been going on for years.

"The NAWSA has a card file on every politician in the country," Betty said. "We copied their system when Miss Paul formed the Woman's Party, and now we have an even better system than the NAWSA does. We know everything about the Tennessee legislators, their voting records, of course, but also all about their personal lives and any scandals associated with them. We can search through those records to see if there is anything we can use."

"For blackmail?" Elizabeth asked with a worried frown.

"That's what the Antis will claim," Anna said.

Freddie nodded. "They're already throwing that word around."

"Is blackmail any worse than bribery?" Betty asked bitterly.

"It is if you're the ones on the side of right," Elizabeth said. The other three stared at her in surprise. Freddie and Anna knew her background, so naturally they would be surprised to hear her arguing for doing right, but Betty was simply amazed at her logic. "Think about it," Elizabeth continued. "I know the Antis believe they are right, but look at who opposes us: the liquor people, the railroads, the steel and factory men. Why do they oppose us? Because they're afraid that if women get the vote, they'll put an end to their corruption and force them to stop child labor and pay their workers a decent wage. We don't just want the vote. We want to make our world a better place, and that's why they don't want us to vote."

Elizabeth could actually see the change come over her three companions. They straightened in their chairs and their faces took on the glow that the disappointments of the past few days had extinguished.

"We *are* the ones in the right," Anna said. "We need to take the high ground."

"But if it's not working . . ." Freddie reminded them.

"Then we may have to stretch the truth a bit sometimes," Elizabeth said, "like I did just now."

Betty frowned. "I heard that a legislator asked Mrs. Catt's friend, Harriet Upton, to promise him a post office in his district if he supported ratification. She refused, of course, so he pledged his vote to the other side."

"But why couldn't she have agreed?" Elizabeth asked. "In any case, Harriet Upton and even Mrs. Catt don't have the power to build a post office, no matter what they might promise."

"And after we have the vote, we might even be able to give that man his post office," Freddie said with a grin.

"But will Miss Sue agree to let us, uh, *stretch the truth*?" Elizabeth asked Betty, who knew their leader much better.

"Miss Sue has all the signed pledges that we gathered in the past month. She is threatening to publish the list of names so any man who changes his vote will be humiliated," Betty said. "The Antis call that blackmail, but I don't think Miss Sue sees it that way."

"But that's not quite the same as lying," Freddie said. "Revealing the names of the men who pledged is perfectly true."

"But if the Antis consider it blackmail, we're back to the question of whether blackmail is worse than lying," Anna pointed out.

"Then let's let Miss Sue decide," Betty said, rising to her feet. The others followed suit and let her lead the way to Miss Sue's suite.

They found her deep in conversation with Anita Pollitzer and Catherine Flanagan. Elizabeth reminded them of Anna and Freddie's names since they had only met them once.

"Miss Sue, we need some advice," Betty said.

"We all need advice," Anita said impatiently, "but we have more important things to think about just now. Miss Sue has uncovered the conspiracy behind the Antis' shenanigans."

"Conspiracy?" Betty echoed.

"Yes, sit down and we'll explain it," Miss Sue said.

"And see if it makes as much sense to you as it does to us," Catherine said.

When everyone had found a chair, Miss Sue said, "We know that the Louisville and Nashville Railroad has long held the Tennessee legislature in a stranglehold, and we believe that the L&N somehow convinced Seth Walker to change his allegiance from pro-suffrage to anti."

"Probably by offering him a lucrative contract, since he already does legal work for them," Anita added.

"Yes, well, we also know that someone convinced Edward Stahlman, a longtime supporter of suffrage, to work against us, and Stahlman started his career in L&N and worked his way up from cart driver to vice president, so we know where his loyalties probably are."

"He's been working very hard against us since he made that

awful speech at the public meeting, too. They say he's already turned many of our pledged legislators," Catherine said, her anger obvious, "and his newspaper is publishing the most outrageous lies."

"He is now the most effective lobbyist the Antis have," Miss Sue said, her disappointment plain. "All those years of lobbying on behalf of the L&N gave him the experience, and we suspect that he, too, was influenced by them to switch sides."

"But whom did they conspire with?" Anna asked.

"It is a rather complicated theory, but this is what we think is happening. The L&N is owned by the Connecticut-based Atlantic Coast Line holding company. If we are correct, they are financing the Antis here in Tennessee to help Connecticut Senator Frank Brandegee get reelected. He has a powerful position on the Senate Interstate Commerce Committee where he provides many favors for the L&N and other railroads owned by Atlantic Coast Line, and they don't want to lose his support."

"Brandegee is also an avid anti-suffragist," Catherine said. "He and his cohorts, James Wadsworth and George Moses, helped block the Susan B. Anthony Amendment in the Senate for years and all three of them are up for reelection this year."

"Oh, I see," Elizabeth said. "They're afraid if women get the vote, they'll lose the election."

"Of course, they will," Betty said almost gleefully. "Women won't vote for any of them."

"These three men are also Republicans who made sure Warren Harding was nominated for president," Anita added. "We think that explains Harding's horrible letter to Judge Tillman. He's pledged to support suffrage, but he's afraid to be too open and offend his sponsors, so he's waffling."

"This really is complicated," Freddie murmured.

"And you haven't heard it all yet," Miss Sue said gravely. "The governors of Connecticut and Vermont are firmly under the control of the Atlantic Coast Line and don't want to see these senators defeated, either. This is most likely why the governors of both states have refused to call a special legislative session to vote on ratification."

"And why it has come down to Tennessee alone to save it," Elizabeth concluded.

"Exactly. So, what do you think?" Miss Sue asked. "Does our theory make sense?"

Elizabeth and her three friends exchanged a glance and all of them nodded their heads. "Unfortunately, it makes perfect sense." In the way a perfectly executed con made sense, although Elizabeth wasn't sure who was the mark in this case. Usually, the mark got cheated out of his money, but the legislators were the ones receiving the money or political favors or whatever else they were being offered. But it was definitely the businessmen who were in charge of the con, and in the end, they were getting what they wanted, too—the opportunity to make even more money because of the favors the men they controlled could grant.

Then she had a sudden moment of clarity in which she realized that it was the women who were being conned. They weren't being cheated out of money, but they were definitely being cheated. She thought of all the powerful men who had betrayed them already and how many others there must have been down through all the years they had been fighting for equality.

Life, she knew, was often unfair, but usually it was random and unexpected, so there wasn't much she could do about it. This, however, was organized and predictable, and if she could figure it out, maybe she could do something about it. That was, she realized, why Miss Sue and the others were in this very room.

The other women had been talking while she was having her epiphany. They were confirming Miss Sue's opinion that her theory was correct. Miss Sue was going to telephone Miss Paul in Washington City and tell her what they had discovered. Elizabeth couldn't see that it would make much difference in the way the Tennessee congressmen voted this week, but even if they could sway just one or two, it might be enough.

"Before you telephone Miss Paul," Betty was saying, "Elizabeth had an interesting experience down in the lobby just now that made us wonder about a different way of approaching the legislators."

"Did she?" Miss Sue asked with interest. "And what is this different way?"

Elizabeth could have groaned. She was no longer sure her idea was a good one, because not only did they have to be clever, but they also had to be careful. If anything went wrong or they were found to be doing anything unethical, it could cost them the vote. Well, she would at least run it by Miss Sue, whose judgement wouldn't be colored by years spent as a grifter. Miss Sue could fairly rule on the issue.

GIDEON WAS PACING THE THIRD-FLOOR HALLWAY AGAIN the next morning, and mercifully, things seemed to be relatively quiet, probably because it was Sunday and a lot of people had gone to church. He'd heard about the ministers who had been escorted up to the Antis' so-called museum on the second floor yesterday to see the *Woman's Bible* and to hear all the Anti propaganda. After that visit, more than two dozen of them had signed a letter condemning the bible and Woman Suffrage. The Antis were practically crowing.

Tom Riddick had called a meeting in his room, so Gideon was doing double duty, guarding both Mrs. Catt's door and Riddick's as well. Joe Hanover was also in attendance at Riddick's meeting. Riddick was still the chair of the Amendments Committee, but he was deferring to Joe Hanover as floor leader because Joe had so much experience at this, and Riddick had none.

They were, Gideon understood, trying to figure out a strategy to get the amendment released from committee with a recommendation for passage so they could finally hold a vote before more legislators changed their minds. The question was whether they should hold the vote sooner or later—which schedule would give them the best chance of passing it?

Unfortunately, no one knew the answer to that question.

Gideon had chased off some Anti spies earlier, and things had been quiet since then, but suddenly a man came off the elevator in a great hurry and rushed to Tom Riddick's door.

Gideon managed to intercept him. "You can't go in there."

"But I have to see Tom. I got a telegram. My wife is sick and—"

"Who are you?" Gideon asked, sensing the man's panic was real.

He gave his name and identified himself as a Tennessee congressman. "I promised Tom I'd vote for ratification, but now my wife is very sick, maybe dying, and I have to go to her."

Gideon nodded his understanding. This was a crisis only Joe and Tom could solve. Gideon gave the coded knock they had decided upon so they would know he was the one seeking admittance.

Tom Riddick opened the door and Gideon started to explain, but the man was too upset to stand on formalities and he pushed his way into the suite so he could make his case. Tom thanked Gideon and closed the door.

Gideon had just resumed his vigil when another man came off the elevator in a similar state of panic. "I have to see Tom," he said. "I just got a telegram. My son was seriously injured in a motorcar accident. I have to go to him at once."

Gideon got a bad feeling about this coincidence, although tragedies did happen. Accidents did happen. People got ill every day and doctors often couldn't do anything for them. These men were genuinely upset, so they weren't lying to get out of doing their duty, but how odd that two of them had received bad news at the same time.

Tom Riddick had just answered Gideon's knock when a third man came off the elevator and hurried down to where the second man was explaining his plight.

"Tom," the third man cried, "my house is on fire. I just got a telegram and—"

"Come in, all of you," Riddick said in exasperation.

Joe Hanover had been trying to calm the first man, and he looked up in surprise at the two new arrivals. The three other men in the room for the meeting had all stepped back as if unwilling to get involved in the crisis.

"An injured child," Riddick said to Joe, "and a house on fire."

"What's going on?" the second man asked, completely bewildered.

"An unlikely series of tragedies," Gideon said.

"But you don't understand," the first man said. "My wife is dying."

"Was your wife ill when you left for Nashville?" Gideon asked.

The man frowned his disapproval of Gideon's interference. "No, she wasn't."

"Would your son have been riding in a motorcar for any reason?" he asked the second man.

He shook his head.

"My house definitely wasn't on fire when I left for Nashville," the third man said impatiently. "Tom and Joe, I have to go. I know I promised to vote for ratification, but you can't expect me to—"

Gideon turned to Joe Hanover. "The Antis. They're trying to break quorum or at least send enough Suff votes home that it won't pass."

"My thought exactly," Joe said. "Listen, fellows, I know you're upset. You've gotten terrible news but give me a minute. Last night, I started getting telephone calls in my hotel room from women with very soft voices. They told me they had important information that would help us pass the amendment and would I come to room such-and-such and they would tell me."

"And if you'd gone to that room," Gideon said, "you would have been greeted by a scantily clad young woman and a photographer, and the photo would have appeared in Edward Stahlman's newspaper this morning."

Joe Hanover nodded resignedly. "Yes, that is what I thought would happen, and now our pledged representatives are being summoned home by telegraphed reports of illness and tragedy. Can I ask you fellows to do one thing before you hop on the next train for home?"

The three men exchanged glances and, somewhat reluctantly, they all nodded.

"Telephone home to make sure your telegrams are really from your families. If they are, you can go with our blessing, right, Tom?"

"Of course, but I think you're going to hear only good news. Use my telephone. I'll pay the charges."

The men took turns using the telephone. The long-distance connections took a while, but each man learned to his relief that their telegram had been a hoax.


To elizabeth's relief, Miss Sue had seen nothing wrong with promising political favors to legislators who supported ratification when Elizabeth had shared her story with her last night. Politicians did that every day, and no one would be surprised if the favors never materialized.

The women had pulled out the list of delegates and Catherine Flanagan consulted her card file as they pored over the list, looking for anyone they thought might be leaning their way or at least undecided. Elizabeth wanted to help but found she could hardly keep her eyes open. Miss Sue had sent her off to get some sleep, promising that the rest of them would go through the cards that night and have a list for everyone in the morning.

Now she was back in Miss Sue's suite and ready to work again. Betty, Anita and Catherine were already there. Betty handed her a list.

"Harry Burn," Elizabeth said with disgust, seeing his name near the top. "What was it he said to you, Betty?"

"That he wouldn't do anything to hurt us," Betty said, "but he wouldn't pledge to vote for us, either."

"Who was originally assigned to him?" Miss Sue asked.

"I was," Anita said with a trace of bitterness.

"Has he ever actually said he'd support us?" Miss Sue asked.

"I'm not sure. I never got to speak with him directly when we were traveling the state and looking for all the delegates at home. You see, Burn lives in Niota, which is a tiny little town, less than five hundred people. The train does stop there, but his house is a long way from the depot, and I couldn't afford to hire a car to take me." Everyone nodded their understanding. "Since I couldn't get to him, I asked his party chair to telephone him. I didn't get to speak to Burn myself, but the party chair told me Burn would support us."

"So we thought his vote was secure," Catherine said with a sigh.

"Isn't there any way we can influence him?" Elizabeth asked.

"I don't suppose he has a nice juicy scandal we could promise not to reveal."

"Hardly," Anita said. "He's only twenty-four, the youngest delegate in the House, and he supports his widowed mother and two younger sisters."

Catherine consulted her file card. "He works two jobs, as a Southern Railway agent and at a bank."

"Ah yes, a paragon of virtue," Elizabeth said. "He should be easy prey for the Antis since he probably needs a better paying job to support his family."

"He's also reading the law at night under Herschel Candler," Catherine said.

All the other women groaned.

"Too bad Burn wasn't in the Senate that day to hear Candler's horrible speech," Anita said. "That might have changed his views."

"For all we know, Burn might agree with him. Men tend to be loyal to their mentors," Elizabeth said.

"What else do we know about his family?" Miss Sue asked.

Catherine looked at her cards again. They waited uneasily as she read through all the notes written there. "His mother is a suffragist!" she crowed in triumph.

"Then how can he in good conscience vote against us?" Betty asked of no one in particular.

"Who knows why men do anything?" Miss Sue asked with a small smile. "But perhaps someone should remind Mr. Burn of his mother's views."

"I'll hunt him down and do just that," Anita said.

"How many votes do we really need?" Elizabeth asked.

Miss Sue shook her head. "When I arrived here, I had sixty-two signed pledges in support of ratification."

"But that's wonderful," Freddie said. "We only need fifty, don't we?"

"Yes, but many of those sixty-two have since changed their minds or, should I say, have been encouraged to change their minds. At last count, we have between forty and forty-three firm votes and about a dozen more possible."

"And the Antis are claiming that some of the men we are counting as firm votes have also pledged to the Antis, so we can't really be sure of anything," Catherine said.

"Then all we can do is go over our list again and track down everyone we think might support us and ask them one more time to pledge," Miss Sue said. "We'll have today and all morning tomorrow because the House isn't going to convene until two o'clock."

The women began the arduous task of deciding who on their list might be swayed.

WHEN THEY HAD DIVIDED UP THE LIST, ELIZABETH AND the other women set out to locate their assigned legislators. This took the entire day as they scoured the city, following up rumors and tips provided by Suff legislators. Freddie and Anna had joined them, and Elizabeth had paired up with Betty, but by that evening, none of them had gained a single vote.

As she and Betty entered the Hermitage lobby through the ladies' entrance, Elizabeth noticed that reporters now seemed to outnumber the legislators since most of the lawmakers who were still in town were either hiding out in the Jack Daniel's Suite or had left the hotel completely, which was why they had been out all day.

Elizabeth saw that Josephine Pearson, the leader of the Antis, was holding forth to a group of reporters in one corner and Seth

Walker, the House Speaker, had his own group in another. "Look, they're probably bragging about how they are going to win," Elizabeth said to Betty. "Miss Sue needs to make a statement."

They hurried upstairs and found Miss Sue going over her lists once again. "Did you have any luck?" she asked when they entered.

"No, but all the Antis are downstairs giving statements to the press," Elizabeth said. "You need to go down and assure them that we are going to win the vote tomorrow."

"I can't lie well," Miss Sue said in dismay. "How can I make them believe we are confident we'll win?"

Given more time, Elizabeth could have taught Miss Sue how to lie perfectly well, but they didn't have that time. "Just smile and throw your shoulders back and think about all the women who fought for this for decades."

Miss Sue gave her a sad little grin. "Let me make sure I'm presentable."

When Miss Sue felt she was ready, the three women went down in the elevator.

Elizabeth gave Miss Sue a moment to compose herself and then whispered, "Remember, we are going to win!"

Then Miss Sue stepped out into the lobby so the reporters could see her. As soon as they did, they left Miss Pearson and Walker and surged toward her. To her credit, she didn't flinch, and she did manage a smile of sorts. They were shouting questions at her, and when they finally fell quiet, she told them the outcome was as yet undecided, which made Elizabeth wince, but she bit her tongue and kept smiling and nodding at Miss Sue as she continued. "We have the votes pledged," she said, "and many of these pledges are in writing, and in my possession."

The reporters wanted names, but Miss Sue declined to give them. She answered other questions as best she could, growing more confident as she replied. Gideon would have been impressed by how she managed to convey a certainty of victory without actually lying. Miss Sue knew the pledges she had were old and some were already worthless, but she wasn't going to admit that.

When the reporters had finished with Miss Sue, the women went out in search of legislators again. The ones they found were in no condition to decide anything, however. All of them had been imbibing rather freely in the Jack Daniel's Suite and some had become belligerent and argumentative. Others apparently forgot they were gentlemen and made inappropriate remarks to some of the ladies. Finally, Miss Sue told the women to go to their rooms and get a good night's sleep. The morning would be busy.

Anna and Freddie had already gone upstairs. Betty and Elizabeth headed to the elevators.

"Miss Paul's statement revealing the L&N conspiracy should be in the newspapers tomorrow," Betty said.

"I just hope it will scare off these men who are bribing the representatives," Elizabeth said.

"Yes. All these mysterious men loitering in the lobby are certainly suspicious. Like that one there." Betty jerked her chin in the direction of a man who had just come into the lobby.

Elizabeth nearly choked. She had half expected it to be the Old Man, but it was even worse. Her brother Jake was scanning the lobby as if looking for someone. What was he doing here? And why had he shown up *now*? His gaze met hers for a moment, but he gave no sign he recognized her. She raised her hand to her face and gave him the signal that told him not to know her because she was working. It was a lie, and he probably knew it, but he'd honor her wishes.

"Oh, he's not one of the men from the railroad or the liquor people," Elizabeth said with confidence.

"How can you know?" Betty challenged.

"His suit, for one thing," Elizabeth said, surprised but relieved by the evidence. "The men working against us for all the industries are well paid and well dressed. This fellow is wearing a ready-made suit that doesn't even fit him, and he needs a haircut."

Indeed, her usually dapper brother was dressed disgracefully in a shabby suit he had obviously borrowed from someone a little shorter than he was, and his hair had apparently been cut by a blind barber.

"Well, he's also not a legislator, so who could he be if he's not working for some sinister outside company?" Betty asked, still not convinced.

"I'd guess he's—and this is just a guess—that he's a revenue agent," Elizabeth improvised. "They aren't paid very well, which would explain the suit, and someone must have reported the Jack Daniel's Suite, so that would explain why he's here."

"Elizabeth, that's very clever," Betty said. "And it also makes perfect sense. Shall we point him in the right direction? I'd love for the revenuers to raid the Antis."

"It would be embarrassing, but since they're giving the liquor away, I don't think they'd get in any trouble. I also don't think Miss Sue would want us to get involved. There are plenty of other people who can show him the way."

"You're right. Let's go up and try to get some rest."

MOTHER BATES WAS ASLEEP WHEN ELIZABETH RETURNED to their suite, and Gideon wasn't back yet. She knew meetings were going on all over the hotel, so Gideon was probably busy keeping spies away. She lay awake for a long time, unable to sleep for worrying about the session tomorrow. Would the House vote or would Seth Walker find a way to delay things again? They were losing supporters every day. They couldn't wait much longer. And when she got tired of worrying about the session, she wondered why Jake was here and what trouble he was going to cause her.

Elizabeth jumped up when she heard the door to the hallway open. She threw her arms around Gideon and kissed him because she knew he'd been on guard duty all day and he deserved a reward. "You are my hero."

"Not much of a hero, but we did figure out the Antis' latest strategy. You won't believe it."

"Before you tell me, have you eaten anything?"

"I grabbed a bite earlier, and the kitchen is closed now anyway."

Elizabeth sat down on the bed, and Gideon told her about the phony telegrams as he undressed and got ready for bed.

"Joe Hanover has been getting a lot of telephone calls in the middle of the night, too," he said. "I think part of the strategy is to make sure he doesn't get much sleep."

"Let me guess, the calls are from women wanting to meet with him," Elizabeth said. That was a con that even had a name, the badger game.

"Yes, but he could just ignore those calls. He also got calls from men threatening him."

"How awful!"

"Yes. He tried to brush it off, but Tom Riddick telephoned the governor, and the governor assigned a policeman to guard Joe until all of this is over."

"Thank heaven. I wonder if other legislators are getting threats as well."

"From what Joe is hearing, they are. The men who refused to take bribes are now getting threats of losing their jobs or having their mortgage foreclosed or their businesses ruined."

"That's awful! Could the Antis really do things like that?"

"Who knows? I'm sure they could at least try. The men behind this are very rich and powerful, and most of the representatives are just ordinary working men or farmers. They only make a pittance for being an elected representative, so they need their jobs."

"And what can the Suffs offer?" Elizabeth asked sadly. "We can't afford to bribe them. We can't even afford to hire a car to find them." She told him about Anita Pollitzer's efforts to visit Harry Burn in his hometown.

"Don't worry, Anita will find him in Nashville," Gideon said. "We're going to win this thing."

"What makes you think so?" Elizabeth asked.

"Because we have to," he replied. "Let's try to get some sleep. Tomorrow will be a busy day."

But Elizabeth had to tell him one more thing before they could sleep. "Jake is in town."

"In Nashville?" Gideon asked in surprise. "What on earth? Oh, he's probably here to help your father."

"I'm not sure. Betty saw him and thought he was one of the men working for the railroads, but he's dressed very poorly, like he's a simple working man. I told Betty he was probably a revenue agent or something."

Gideon laughed at that. "Just don't let him draw you into his game, whatever it is. We have too much to do already."

"Don't worry. I'm saving all my skills for ratification. I just hope I have a chance to use them."

Elizabeth had no idea how long they had been asleep when the telephone rang. The room was still dark, though, so it hadn't been long. Gideon answered the call, not bothering to hide his annoyance at being disturbed.

Elizabeth couldn't tell much from Gideon's end of the

conversation, but he closed by saying, "Give me a few minutes to get dressed and I'll be right there."

"Who was that?" Elizabeth asked when he had hung up.

"Mrs. Catt. She knows she can trust me from the incident with the whiskey bottle. They found a drunken representative staggering down their hallway. He's one of ours, so she needs help getting him safely to his bed."

"Poor Mrs. Catt," Elizabeth said as Gideon began pulling on his clothes. "I'm sure she didn't think she'd have to deal with drunken men again after Prohibition passed."

"I think we'll always have to deal with drunken men."


G IDEON ARRIVED AT MRS. CATT'S SUITE TO FIND A MAN SIT- ting on the floor outside her door. He was slumped over and barely conscious. Mrs. Catt and Miss Upton had been watching for Gideon and they opened the door when he arrived. They were both in their nightclothes.

"We couldn't bring him into our room," Harriet said. "The Antis would have a field day with that if anyone found out."

"I understand completely. Do we know what room he is in?"

"He may have a key. We haven't tried to search him, for obvious reasons," Mrs. Catt said in disgust.

Gideon checked the man's pockets, and he did have a key. "He's on the fifth floor. I'll see if I can get him on his feet."

"He must sober up," Mrs. Catt said. "If they hold the vote tomorrow, we'll need him."

"Yes, you will. I'll do my best."

With great difficulty, he got the man upright, and Gideon pulled one of the man's arms over his shoulder. He protested weakly, but he did manage to stumble along as Gideon half dragged him down the hallway to the elevator. Gideon briefly considered knocking on Tom Riddick's door as they passed to ask for help, but if the man was lucky enough to be getting some sleep, Gideon didn't have the heart to wake him.

The wait for the elevator seemed interminable, but at last the doors opened and there stood Jake Miles looking as surprised as Gideon was.

"What are you doing?" Jake asked, frowning at the drunken man leaning on Gideon.

"I'm taking this fellow to his room, and you're going to help me." Gideon began to haul his companion into the elevator. Jake made no move to help, but the operator jumped up and took some of the man's weight.

"I was just going up to bed," Jake protested.

"Then you don't have anything better to do. Five, please," he added to the operator who nodded. "And this other gentleman will be getting off with us whether he likes it or not."

Jake knew better than to talk in front of the operator, so he didn't say another word until they had gotten out and the doors had closed behind them. "Aren't you going to ask me what *I'm* doing here?" Jake asked, pulling the man's other arm over his shoulder so he could help Gideon get him to his room.

"Elizabeth assumed you were helping your father."

"Oh. Well, yes, that's what I'm doing."

"I don't think he's been having much luck."

"I guess you haven't talked to him lately, then."

Gideon looked sharply at Jake, but he seemed perfectly sincere. "Good. Then he should be making a big donation to the Suffs."

"I have to make roll call," the man they were carrying mumbled when they had reached the door to his room. "Can't miss it."

"You won't miss it," Gideon assured him.

"They said I would," the man moaned. "They said I'd be too hung over to get there."

Now wasn't that interesting? Were the Antis really hoping to ply the pro-ratification legislators with drink so they would miss roll call the next day? Sadly, it was a good plan and another way to break the quorum. "You're in luck, my friend, because the House isn't meeting until afternoon tomorrow. We'll have you sobered up and fit by then."

"What do you mean, *we*?" Jake asked.

"Didn't I tell you that you're helping me? You owe it to Elizabeth."

"I do? Why?" Jake asked with a thunderous frown.

"I don't know, but she'll think of something."

# CHAPTER NINE

THE NEXT MORNING, AFTER ONLY A COUPLE HOURS OF SLEEP, Gideon wanted to go to the dining room for breakfast since he had to share with the other members of the Men's Ratification Committee what he had learned about the Antis' plans for fostering hangovers in the Jack Daniel's Suite. They found the crowded lobby and the dining room littered with copies of a broadside that was being handed out by Anti women sporting their red roses.

Gideon glanced at the one he had picked up and then immediately crushed it into a ball for trash.

"What does it say?" Mother Bates asked Elizabeth, who was actually reading the one she had.

"They're trying to frighten the legislators with the race issue again," she said. "They say, 'Woman Suffrage means a reopening of the entire Black Suffrage question; loss of state rights; and another period of Reconstruction horrors, which will introduce a set of female carpetbaggers as bad as their male prototypes of the sixties.' There's more of the same, but that's the main point."

"They're always trying to fight the War Between the States over again," Gideon said. "You'd think they would want to move forward."

"People hate change," Mother Bates said, "and they also tend to romanticize the past."

"Not all of us do," Elizabeth said.

"No," Mother Bates said, "thank heaven."

"Their timing is excellent, though," Gideon observed. "The legislators who left town for the weekend will all be arriving back this morning, and they'll be greeted with this." He held up the wadded-up broadside he still held.

They were distracted by two men nearby who had suddenly started shouting at each other. Elizabeth recognized one as a ratificationist, but from the way they were arguing, the other one was an Anti. The Anti shoved the other man, who staggered backward a few steps and then charged forward, ready to return the favor.

Gideon managed to step between them before he could. He pushed the men apart and yelled, "Gentlemen, you've forgotten yourselves."

They seemed a bit chagrined at his chastening, but they were both obviously still furious.

"This isn't the place for a physical altercation," Gideon reminded them. He glanced over his shoulder at Elizabeth. "Take Mother into the dining room. I'll find you there."

Elizabeth took her mother-in-law's arm, but they hadn't even reached the door to the dining room when they heard raised voices again. They looked back to find another pair of men ready to come to blows.

"We should have eaten in our room," Mother Bates said.

Elizabeth saw Betty Gram and Anita Pollitzer at a table and hurriedly guided Mother Bates to join them.

"Is Gideon with you?" Betty asked, looking to see if he was following them.

"He's breaking up a fight in the lobby," Elizabeth told them. "He'll be along soon."

"A fight?" Anita echoed in dismay. "I knew things were getting tense, but I can't believe men would actually come to blows."

"Everyone is tired and on edge," Mother Bates said. "The heat isn't helping, either."

"Have you seen this?" Elizabeth asked, laying the single sheet with its harmful message on the table.

"Oh yes. It's a nice welcome for the representatives returning to town this morning," Betty said. "At least the newspapers are reporting on Miss Paul's statement. She told the press all about the conspiracy last night."

"She even confirmed Betty's accusations that Seth Walker had changed his mind on suffrage because the railroad offered him a lucrative contract," Anita said with a grin.

"I just hope he doesn't sue us all for defamation," Betty said, half in jest.

"I'm sure Mr. Walker doesn't want anyone looking too closely at his recent business dealings," Elizabeth said. "Have you heard the latest trick the Antis are trying?"

While they waited for Gideon to finish his peacekeeping mission in the lobby, Elizabeth told them about his encounter with the drunken representative the previous night.

"You have to admit, it could work," Anita said.

"Yes, and they would only need to succeed with a few of our delegates to secure the vote," Elizabeth said.

"We'll have to be extra vigilant today and make sure all of our men make it to the chamber on time," Betty said.

"The Men's Ratification Committee will be doing just that,"

Gideon said, pulling up a chair to join them. "I just saw our chairman in the lobby. He's going to spread the word."

"Does anyone know if they'll be voting today?" Anita asked. "Miss Sue hasn't been able to find out anything."

"That depends on whether the committee has met yet, and I haven't heard any news about that," Gideon said. "The House can't vote on it until the committee votes on whether to recommend it."

"That's not quite true," Betty said. "Miss Sue said they could force it out of committee, but that would take a two-thirds vote."

"And if we had that many votes, we could have passed it by now," Elizabeth said.

Betty sighed. "Exactly."

The waiter had arrived with their food, so they took a few minutes to enjoy it while they considered the battle still ahead.

A few minutes later, they saw Joe Hanover hurrying through the room. Gideon flagged him down as he passed their table. Elizabeth couldn't help noticing how exhausted Joe looked, as if he hadn't slept at all. He probably hadn't.

"Any news?" Gideon asked, eyeing the strapping policeman with Joe.

Joe nodded to the ladies whom he had come to know well in the past week and introduced Captain Paul Bush of the Tennessee State Police, whom the governor had appointed as Joe's bodyguard. "Only bad news, I'm afraid. Overnight, some Democratic newspaper publishers visited the governor. They warned him that if he didn't back off his support of the amendment, they would turn on him in the upcoming election and support his Republican opponent."

They all knew what a powerful threat that would be. Governor Roberts had already delayed calling the special session for fear he would lose the primary. Getting reelected was always going to be his first priority.

"Do you think Roberts will fold?" Gideon asked.

"I'll be happy if he just doesn't go to work for the Antis," Joe said.

Sadly, at this point, about all they could wish for was for Roberts not to betray them.

ALTHOUGH ROSE PETALS OF BOTH COLORS COVERED THE Hermitage lobby floor, the mood was anything but romantic as Elizabeth and the other women tried to talk to legislators. It seemed every conversation taking place ended with raised voices and sometimes raised fists. No one dared attack Joe Hanover because of his large bodyguard, but Captain Bush had to break up more than a few random fights between others.

"What is wrong with these men?" Elizabeth asked in disgust after being insulted by a delegate who had no intention of supporting the amendment. "Why are they so angry?"

Mother Bates smiled wisely. She had been resting for a few minutes in a corner of the lobby and Elizabeth had sought her out. "Some of them are probably angry either because they really believe women should have the vote or because they are really afraid something bad will happen if women do get the vote, and they are frustrated that so many others won't see things their way."

"You said only some of them feel that way, though. Don't all of them have to believe either one way or the other?" Elizabeth asked.

"Not really. I'm sure at least some of them don't particularly care if women get the vote or not, and without conscience to guide them, they have to decide not on the basis of what is right or wrong but on what is best for them personally."

"But wouldn't they know what that is and just vote accordingly?"

"Not always, and not in this case at all. Think about it. Both major political parties have officially announced support for the Susan B. Anthony Amendment, but can the Tennessee politicians really trust in their support? You heard Governor Harding's letter to Judge Tillman, and his latest statements are equally as anti-suffrage. So, who knows how the Republicans are really leaning? So far, the other presidential candidate . . ."

"Cox," Elizabeth supplied when Mother Bates couldn't recall his name.

"Yes, Cox. He seems to be holding fast to his party's line, but can we trust him not to change if it suits him? As a result, no one trusts their party's presidential candidate to stand by them."

"I see what you mean," Elizabeth said thoughtfully. "Locally, things aren't much better, either. Governor Roberts isn't as committed as we would like, and his only real priority is getting re-elected."

"If sabotaging the amendment will accomplish that, I believe he will not hesitate," Mother Bates confirmed.

"And all the legislators have most likely been offered bribes of some kind—either money or favors or both—and those who didn't accept are now being threatened, sometimes with their personal safety."

"And every one of them must stand up in the Capitol and cast their ballots so everyone knows which side they took. They are all under a tremendous amount of pressure."

Elizabeth frowned. She didn't want to feel sorry for the legislators, especially the ones who refused to support suffrage, but Mother Bates was right, they *were* under a lot of pressure. Some would even vote against their personal beliefs in order to win favor with their party leaders or to protect themselves or their families from retribution. "Still, they can't really know which is the right side, can they? I don't mean the difference between right and wrong, because it's obvious some of these men don't care a fig for that. I mean the right way to vote to protect themselves and whatever it is they need to protect, because what if the side they support loses anyway? Will they still be rewarded? And will those on the winning side be punished by the losers?"

"I'm certainly not an expert in these matters, dear, but I suspect a lot of the threats are just that and no more."

"I hope you're right," Elizabeth said, although she wouldn't mind seeing a few of the men who had betrayed them suffer a bit for their perfidy.

Before Mother Bates could reply, a tussle broke out between two men nearby. One man shoved the other and the other shoved him back while they each called the other names that newspapers wouldn't print.

"Gentlemen, there are ladies present," Mother Bates informed them in her no-nonsense voice.

Both men turned to look. One frowned sheepishly, but the other just scowled. "You're no ladies. You're suffragettes."

"You take that back," the other man cried and punched him right in the face.

Someone screamed and Elizabeth grabbed Mother Bates by the arm and hauled her up and out of the way as the two men started trading blows in earnest. Fortunately, other men hurried to break up the fight, and Gideon was among them. He escorted his two women a safe distance from the now-parted combatants who were still hurling verbal invectives even if they couldn't strike any blows.

"I think you may have forgotten the other factor in all this unpleasantness, Mother Bates," Elizabeth said, shaking her head. "Alcohol."

"Yes, those two men did smell rather potent," she agreed.

"Are you all right?" Gideon asked. He looked exasperated and more than a little alarmed.

"We're fine," Elizabeth assured him.

"That man was yelling something at you. I hope it wasn't too awful," Gideon said.

"Not really. Your mother made the mistake of reminding them there were ladies present, and he said we weren't ladies, we were suffragettes."

"I was going to tell him that we prefer to be called suffragists, but Elizabeth pulled me away too quickly," Mother Bates said quite calmly. The incident hadn't disturbed her at all.

Gideon just shook his head. "This is no place for you. It's getting too dangerous."

"It's time to head over to the Capitol in any case," Elizabeth said. "We want to be sure to get a seat."

"Yes, now that the Senate has approved ratification, no one will want to observe their session," Mother Bates said. "Everyone will be crowding into the House chambers to see the drama play out there."

"I'll go find Anna and Freddie. They won't want to miss it, either," Elizabeth said.

THE HOUSE GALLERY WAS STILL ALMOST FULL WHEN THEY arrived, and lots of visitors were already prowling the floor in hopes of influencing a legislator or two before the session started. The crowd was about evenly divided between those wearing red roses and those wearing yellow. Tensions were high here, too, but the insults were mostly being whispered and no one re-sorted to physical violence, probably for fear they would be thrown out and miss all the fun.

"So much for the plot to get legislators to miss roll call," Eliz-abeth whispered to Gideon after the meeting had come to order and the roll had been taken. She had brought along pen-cil and paper so she could keep her own tally of the votes. "I counted ninety-five of the ninety-nine representatives in their chairs."

"The Men's Committee has been working really hard to make sure nobody tries to leave town," Gideon said.

"Does this mean they'll vote today?" Freddie asked.

But Seth Walker stepped up to the podium again before any-one could answer her. He announced that the Committee on Constitutional Affairs and Amendments had not yet met to vote on whether or not to recommend ratifying the Susan B. Anthony Amendment. Then he adjourned the session. Everyone heaved a sigh, either of disappointment or relief.

"Quick, ladies, we've got every one of the representatives right here," Elizabeth said, exaggerating only slightly. "Now is our chance to corner the ones we haven't seen yet."

Freddie, Anna and even Mother Bates were quickly on their feet and hurrying down the stairs to meet the representatives as they exited the chamber. Others had had the same thought and the corridor became choked with Suffs and Antis, distinguish-able by the color of rose they wore.

As each man came through the door, he was accosted by a group of women determined to get his pledge to vote either for or against ratification. There were almost a hundred representatives, but there were many hundred women to meet them. Men found themselves cornered by whole conclaves, and as soon as they managed to extricate themselves, they were surrounded by another group.

Elizabeth and her cohorts quickly mastered the art of spotting a legislator just breaking away from another group of women and herding him into their clutches. Mother Bates did most of the talking, since the men were apparently loath to be rude to a matron, but if one *was* rude or tried to get away too quickly, Elizabeth jumped in. The more docile victims heard Anna's spiel, followed by Freddie's urgent pleas.

As the representatives worked their way out of the building, they met even more women on the sidewalks leading to the Hermitage and the side streets leading to other places of refuge for the representatives.

The Antis were shrill and the Suffs were determined. Elizabeth didn't want to think of them as desperate, but she could sense that, too. No one, Suffs and Antis alike, knew exactly which of the representatives was going to support them, so everyone had to speak to every man in hopes of confirming or influencing his vote.

As the legislators gradually made their way down the sidewalk and back to the hotel, small groups began to form as people started to argue. Then, curious spectators spontaneously gathered to watch, the way people did to watch a dog fight or a brawl. They even shouted comments and suggestions to those arguing, which only made the combatants angrier.

"This is a circus," Elizabeth complained as she and her group finally reached the hotel.

"Does that mean we are the clowns?" Anna asked, only half in jest.

"I'm afraid so," Mother Bates said. "But our act isn't over yet. Look how many legislators are still in the lobby. I thought they would have gone to their rooms to hide."

"Then we better get to work," Elizabeth said.

"I'll see if I can find out when the Amendments Committee is meeting," Gideon said. "They'll probably want me and other members of the Men's Committee to stand guard outside."

"Yes, go," Elizabeth said. "Just make sure the Amendments Committee recommends approval."

"I'll do what I can," he promised before disappearing into the crowd.

"Does anyone see Harry Burn?" Elizabeth asked. All the Party leaders had agreed that the son of a suffragist mother should be supporting ratification, but even Anita had not yet been able to get him to pledge.

"Is that . . . ? No," Freddie said with a frown. "That's not him. Everyone keep an eye out for him, though. Come on, Anna. Let's see who will talk to us."

The two women stepped into the fray.

Elizabeth turned to her mother-in-law. "Shall we?"

By now every man in the House of Representatives had been lectured time and again by both Suffs and Antis, but the Suffs couldn't risk missing any chance to win someone over. Mother Bates had the advantage of looking rather matronly and harmless, unlike a lot of the Antis who simply looked angry and assertive. The legislators didn't cringe away when Elizabeth and Mother Bates approached them, at least. Mother Bates always started by asking, "Are you married, young man?" no matter how old the fellow was.

Most of them admitted to being married, so then she asked, "Do you respect your wife?"

Sometimes they were confused. They might not have ever considered that question, but Mother Bates got them to thinking. "Your wife has the most care of your children, doesn't she? Do you trust her to raise them well?"

They had to admit they did.

"Then you must trust her judgement and good sense."

When they admitted to that, she had them and went into her speech about women also being able to decide who should govern them.

If a man was unmarried or had no children or was simply dismissive of his wife's good sense, Mother Bates asked him if his mother was still alive. Few men would accuse their mothers of not having good sense.

If the man was dismissive or insulting, Elizabeth stepped in and shamed him for being rude to a lady. She was good at defending Mother Bates because she loved her so much.

But some of the men could not be shamed. A few genuinely believed that allowing women to vote would mean the end of civilization or something very like it. Never mind that women in many states already had limited suffrage, even in Tennessee, and nothing untoward had happened.

Others pointed out that allowing women to vote would double the number of people of color casting ballots, which would lead to the overthrow of the white race. Since there was no reasoning with these people about equality for all, they didn't waste time trying.

Gradually, the legislators wearied of the arguments and began to slip away. Some, no doubt, went to the Grill Room where women weren't allowed and they wouldn't be harassed. Others probably went to the Jack Daniel's Suite where they would have to listen to the Antis argue, but at least there they would have the comfort of all the alcohol they would need to dull the edges. The rest found refuge in their hotel rooms or in a meeting where legislators were trying to organize for the fight they knew was coming.

Gideon eventually returned. "The Amendments Committee isn't meeting until eight o'clock tonight."

Elizabeth sighed. "A lot can happen between now and then."

"We're keeping a close eye on our people," Gideon assured her before going off to do just that.

Elizabeth was scanning the room, looking for anyone they hadn't spoken with yet when she saw Anne Dallas Dudley. The poor woman looked stricken and had sunk into a chair near the wall. Elizabeth went straight to her.

"What's happened?" she asked, knowing it must be very bad. "Is it Lon McFarland again?" Had he threatened her or done something even more outrageous than cutting his own tie?

Anne smiled sadly at that. "No, McFarland can't bother me. It's the Nashville-Davidson County delegation. Seven men from my home district whom I personally recruited and who were firmly pledged for ratification. Five of the seven of them have gone over to the Antis. They betrayed us."

"Oh, Mrs. Dudley, I'm so sorry," Elizabeth said, her stomach in a knot at the horrible news. *Five votes lost!* They couldn't afford to lose even one. "What does Mrs. Catt say?" Anne Dudley was not just a member but a leader in the NAWSA, so she would know.

"She's naturally upset, but as always, she wasn't surprised. This has happened so many times. I'm starting to wonder if we can trust any of the pledges that we have."

Elizabeth was wondering that, too. She needed to tell Miss Sue this news right away. "Can you tell me who they are? The Party is keeping its own count, too, and they'll want to know."

Anne shared the names. "Tell them I'm sorry. The women, I mean."

"It's not your fault. You did all you could."

"Evidently, I didn't," she replied sadly.

Mother Bates had followed Elizabeth and heard the conversation. "Miss Sue will probably be holding meetings in her room. We should tell her right away."

GIDEON WAS ON HIS WAY TO TOM RIDDICK'S ROOM ON THE third floor when a group of well-dressed men got on the elevator with him. He'd never seen any of them before, and he noticed they had fallen completely silent when they saw he was there to overhear them. They had pushed the button for five, so Gideon stayed on with them and turned the opposite way down the hallway, stopping at a random room door so he could glance back and see where they had gone.

They had also stopped at a room door and knocked. The door opened and after a brief conversation with the occupant, they went inside. Gideon was pretty sure the occupant of that room was one of the leaders of the House Republicans.

He waited a minute or two and then walked silently down to the door they had entered. The transom was open to help circulate the air and make the room bearable in the heat, so Gideon had no trouble hearing the conversation inside. He realized he was behaving like an Anti spy, but his mother would say something like "All's fair in love and war," and Elizabeth would kiss him and tell him he was a hero, so he managed to overcome his natural instinct to do the right thing and listened to every word.

The men inside were introducing themselves. They were the publishers of Democratic newspapers, the same ones who had visited and threatened Governor Roberts overnight. They now had a different offer to make to the Republicans. If the Republicans could organize their representatives to vote against ratification, the Democratic newspapers would support all the Republican candidates, from Harding on down, in the upcoming election.

It was, Gideon had to admit, a tempting offer. Newspapers were just about the only way people could learn about the candidates in an election unless the candidate made a personal appearance in their town. Having a newspaper that normally endorsed Democrats suddenly change parties would be quite a powerful recommendation.

Gideon waited, straining every muscle to hear the response. A long silence fell, and when the representative finally replied, he spoke softly. So softly in fact that Gideon couldn't make out what he was saying, no matter how closely he listened. Was he agreeing? Was he refusing? Or was he negotiating?

From what the publishers were saying back to him, Gideon gathered that the representative had not committed himself. They were urging him to discuss the offer with his cohorts. They were sure he'd find them agreeable to such a generous offer.

Gideon wanted to pound on the door and tell the representative that these men had made a similar visit to the governor, only that time they had threatened to withdraw support from Roberts unless he complied. Gideon realized they could carry out both the threat and the promise at the same time, but they would need Roberts to refuse their offer and be punished by having the Democratic papers support his Republican opponent, while the Republicans would have to agree and be rewarded with full support. If either of them chose the opposite option, the publishers wouldn't be able to keep their promise to someone. Had Roberts already refused? No one was really sure. Would the Republicans accept the offer and instruct their people to oppose ratification?

Gideon realized the publishers were taking their leave. He couldn't be found eavesdropping. He hurried to the stairway door and had just stepped inside when he heard the publishers coming out into the hallway.

He started down the stairs. He had to warn Tom Riddick and Joe Hanover about what was happening.

MOTHER BATES CHOSE TO REMAIN IN THE LOBBY TO SEE IF she could speak with any more legislators while Elizabeth went up to Miss Sue's room to tell her what they had learned from Anne Dudley.

Miss Sue's door was closed and locked, so she had to knock. Miss Sue greeted her somberly, as if she already knew the news.

"You've heard, then?" Elizabeth asked when the door was closed behind her.

"Yes, we've heard," Anita Pollitzer said.

Elizabeth hadn't noticed her sitting slumped in the corner of the sofa, a handkerchief clutched in her hand as if she had been weeping. Elizabeth wanted to weep, too. "I know losing five votes is a blow, but maybe there's time to turn them back. I have their names and—"

"What are you talking about?" Miss Sue asked in alarm. "Which five votes did we lose?"

"You said you knew," Elizabeth said, confused.

"We knew that Jesse Littleton has come to Nashville and he's working for the Antis," Miss Sue said.

Anita groaned as if this news gave her physical pain.

"Who is Littleton?" Elizabeth asked.

"The former mayor of Chattanooga and Governor Roberts's opponent in the primary," Miss Sue said.

"And he swore to me that he was a suffragist," Anita said bitterly. "I can't believe how these men can lie right to your face."

Since Elizabeth had once earned her living as a liar, she made no comment.

"I should have known. He did promise, but something about him, I just didn't trust him completely," Anita continued.

"Another betrayal," Elizabeth murmured.

"What were you saying about us losing five votes?" Miss Sue said. "Has Littleton already done that much damage?"

"I don't know who was responsible, but Anne Dudley was down in the lobby a few minutes ago looking as distraught as Anita is. She told me five of the seven Nashville-Davidson County delegation have switched allegiance."

"Luke Lea was supposed to keep an eye on them," Miss Sue said, naming the publisher of the *Nashville Tennessean*, which was a rival newspaper to Edward Stahlman's *Banner*. Had Lea betrayed them, too? Or had he just gotten careless?

"Well, he obviously didn't keep an eye or anything else on them," Anita said.

"Did you say you have their names, Elizabeth?" Miss Sue asked.

"Yes, if you think it will do any good to try to win them back."

"It can't hurt to try. If we keep working, we may yet win, but if we give up, we are sure to lose."

Elizabeth hadn't thought about it that way, but she was right. Miss Sue wrote down the names Elizabeth reported.

Miss Sue looked at the list and sighed. "These men were the base of our Democratic support. How many others will they convince to switch allegiance?"

"None if we can get them to switch back," Elizabeth said.

Before anyone could reply, someone else knocked on the door.

Miss Sue admitted an agitated Betty Gram. She didn't even bother to greet them.

"Have you heard? Judge Lester has come to Nashville to help the Antis."

Miss Sue frowned. "Isn't he the one who—"

"—who helped defeat ratification in Maryland," Betty finished for her. "Oscar Lester. He's a famous legal scholar or something. He knows all the legal tricks to pull."

"I guess he's just in time to instruct Seth Walker on how to avoid voting on ratification," Elizabeth said.

"Not that he needs any instruction," Anita said.

"We must let Tom Riddick and Joe Hanover know. The Amendments Committee is meeting this evening," Miss Sue said. "That is when they are most likely to pull some shenanigans. If the committee doesn't recommend the amendment, it may not come to a vote at all. Betty, can you find them?"

"I'm sure I can."

She was already heading for the door when someone else knocked. Betty opened the door to Catherine Flanagan. She was carrying a newspaper, making Elizabeth think she had seen something of interest she wanted to share, but she said, "Do you know what Charlotte Rowe has done?"

Miss Sue looked as if she had received a knockout punch. She sat down quickly in the nearest chair. Anita groaned again. Betty sighed. Elizabeth said, "Is she going to sue you for defamation?"

"Not that I know of, but she announced that she would defend any man whom Miss Sue exposed for having violated his pledge. She claims she has an information file like ours, only hers is dirt she has collected on the Suffs. She says she will share it with any man who is subjected to Miss Sue's *blackmail*, so he can use it in retaliation."

"What dirt could she have on us?" Catherine scoffed.

A chill went down Elizabeth's spine. She certainly had secrets she wouldn't want exposed, but she also wasn't a well-known leader of the suffragists. Surely, exposing her wouldn't be a priority. Besides, no one knew about her questionable past. Still, Elizabeth recognized the real danger. "The Suffs lead such virtuous lives, it's unlikely she has any real information, but she doesn't need it. She can simply lie. By the time the truth comes out, it will be too late."

"Which is enough of a threat to keep me from revealing the names of the men who have pledged to support ratification," Miss Sue said wearily.

"But no one needs to know you won't really do it," Elizabeth said.

"That's right! Elizabeth, you are so clever," Betty said with genuine admiration. "The possibility that she *might* do it should keep most of the legislators in line, and as long as she doesn't actually do it, we don't have to worry about Charlotte Rowe seeking revenge with her lies."

"Is that the afternoon paper?" Betty asked, nodding toward the newspaper Catherine still held.

She looked down at it as if she wasn't quite sure. "Yes," she finally said with disgust. "Stahlman's *Banner*. He reported Harding's latest statement."

"Oh dear," Miss Sue said, speaking for all of them, if their expressions were any indication.

"Yes, well, Harding still doesn't seem to realize he is supposed to support ratification." Catherine handed the newspaper to Miss Sue.

Harding's remarks were on the front page.

"What does he say?" Anita asked after Miss Sue looked up from perusing the article.

"He warns that if Tennessee ratifies the amendment, all the

legal issues surrounding it would throw the results of the November election into question."

"That's exactly what the Antis are claiming!" Betty cried.

"What else can go wrong today?" Anita asked in despair.

"Don't ask that," Elizabeth said. "The Amendments Committee still has to vote this evening."

# CHAPTER TEN

MISS SUE GAVE EACH OF THE WOMEN AN ASSIGNMENT. ELIZabeth was to find Joe Hanover and make sure he knew everything they had just learned. She and Betty stopped at Tom Riddick's room, which was Betty's assignment, and found him meeting with a few legislators, but none of them was Joe Hanover. Betty stayed to pass along the information to Riddick while Elizabeth chose to use the stairs to go up one floor to Joe's room.

She had gone up one flight when she heard the door she had used open and close again. She glanced over the railing and saw a man starting up the stairs. Who was he? Was he following her? She couldn't see his face because the brim of his straw boater shielded it. He started taking the stairs two at a time and Elizabeth realized he was trying to catch up to her.

What did he intend to do? She'd seen too much violence today to take a chance. She lifted her skirt and started running up the stairs. If she could get out of the stairwell, at least someone would hear her scream.

She had just reached the door when the man called, "Lizzie, stop!"

Only two people in the world called her Lizzie. She turned to see her brother bounding up the second set of steps to reach her.

"Are you following me?" she asked with a frown.

"I've been trying to catch you alone."

She couldn't complain. She knew she needed to find out what Jake was doing here so she would know how to behave around him. "We can't talk here. Anybody might come along. Let's go to my suite." She gave him the room number and told him to give her a five-minute head start.

"This is nice," he said when she admitted him to their suite. "I've got a closet on the west side of the hotel. You could fry eggs on my bed in the afternoon."

"I guess that's all a revenue agent can afford," she said.

He registered surprise. "How did you know I'm a revenue agent?"

She registered surprise right back. "I didn't. Is that the tale?"

"Well, I'm undercover. I'm pretending to be the Old Man's chauffeur while I gather information about him."

"That explains your outfit," she said, looking him over with disdain.

"Don't make fun. I think I did a good job of looking down and out."

"So, you're pretending to be a revenue agent who is pretending to be a chauffeur."

Jake smiled his approval. "You always were a clever girl."

Clever enough to be able to figure out how the Old Man was probably going to end the con and get away clean, and how Jake would factor in it. But she didn't care anything about that.

"The Old Man said to thank you for that tip on Lon McFarland," Jake said.

"Oh, good. I'm glad that worked out." She hoped the Old Man had taken that coward for a bundle. "Tell him I'll expect my cut for the Woman's Party. Is there anything else I need to know?"

"Just be sure Gideon and his mother don't know me."

"They understand how all this works."

"I'm not sure Gideon does. He made me help him with a drunk last night."

"He did?" Elizabeth said in delight. "He didn't mention it. That was very nice of you, Jake."

Jake scowled. "He told me you'd return the favor."

Elizabeth knew a lie when she heard one. "I can't imagine he said that."

"Well, you *should* return the favor. Sobering up that drunk took half the night."

"I'm sure it wasn't the first time you were up late, and you were doing a good deed. That will help balance the scales on Judgement Day."

Jake rolled his eyes. It would take more than one good deed to do that, and they both knew it. "The Old Man wants to know if you have any more names for him, and to warn you that he's not having much luck getting his marks to support your amendment, whatever that means."

"Don't tell me you have no idea why we're here," Elizabeth said in disgust.

He grinned mischievously. "Something about women getting the vote, although I could never figure out why they'd want it."

He knew perfectly well why they were here. He was just trying to annoy her, like brothers do. "Why did you really need to meet with me? And don't tell me you're just passing along the Old Man's message."

He looked a little sheepish, but he said, "I wanted to know if you needed me for the con you're running here."

"I'm not running a con," she said in surprise.

He shook his head in mock dismay. "Lizzie, you've got Freddie and Anna here. You've got wicked politicians who need to be taken down a notch. You've got secret operatives with sacks of money to give away. If you aren't running a con, you're crazy."

"I told you, I packed it in. I haven't run a con in over a year," she reminded him.

"Is that really true? I thought maybe you just didn't let me in on the action."

"It's really true. Although . . ."

He perked up at that. "Although?"

Elizabeth sighed. "I keep thinking there should be something I could do to help get the amendment ratified."

"If you do and there's any money in it, let me know. I'll be glad to help."

"You're so generous," she said sarcastically.

"We're family, Lizzie. We have to stick together," he said unctuously.

She didn't bother to respond to that. "If that's all, I have work to do."

"That's all. Don't forget me." He gave her his room number. "But you'll probably find me in the hotel lobby, trolling for marks."

Hopefully, she wouldn't need that information.

TOM RIDDICK HAD ASKED GIDEON AND A FEW OTHER MEMbers of the Men's Ratification Committee to stand guard outside his hotel room while the Amendments Committee met there that evening to vote on whether to recommend the amendment to the entire House for a final vote. After the violence that had been breaking out all day, he didn't want to take any chances.

The committee consisted of eighteen men chosen from both parties and Speaker Seth Walker, who was an ex officio member of all committees. Naturally, he had chosen to attend this meeting in person. The room was stifling, so they had to leave the door open, which allowed Gideon and the other guards to hear everything that was happening.

As the eight o'clock hour approached, Joe Hancock, who was also a member of the committee, came out. "Bates, two committee members aren't here yet. Both are pledged to support ratification, but they may be trying to duck this meeting. Can you fellows round them up?"

"We certainly can," Gideon said, seeing nods from the other guards.

Joe gave them the names of the two missing men, and Gideon sent a guard off to find one while he went to find the other. It wasn't very difficult.

Gideon got his room number from the front desk and the man answered the door when Gideon knocked. He was in his shirt-sleeves.

"It's time for the committee meeting," Gideon said with a friendly smile.

The man pretended to be surprised. "Is it? I must have lost track of the time."

"Better hurry," Gideon said. "Don't want to miss the vote."

"Thanks for letting me know." He started to close the door.

Gideon threw up his hand to keep the door from closing. "I'll walk back with you since I'm helping out there anyway."

The man's face fell. He'd obviously been planning to ignore Gideon's reminder and skip the meeting altogether. "Just let me get my suit coat."

When he was suitably dressed, the two men headed for the elevator.

"Joe Hanover says you're pledged to vote for ratification," Gideon said. "We really appreciate your support. It's going to be a close vote."

"Yes," he said with little enthusiasm. "It's going to be close."

A NICE SOUTHERN GENTLEMAN GAVE MOTHER BATES HIS chair in the lobby, which was rapidly filling up with legislators and lobbyists and Suffs and Antis and mysterious men who wouldn't tell anyone who they really were. Hundreds of people were gathered, spilling out into the corridors and public rooms, anywhere they could find a place to stand. All of them were there to hear the report from the Amendments Committee meeting upstairs.

The buzz of conversation quickly became a roar, making Elizabeth wonder how anyone would be able to get their attention to make the announcement when the time came.

"How long do you think it will take?" Freddie asked. She and Anna were fidgeting with nervous energy.

"Not long if one side wins the vote," Elizabeth said. "If it's a tie, then they'll have to try to convince someone to change his vote. That could take a while."

"Having seen these men in action," Mother Bates said wearily, "it could take all night."

They all laughed at that, as did some of the people standing nearby.

"And if the committee votes to recommend," Anna said, "that means they will probably hold the vote of the full House tomorrow."

"That's right," Elizabeth said. "There would be nothing else to do."

"Except argue for hours," Mother Bates said.

No one contradicted her.

W HEN GIDEON AND HIS CHARGE ARRIVED AT TOM RID-
dick's room, they found the guards doing their best to
hold back a growing crowd. They had heard that the lobby was
full of people who had come to hear the committee's decision,
and apparently, the most enterprising had come straight to the
source. Most of them were reporters.

Gideon was pleased to learn the other missing committee
member had also been delivered, and Riddick called the meeting
to order. Because Gideon and his friends had been pushed back
by the crowd, they were practically in Riddick's doorway and
could hear everything happening.

Riddick told the delegates that since they had certainly already decided how they would vote, there was no reason to debate. He started calling the roll. Gideon kept track of the aye
votes on his fingers. They needed at least ten votes for recommendation.

But they only got nine.

Since Walker didn't have a vote, the vote was tied. What
would happen now? Gideon looked over his shoulder to see how
Riddick and Hanover were taking the news and if they had a plan
for foiling whatever parliamentary maneuver Seth Walker might
have planned.

But Gideon couldn't see Riddick or Hanover from where he
was standing. He could only see Walker, and Walker gave one of
the committee members some kind of sign with his hand. It was
so quick, Gideon wasn't even sure he'd seen it until that man said,
"Mr. Chairman, I would like to change my vote from nay to aye."

If Riddick was surprised, he gave no indication. "That changes the vote to ten to eight in favor of recommending ratifying the amendment. The motion passes."

Gideon noted that he didn't exactly sound jubilant over the success. He didn't have any reason to, either. A tie vote indicated how close the final vote in the House would be, and Walker wouldn't be signaling anyone to change their votes there.

As soon as Riddick adjourned the meeting, Joe Hanover left without making a statement to the press. Walker, however, stepped out looking as pleased as if he had stopped the committee from recommending passage.

"We've got 'em whipped to a frazzle," Walker told the press. "We have ratification beaten, that is all there is to it."

Riddick asked Gideon and his friends to accompany him to the lobby so he could announce the committee's decision. The reporters had scattered as soon as they had the quote from Walker, and the other spectators had gone on ahead to tell their friends.

In the elevator, Gideon told Riddick about Walker's signal to the man who had changed his vote.

"I thought it must be something like that. Walker probably thinks the close vote tonight indicates it will be just as close in the full House, and he's right. He wants the vote to happen as quickly as possible, so no one has a chance to change their minds."

"That could work in our favor, too," Gideon said with more hope than certainty.

"Maybe," Riddick said, "but did you notice Banks Turner voted against recommendation? He's been one of Governor Roberts's closest allies, so that means he may have already changed his allegiance."

"Do you think the governor has, too?" Roberts had every reason to fear retaliation if he continued to support ratification.

"I guess we'll find out tomorrow," Riddick said.

LIZABETH WAS PROUD TO SEE GIDEON BESIDE TOM RIDDICK when he emerged from the elevator, but could they be done already? It wasn't even eight thirty. A buzz went through the crowd as people began to notice he had arrived. She saw Gideon say something to Riddick and they moved to one of the staircases that led to the loggia. Riddick climbed up a few steps so he could be seen.

After a few more minutes, the crowd fell silent, and Riddick announced that the committee had voted to recommend the amendment to the House for ratification. The bill would be presented to the full House tomorrow.

The announcement was met by cheers and whistles from the Suffs and hisses and boos from the Antis.

"Tomorrow is the day," Anna said, smiling radiantly. "After seventy years, and we'll be here to see it." She touched her prison pin reverently.

Elizabeth couldn't share her enthusiasm. She kept hearing Tom Riddick's announcement over in her head. He hadn't sounded triumphant, the way a man who has won a battle sounds. He sounded almost resigned.

"Those men must be exhausted," Mother Bates said as if reading her mind. "Mr. Riddick and Mr. Hanover and the others. They look like they haven't slept in days."

"They haven't," Gideon said. He had left Riddick to the other guards for a few moments. "Are you ladies all right?"

"We are now that we've heard the good news," Freddie said.

But Gideon was watching Elizabeth. "You don't look as happy as I expected."

"Neither do you. Is there something we should know?"

Gideon glanced around. No one was paying any attention.

The crowd was either dispersing or closing into small groups to discuss what had happened. He told them about the close vote and Walker's contrivance.

"But why would he want the committee to recommend it?" Anna asked.

"Probably because he thinks it cannot pass in the full House and he wants the defeat to be public. He could have left the committee deadlocked and let the bill die, but he wants the public to see him defeating it."

"How venal of him," Mother Bates said. "Especially since he was an avid suffragist until just a few days ago."

"He must have been offered quite a lucrative contract by the L&N," Freddie said.

"Shhh," Elizabeth teased. "You don't want to get in trouble like Betty Gram did."

"I wouldn't mind that kind of trouble," Freddie teased back.

"Ladies," Gideon said, "may I suggest you get a good night's sleep tonight? I don't think this lobby will be safe for you this evening once the legislators finish up in the Jack Daniel's Suite, and tomorrow promises to be a busy day."

"Aren't you coming?" Elizabeth asked.

"I'll be along. I just want to make sure I'm not needed for anything."

"And if you are?" Elizabeth asked with a smile.

"Then I won't be along."

ELIZABETH SLEPT SO SOUNDLY THAT SHE NEVER HEARD Gideon come in that night. She decided to let him sleep for a while, since she and the other Suffs were going over to the Capitol at dawn to decorate. She bathed and dressed quietly and left the suite without disturbing either her husband or her mother-in-law.

The other women were just gathering when Elizabeth arrived at Miss Sue's suite. Anna and Freddie were already there. Elizabeth grabbed an armload of yellow satin and followed the others out of the hotel and down the block to the Capitol. The NAWSA had already hung a huge swath of golden cloth between the columns on the building's portico, a very welcoming sight.

Elizabeth and her group went up to the House gallery where other Suffs were already at work. They set about hanging the purple, white and gold banners of the Woman's Party next to the Tennessee suffrage organizations' saffron standards.

Elizabeth was leaning over the railing, securing one of the banners, when the world suddenly started spinning.

"Are you all right?" Anna asked, grabbing her and pulling her back. "You looked like you were going to faint."

Elizabeth sank down into one of the gallery chairs and blinked until everything settled again. "I'm not going to faint," she said, more as a wish than an affirmation, but after a few more seconds, she felt steady again. "I must have gotten dizzy from leaning over."

"Then don't lean over. Did you have any breakfast?"

"No, I was too excited to eat."

"We're all excited," Anna said. "That's no excuse."

"I promise I'll eat something when we go back to the hotel. Oh, look!" Elizabeth exclaimed, standing up to see better.

One intrepid Suff had climbed up and was attaching an enormous yellow sunflower to the eagle sculpture that spread its large wings above the Speaker's chair.

"That will serve to remind Seth Walker of where his loyalties should lie," Anna said.

"Only if it falls on his head," Elizabeth countered.

Ignoring Anna's admonitions to take it easy, Elizabeth got up and helped the other women finish their decorating, although she was careful not to lean over the railing again. When the House chamber looked like a suffrage convention, they started back to the hotel.

"Look at all these people. We'll have to come back soon if we want to get a seat," Elizabeth remarked. Crowds were already starting to gather for the ten-thirty session.

As they reached the hotel, a carload of what looked like female factory workers, all wearing red roses, pulled up.

"Isn't this exciting?" one of them asked Elizabeth and her friends. "Our boss gave us the day off to come."

"Only because he's afraid if you get the vote, you'll want higher wages," Elizabeth said.

"And that's just one of the things we'll get for you once we win this fight," Betty Gram said. "When women get the vote, we'll fight for all of your rights."

But the women didn't seem pleased at all by that possibility. They scurried away in alarm.

A woman wearing a yellow rose was coming down the sidewalk, holding the hand of a girl who appeared to be about ten years old. Seeing that Elizabeth and her friends wore the purple, white and gold of the Woman's Party, she said, "Thank you for coming. I've brought my daughter so she can see this happen."

Elizabeth's heart ached. She hoped the girl and her mother weren't disappointed.

"You need to get something to eat," Anna whispered to Elizabeth, taking her arm to lead her inside.

Catherine Flanagan had already gone into the hotel, but before Anna and Elizabeth reached the door, she came rushing out holding a newspaper and looking furious. This was getting to be a habit. "Look at this," she demanded, handing the newspaper to Miss Sue.

"What is it?" everyone asked, crowding around to see.

Catherine had folded the paper open to a boxed and boldfaced advertisement. Miss Sue read it aloud:

## AN APPEAL TO THE CITIZENS OF NASHVILLE

*Will you, by your presence in the Capitol this morning, help to DEFEAT the Susan B. Anthony Amendment? This is the most important issue that has confronted the South since the Civil War. We appeal to you in the name of Tennessee, in the name of the South to help us maintain a righteous cause. Wear a red or pink rose. Show your loyalty to the people of your own land. In the name of millions of Southern women we appeal to the unquestioned chivalry of the South.*

"That certainly explains all these spectators," Betty said.

"I need to warn my mother-in-law, so she'll leave early enough to get a seat," Elizabeth said.

"We'd like you to join us on the floor today, Elizabeth," Miss Sue said. "We'll be lobbying the legislators right up until the vote is taken, and you are so good at it."

"She'll be honored," Anna said with a grin when Elizabeth couldn't find the words to express her gratitude.

"Thank you" was all she could manage.

"I'm going to make sure she gets some breakfast, but she'll be at the Capitol in plenty of time," Anna promised. She and Freddie each took one of Elizabeth's arms and escorted her into the hotel.

The dining room was chaos, so they went up to Elizabeth's

suite. Gideon and Mother Bates were up and dressed. They ordered breakfast for all of them and shared what they knew and hadn't had an opportunity to discuss until now.

"Miss Sue asked Elizabeth to help her work the floor today," Anna reported when Elizabeth failed to mention it.

Gideon was thrilled and Mother Bates practically glowed with pride. Elizabeth felt an urge to cry, which was a very unusual feeling for her. She decided to distract them and herself.

"You should know that Jake is here," Elizabeth said, "although Gideon already knew this."

He managed to look a little guilty. "I guess he complained to you about me. I needed help with that drunk legislator, and I saw him in the elevator."

"Why hasn't he come by to say hello?" Mother Bates asked.

"He's working," Elizabeth said, putting emphasis on the word "working."

"Oh," Mother Bates said, and that was that.

"He also made sure I knew he was willing to help if I'm running a con here, but of course, I'm not."

Freddie sighed. "I miss those days."

"So do I," Mother Bates said with a grin.

"Stop it!" Elizabeth said. "The Antis are looking for scandals to hurt the Cause. What do you think they would do if they knew about me?"

"Not to mention how it would hurt Elizabeth personally," Gideon said.

"Gideon is right," Anna said. "Even though I miss those days, too."

Elizabeth groaned. "I just wish I could think of a con that would help."

"Yes, I don't think our pretend papa recruited a single mark to the Cause," Anna said.

"Although Jake told me he did take Lon McFarland," Elizabeth said.

"The one who cut his tie while Anne Dudley was straightening it?" Freddie asked in delight.

"And the one who didn't even vote in the Senate," Elizabeth said. "Yes, that one."

Their breakfast arrived and Elizabeth realized she was starving, which was very different from the way she had felt this morning when the thought of food had revolted her.

"If you're working the floor today, maybe you'll finally get Harry Burn to pledge," Mother Bates said.

"I'll certainly try," Elizabeth replied.


G IDEON ESCORTED HIS MOTHER, ANNA AND FREDDIE TO THE Capitol as soon as they were finished eating. It was going to be a long day, and seats would be claimed early. He didn't want his mother to have to stand the whole time. They were fortunate to find places in the rapidly filling gallery where Suffs and Antis alike were already arguing over saving seats.

"Where will you be, dear?" his mother asked.

"I'll be roaming around the hallways, looking for trouble."

"That doesn't sound like you, Gideon," Anna teased.

"Don't worry. I'll be looking to stop it."

"Let's hope you can," his mother said.

Gideon hoped so, too.


E LIZABETH JOINED MISS SUE, BETTY AND ANITA POLLITZER in Miss Sue's suite after breakfast. They had to review their list of legislators one last time before heading out to remind themselves of which men they needed to keep an eye on,

"We need to watch Banks Turner," Miss Sue said. "He is one of Governor Roberts's closest allies and he should be supporting suffrage."

"But someone must have gotten to him with either a promise or a threat since he voted against recommending ratification at the committee meeting," Elizabeth reminded them.

"We'll ask Governor Roberts to speak to him," Miss Sue said. "I expect the governor will be on the floor with us today. The Democrats are putting a lot of pressure on him to make sure the amendment passes."

"And let's not forget Harry Burn," Betty said.

"How can we?" Anita asked. "He's so handsome."

They all laughed at that.

"Yes, he's adorable," Elizabeth said, deciding that as the only married woman in the group, she should be sensible. "And young—"

"He's just my age," Anita mused.

"You're twenty-five," Betty reminded her. "He's only twenty-four."

"Harry Burn should also be voting for suffrage," Elizabeth said sternly. "His own mother is a suffragist."

"I'll be sure to mention that when I see him this morning," Betty said with a sassy smile.

When Miss Sue was satisfied that they all knew their assignments, they headed out to the Capitol. The crowds outside had grown since they had returned from decorating. All sorts of people were heading to the Capitol, and far too many of them were wearing red roses. Elizabeth had been in Nashville for nine days, and she thought by now she knew by sight all the legislators and the Woman's Party volunteers, and the NAWSA volunteers, and even the Antis. But she had never seen any of these people before.

"Is this because of that advertisement in this morning's papers?" Betty asked.

"Partly, I'm sure, but have you noticed our news stories are now on the front page?" Miss Sue said.

"That's true," Anita said. "Before, we've always been relegated to the women's section of the papers."

"But now we're national news," Elizabeth realized. "What they decide today will affect the entire country."

"And we might suffer a humiliating defeat," Miss Sue warned. "A lot of these people are here to see that. No matter what happens, we must retain our dignity."

That sobered all of them. They had reached the Capitol and went up to the second floor where the House and Senate chambers were located. The area behind the brass rail where spectators were allowed to stand was already full and the crowd was spilling out into the hallways.

"What's that?" Elizabeth asked, seeing a very unusual item had been added to the chamber's decor since they had been here decorating earlier.

When Miss Sue had seen it, too, she said, "They did it! The Tennessee Suffs were trying to locate a replica of the Liberty Bell to ring when the amendment passes."

Now Elizabeth could see that it did, indeed, look like the famous bell. It was much smaller than the original, probably half the size, and the crack was merely painted on, but the intent was clear: A victory today would mean liberty for all women.

Miss Sue led them out onto the floor itself where the lobbyists had direct access to the legislators. Elizabeth decided to use her mother-in-law's technique of asking each man she approached if he was married. She didn't call them "young man," since she was younger than any of them. Instead she called them "sir," since

Southern men liked getting respect, especially from Yankee women.

In between each conversation, she would look for Harry Burn. She desperately wanted to speak with him about his mother. This would be her last chance before they convened to vote. But Harry Burn must have realized how important his vote was and that he would be mobbed by lobbying females, Suffs and Antis alike, so he didn't enter the chamber until the very last minute.

To Elizabeth's dismay, he wore a red rose on his lapel.

He was also on the other side of the room from where she was. By then most of the legislators had taken their seats, nearly a hundred of them, and the aisles were clogged with more than twice that many lobbyists eager to win support for whichever side they represented. She tried desperately to make her way to Burn, but no one wanted to let her by.

Fortunately, Betty and Anita had managed to buttonhole him. They were speaking urgently because Seth Walker was pounding his Speaker's gavel to call the session to order. Burn replied, but judging from the women's expressions, he didn't pledge his support.

Speaker Seth Walker looked as if he hadn't slept in days, and he probably hadn't. Elizabeth remembered her father complaining that he couldn't con Walker because he was always in meetings. She didn't feel a bit sorry for Walker, though. He had chosen his side.

Walker finally quieted the crowd, and the clerk began the roll call. Ninety-six of the ninety-nine legislators were present, a far better than average turnout. Plainly, everyone knew how important this was.

As soon as the roll call was complete, several representatives began shouting requests. As far as she could tell, they were all Antis, too. It took a minute for Elizabeth to understand what they wanted, and when she did, she had to bite back a groan.

"House Rule #17 states that the only people who can be on the House floor are representatives and guests of the Speaker," one of the legislators said when he had gained the floor. "We demand that all lobbyists and spectators be removed."

A roar filled the chamber as all the Suffs shouted their protests. That would mean Elizabeth and all the other Suff lobbyists could no longer speak directly to the representatives. Of course, the Antis couldn't, either, but they must be confident they wouldn't need to turn any more delegates or they wouldn't have made this demand.

She glanced over to where the spectators already filled the area behind the brass rail. The galleries were packed, too. Where could they go and still see what was going on?

The man who had made the formal request continued when the protests had died down. "I know Rule #17 is rarely enforced, but this is a special situation. How can the legislators do their work with so many people pestering and distracting us?"

This time the Antis cheered their approval.

Speaker Walker agreed with the suggestion, but Joe Hanover jumped up and protested. "There is no reason to ask America to leave the chamber," he hollered. "The people are entitled to petition their representatives in person; we have nothing to hide."

More cheering and jeering, and Hanover moved to suspend Rule #17.

"Oh no," said the representative sitting beside where Elizabeth stood.

"What's wrong?" she asked. She knew he was pledged to support the amendment.

He was shaking his head. "They can only suspend a House rule with a two-thirds majority vote, and the Suffs don't have that many. Neither side does. But this will be a good test to see how many votes each side really does have."

Elizabeth could see it now. Walker had outmaneuvered the Suffs again. After this test vote, he would know how close he was to defeating ratification and could proceed accordingly.

Someone seconded Hanover's motion, and the clerk started the roll call. Elizabeth had carried a pad and pencils in her bag, so she tallied the votes as they came in. Fifty-one voted to allow the spectators to stay and forty-five voted against. This paper-thin majority was far short of the two-thirds majority they needed to overturn a House rule, so the motion failed. Elizabeth wasn't heartened by the count, either. They needed fifty votes to win ratification, and they couldn't count on all of the representatives who voted not to enforce Rule #17 to support ratification, too. The Antis only needed two of those delegates to change their vote.

Now Seth Walker not only knew exactly how many representatives might be sympathetic to ratification, but he also knew who they were.

# CHAPTER ELEVEN

SETH WALKER INSTRUCTED THE SERGEANT AT ARMS TO CLEAR the floor of everyone who was not a representative. The man couldn't use physical force since most of those being ejected were women, but he also couldn't be courteous because all the women were objecting. Vociferously.

"We have a constitutional right to speak to our representatives," Miss Sue insisted. She was the only one of the four of them who could claim that since she was the only one of them who lived in Tennessee.

Plainly, the sergeant at arms didn't care. He was only following orders. "Move along, Miss. You're holding everything up."

But Miss Sue didn't move along. She kept arguing, as did dozens of others who were refusing to leave. Some other Capitol guards came to help, and slowly, they were able to force the spectators standing behind the brass railing to move out into the corridor so the lobbyists could squeeze into the only place on the floor where they were actually allowed to be.

Elizabeth, Betty and Anita managed to work their way over to Miss Sue. They were all furious.

"This is outrageous," Anita said.

"At least it shows the Antis are a little afraid of us," Elizabeth pointed out. "They are the ones who wanted the lobbying to stop, so they must be worried we're winning over too many of the delegates."

"I didn't think of it that way," Betty said, "but it is a small comfort."

"Very small, since we aren't confident we have enough votes," Miss Sue said.

"I saw you talking to Harry Burn," Elizabeth said to Anita and Betty. "What did he say?"

"The same thing he said to you and me," Betty said in disgust. "He can't pledge but he won't do anything to hurt us."

"He's wearing a red rose, though," Anita said, equally disgusted.

If only his mother were here to speak to him.

"What will happen now?" Anita asked Miss Sue. "Do you think they'll want to remove all of us completely?"

"I think they would cause a riot if they did," Elizabeth said, glancing around at the angry faces glaring at Seth Walker from across the brass railing.

Walker was pounding his gavel again, trying to restore order. He finally succeeded, although no one behind the brass rail was happy. He recognized Tom Riddick, who stood up to give the report from the Amendments Committee.

"Isn't it time for the South to quit being the tail end of creation, the backyard of civilization, remaining backward on the march of progress?" he began. He was using all his courtroom and oratory skills to great effect. He said opposing giving women the vote was "a relic of barbarism."

He went on to quote sources as varied as the Golden Rule and the Declaration of Independence. "If women are human beings, why shouldn't the first sentence of the Declaration of Independence apply alike to them?" he asked, receiving approving applause from the Suffs. He went on to address and dismiss the racial issues and the legal issues that had been repeatedly debunked but were still being used as excuses for opposing Woman Suffrage.

Then he held up a sheaf of papers. "I have here the pledges of sixty-two members of this House to ratify the Nineteenth Amendment, right here in black and white, which the people of Tennessee will have the opportunity to read."

"If only they were all still good," Elizabeth whispered to Miss Sue, who smiled wanly.

The crowd went wild at this threat. The Suffs were cheering, and the Antis were hissing and a lot of legislators were looking worried.

Miss Sue must have given him the pledges, or maybe Mrs. Catt had because the NAWSA had their own collection of pledges. Would Riddick be threatened with blackmail, too, the way Miss Sue had been? Somehow Elizabeth doubted it.

"You speak of your conscience?" Riddick concluded. "What about your conscientious objections to violating your pledge?" The Suffs cheered again. "If those men fail to keep faith, and this resolution is defeated, I shall go from this chamber a dishonored man. Ashamed of being a Tennessean, and doubly ashamed of being a Tennessee Democrat!"

The roar that went up as he sat down continued for a long time. It was just the kind of speech they had needed to get the debate started. But it wasn't the only speech they would hear that day, not by a long shot. Both sides were determined to convince their opponents they were wrong and should switch sides.

The debate raged on, as those for and those against ratification made their arguments. Since the arguments had all been made many times before during the seventy years the Suffs had been fighting for Woman Suffrage, no one was likely to be swayed by them at this late date. Still, they had to be made one last time, just in case someone was wavering. In addition to the racial issue, they covered such things as Southern chivalry, states' rights, and home rule. They also occasionally mentioned topics that had been recently covered in the newspapers, like violating oaths of office, the heresy of the *Woman's Bible* and the mysterious men at the Hermitage Hotel who had been using nefarious means to sway the vote.

Since so many of the spectators had been pushed out into the corridors and couldn't hear the speeches, helpful individuals in the section behind the rail would repeat a clever quip or a sharply worded point in a shout for the benefit of those who didn't catch it the first time. As each speaker won the approval of either the Suffs or the Antis, their supporters cheered and whistled and stamped their feet in response. This was followed by an eerie echo as the legislator was quoted to those in hallway exile and they responded in kind.

An elderly representative stood up. "Women are the best thing God ever made, and I honor women above all humankind. But I would not pollute them by allowing them to wade through the filthy waters of politics."

The Antis clapped, but Anita leaned over to Elizabeth and said, "That's Creed Boyer. He swore he'd be a suffragist 'until the cows come home,' and now he's rallying for the Antis."

Boyer was bragging that he had a wife, nine daughters and eight sons. The sons each had a wife, so Boyer had eighteen women in his family who all, he claimed, trusted their menfolk to represent them.

Elizabeth hissed along with all the other Suffs, but they were drowned out by the Antis' cheers.

Speaker Walker recognized George Canale. Elizabeth remembered he was a fruit merchant from Memphis. "As a Southern man, I could not refuse to allow women to shed their refulgent rays across the path of politics in the South," Canale said. Elizabeth winced at the flowery prose, but at least he was a supporter. "Woman is God's chosen creature, and won't she, if taken into our political life, scatter her purity and fragrance into the muddled waters of our political life, and make it as clear as a crystal?" The Suffs thought this was entirely possible.

Percy Sharpe stood up to speak.

"He's one of the Davidson County representatives who defected," Miss Sue told Elizabeth with undisguised scorn. Elizabeth glanced over to where Anne Dudley stood. She was glaring at this man who had pledged to her personally and then betrayed them.

Sharpe claimed he had spent many a sleepless night worrying about the violence that would undoubtedly follow if Black men and women were given the vote. How could he subject his elderly mother to such danger? "I reached the decision that I would never put this thing upon my people," he said. "I will not force Woman Suffrage upon the states which don't want it."

The arguments went on and on.

"Taxation without representation should no longer apply to the women of the United States," urged a Suff supporter.

"This issue has nothing to do with Woman Suffrage," countered an Anti. "It is a matter of the Constitution and the violation of our oaths."

"I would be ashamed to admit that my wife, my mother or my sisters were not as capable of exercising the ballot as I am."

"The so-called elevation of woman in politics means instead her degradation."

"Tennessee must place the capstone on the temple of justice by becoming the thirty-sixth state."

Elizabeth's stomach growled and a glance at her watch showed it was past time to break for lunch. The representatives would be hungry, too, and then they would get grouchy. How long would they keep this up?

G IDEON AND HIS FRIENDS FROM THE MEN'S COMMITTEE had been asked by Joe Hanover to stand at the doorways to deal with any problems that might arise after Walker had ordered the floor cleared of lobbyists. From his post, Gideon had a clear view of the chamber and had been watching the legislators carefully to see if any appeared distressed or possibly violent. So far, he had only noticed a few who looked worried.

Then, in a pause between speakers, he saw a page delivering a telegram to one of the representatives. The man looked alarmed, as well he might since telegrams delivered unexpectedly rarely brought good news. He opened and read it and all the color drained from his face. Obviously, he had received bad news. He jumped up and hurried over to where Joe Hanover sat. The two men had a brief conversation.

Gideon could easily imagine what had happened. The fellow had received bad news from home and had been summoned home immediately. Was it a real crisis, though, or one manufactured by the Antis? Virtually all of the telegrams had proven false. From the way Joe Hanover was frowning, he was wondering the same thing.

Joe glanced around and saw Gideon. He said something to the man who had received the telegram and the two of them came over to where Gideon was standing.

"Bates, this is Charlie Brooks," Hanover said. "He just got a telegram from his wife's doctor, telling him she is gravely ill and begging him to come home immediately."

"Are you sure your wife is really ill?" Gideon asked. "A lot of men have received phony messages to trick them into leaving."

"I'm sure," Brooks said. "Ida was ill before I left home but not this bad. The telegram is from the doctor, too, and no one here would know his name."

"But we need Charlie for the vote," Hanover reminded both of them. "They're bound to stop making speeches sooner or later and then Walker will have to bring it to the floor."

"But we don't know when that will be," Gideon said, voicing what they were all thinking. "Where do you live?"

"West Tennessee," Brooks said. "It's a long train ride, and I need to go tonight."

"Do you have a schedule?"

Brooks pulled one from his pocket and they all peered at it, trying to find the latest train that would get him home that night. Gideon checked his wristwatch and realized Brooks's options were limited, but if the speeches ended soon and the vote came immediately after, he could make it.

"Just stay for the vote, Charlie. That's all I'm asking," Hanover said. "You saw how narrow the vote was this morning."

"I know how important this is. I'll stay as long as I can," Brooks promised.

"And meanwhile, I can make a telephone call to check on your wife," Gideon offered, thinking it wouldn't hurt to validate the summons.

Brooks gave him the information he would need to place the call.

A WOMAN WEARING A YELLOW ROSE STOOD NEAR ELIZABETH at the rail. She was trying to get the attention of the sergeant at arms. Reluctantly, he came over to her.

"We have sandwiches and sweet tea for the representatives," she told him. "We would be happy to help distribute them, too."

What a wonderful idea! The NAWSA had the funds for this, and thank heaven they had used them. This would mean the representatives didn't have to adjourn for lunch and they also wouldn't be grouchy.

But the sergeant at arms was shaking his head. "I have strict orders. No one is allowed on the floor except the representatives."

The woman was undaunted. She was a Suff, after all. "Then the pages can distribute them," she said with an accommodating smile. "The men can't work if they're starving."

But the sergeant at arms just frowned and shook his head. "I can't allow that. Speaker Walker will have my head." He turned his back and walked away, ignoring the woman's entreaties.

She was as furious as Elizabeth and all the Suffs of both persuasions who had overheard the exchange.

Elizabeth patted the woman's shoulder. "Maybe if they're hungry, they'll give up on making more speeches and get to the vote."

The woman only sighed.

But hunger only seemed to make the speechmakers more verbose. After a while, they also forgot their dignity. The performances got more and more dramatic as each presenter tried to get more laughs or more applause than his predecessor. They seemed to think they were in some kind of variety show.

After two hours of speeches, Seth Walker rose and turned the Speaker's chair over to Austin Overton so he could move to the floor and be recognized. As soon as the Antis saw this, they broke into applause and gave him an ovation that seemed to last forever.

"This should be interesting," Elizabeth said, earning knowing smiles from her cohorts.

Walker looked like a man on the edge. His eyes were bloodshot and swollen from too many sleepless nights and smoke-filled rooms. Elizabeth wouldn't have been surprised if he was incoherent, but he had been preparing for a moment like this for a long time, and he was ready.

"I thank God I can stand here unfettered and unhampered by political influences or by political aspirations," Walker began. "I resent the statements made by Mr. Riddick that the South is the tail end of creation. I am a Southerner from the bottom of my foot to the crown of my head! We want this to remain a white man's country!"

The race issue again. Elizabeth winced, but the Antis loved it and nearly brought the house down with their cheers.

Walker then started in on his arguments. He addressed the General Assembly's oath of office, which asked them to "not vote for anything injurious to my people." He claimed that passing the amendment would wreak havoc in a state like Georgia, so it would certainly be injurious there.

More of the race issue, obviously designed to frighten representatives into submission.

He held several documents, and they soon realized each one represented one of his points, and he read each in turn. The first was Warren Harding's letter to Judge Tillman saying he could not ask Republicans to go against their oath of office. "I don't know whether Harding or Cox will be elected as president," Walker said, "but if Harding should be elected, you will have an honest man."

Or a very foolish one, Elizabeth thought. Endorsing Harding was also strange, since Walker was a Democrat.

Then he read President Wilson's telegram asking Walker to support the amendment. The gallery roared again, but this time it was the Suffs registering their approval.

To Elizabeth's surprise, Anne Dallas Dudley climbed up on

a bench and began chanting Wilson's name. For such a small woman, she certainly had a big voice.

Wilson was beloved in the South as the Southern president, having been born and raised in Virginia. While the Antis in the Democratic party were angry at his recent support of the amendment, people here still revered him, and the cheer Anne had started went on for several long minutes.

The noise drowned out Walker's speech, so he stopped, waiting until he could claim the floor again. Then he countered Anne's cheer by reading his insolent reply to Wilson's entreaty, and once again the gallery roared, only this time it was the Antis.

"I have been insulted right here in this city," he said, obviously aggrieved. "It has been said that the Louisville and Nashville Railroad had something to do with dictating my attitude."

Elizabeth couldn't help glancing at Betty to see her reaction, and hundreds of others must have done the same thing. To her credit, Betty didn't bat an eye.

Meanwhile, Walker brushed aside these claims that he had been influenced.

"You notice he didn't actually deny that L&N had bribed him, though," Elizabeth said.

Miss Sue had to cover her mouth to keep from laughing out loud.

Walker was now attacking Riddick, who had threatened to reveal the names of those who had pledged to support ratification. "I have right now in my pocket the written pledges of more than a majority of members of this house that they will vote to defeat this amendment."

Elizabeth's mouth dropped open and she could hear others gasping in surprise. This was the first time anyone had said anything about *Anti* pledges.

"Do you think he really does have them?" Elizabeth asked Miss Sue.

"After what he's done, I wouldn't trust him to give me the correct time," she replied.

"But before I would show that paper to a living soul," Walker was saying, "and thus keep any one of these men from voting according to his own conscience, or even threaten to publish the list in an effort to coerce them into voting as they may feel they should not, I would suffer this right arm to be cut off," he shouted, holding up his right arm. "Men of Tennessee, be men today! I don't want Democrats or Republicans. I call upon you as men! In good faith and good morals, we cannot ratify!"

Walker's supporters jumped to their feet, giving him an ovation.

"That was what we in Tennessee call a bearcat of a speech," Miss Sue said sadly.

Elizabeth shook her head in dismay. Walker's speech had lasted nearly an hour and almost everyone in the room had fallen under his spell. With the vote already so close, convincing just one man to change his vote could spell disaster. Could he have done that with his oratory?

When Walker sat down, obviously completely spent, Joe Hanover stood up. He had one last chance to undo Walker's damage.

GIDEON HAD MISSED MOST OF WALKER'S SPEECH SINCE HE'D been at the hotel, placing a call to Charlie Brooks's house. Sadly, he had learned that Mrs. Brooks was indeed very ill. The doctor admitted he was afraid she wouldn't recover. Gideon didn't mention that part to Charlie, not wanting to worry him even more, but he was able to confirm the telegram was real, at least.

When Joe Hanover started speaking, Gideon checked his watch. They still had time to get Charlie to the station for his train if Joe didn't talk too long.

"Ours is the great Volunteer State," Hanover began, "and women from the East, West, North and South are looking to us to give them political freedom." Every Suff in the galleries was leaning forward and smiling down on him with pride. "The entire world today has cast its eyes on Tennessee. This is a moral question, and that's why I am here, voting for this amendment."

The Suffs cheered.

Hanover refuted Walker's claims about the racial issue. Then he attacked Walker directly. "There has been so much said about the constitution of Tennessee and oath of office, but certain interests have sent their lobbyists to ask members of this legislature to violate their pledges!" He had to shout over the boos raining down from the Suffs. "And their agents are down at the Hermitage Hotel right now!"

Gideon was booing along with the other Suffs, but he also noticed that several legislators had left their desks and gathered with Seth Walker behind the Speaker's desk, out of sight. He couldn't hear what they were saying, but they were obviously making plans of some sort. Walker probably knew some parliamentary move to try, and Joe Hanover was stirring his supporters the same way Walker had stirred his. Maybe Walker was afraid Hanover would do a better job of it.

Gideon also checked his watch again. Joe better end soon, or he would lose Charlie Brooks.

"Tennessee never does things by halves for women," Hanover was saying, but like Gideon, he could sense his colleagues were growing restless, so he apparently decided to finish quickly. "What we do for them as Southern men we should have the privilege of doing for other women, that ours may be truly a democracy."

The Suffs gave him an ovation equal to Walker's, but before it had even died down, several legislators were on their feet, clamoring to be recognized.

They were, Gideon realized, the same men who had been conferring behind the Speaker's desk. *They did have something planned.*

Gideon thought they must be eager to hold the vote for some reason known only to them, but when the Acting Speaker recognized Seth Walker, Walker said, "I move this House adjourn until tomorrow morning. The delegates need more time to consider such a momentous decision as this."

Joe Hanover and Tom Riddick sprang to their feet to object and the whole place erupted. The Antis were cheering and the Suffs were objecting, but someone seconded his motion, so they had to take a vote.

Charlie Brooks was growing desperate. He had found Joe Hanover again, and from the way he was pointing at his watch, he was anxious to leave so he didn't miss his train. Apparently, Joe convinced him to stay a little longer because Charlie returned to his seat. Joe, however, came straight over to Gideon.

"We've got to do something for Charlie," Joe said. "If we adjourn, and it's likely they have the votes to do that, then the ratification vote won't be until tomorrow. We'll need Charlie here for that, too."

"I'll run down to the station and see if they have any special trains running or—"

"Take Newell Sanders with you. He's a retired U.S. Senator and he knows everyone in town, so he can probably help. Do you know him?"

"Yes." Gideon had met him at his committee meetings. Gideon was standing under one of the galleries so he couldn't see who was sitting there, but he scanned the opposite gallery and didn't see Sanders. "I'll find him."

He hurried out and up the stairs. Luckily, Sanders was in the other gallery, sitting near the back. Sanders was a dignified elderly gentleman who looked more like a minister than a politician, but if he had been a senator, he knew his way around.

Gideon started to explain Charlie's plight but several Anti women sitting nearby told them to hush, so Gideon led Sanders out into the hall and through the spectators crowding in to hear what was going on.

When he had finished telling Sanders Charlie's tale of woe, Sanders said, "I think I know what we can do." The two men hurried out of the Capitol and on to the train station.

T HIS IS AWFUL," MISS SUE SAID.
"They must think they can sway a few more votes by tomorrow," Elizabeth said, thinking the Antis had once again outmaneuvered the Suffs.

"They know they can. Look how many votes we lost when they delayed the vote over the weekend," Miss Sue said. "This gives them even more time to bribe or intimidate the delegates."

"They know from the vote this morning that we only have a one or two vote majority, if that, so they don't have to change many minds overnight," Anita said.

"Maybe they won't vote to adjourn, though," Betty said.

"And if they do, we know what we have to do," Miss Sue said.

"Yes, flirt with our legislators," Anita said, trying to lighten the mood.

But Elizabeth had thought of something else she could do.

Finally! When they believed the final vote would be held today, there wasn't time, but now . . .

The clerk was calling the roll and the votes were coming in. They saw several of their pledged delegates voting to adjourn. It was heartbreaking.

"Do you think they've switched sides?" Betty asked with a worried frown.

"Let's hope they're just tired and hungry," Anita said. "I know I am."

As the aye votes piled up and it became obvious the ratification vote wouldn't be held until at least tomorrow, Elizabeth thought her plan through. "Anita, how far away does Harry Burn live?"

Anita looked up in surprise. She'd been tallying the votes. "He lives in Niota. It's a little town about two hundred miles from here."

That was a long way, but she could probably get there before dark tonight. "You said the train goes there."

"Elizabeth," Anita said gently, as if explaining to a child, "going to Burn's house won't help because he's here in Nashville."

As if she could have forgotten. "I don't want to see him. That hasn't helped. I want to see his mother."


WHEN GIDEON AND SANDERS RETURNED TO THE CAPITOL, Gideon had to fight his way back to the doorway he had been guarding. The crowds had pushed in closer and closer as the speeches went on. He earned a few shoves and some rude remarks, but at last he was in the doorway. He signaled to Joe Hanover that all was well.

He looked around and saw one of his fellow committee men. "What's happening?"

"The Antis moved to adjourn the meeting," he said in disgust. "They're voting now, and it looks like they'll win."

Which meant the real vote wouldn't happen until tomorrow at the earliest. Gideon angered everyone all over again as he shoved his way back out into the corridor where he had left Newell Sanders. He quickly explained the new problem.

Fortunately, Sanders had a solution.

THE ANTIS WERE CHEERING THE FINAL TALLY, WHICH WAS fifty-two to forty-four in favor of adjourning until tomorrow morning at ten thirty. Did that mean the Suffs could now count on only forty-four votes? No one knew.

But Elizabeth's plans were made.

"You can't go all that way by yourself," Betty was arguing.

"I have someone who can drive me."

"That will take hours," Anita protested.

"You told me yourself the train schedule doesn't work timewise, and then it's quite a distance from the station to his house, so I'd need to hire a motorcar anyway."

"How will you find the house, though?" Betty asked.

"Everyone will know where Representative Harry Burn lives," Elizabeth replied.

"And what will you do when you get there?" Miss Sue asked. She didn't look quite as disapproving as the others.

"Hopefully, I'll bring his mother back with me. She'll be outraged when she finds out he is betraying the Cause."

"And what if she isn't outraged? Or what if she just won't come? She might be elderly or infirm, and she might not want to make a trip like that," Anita said.

"Then I'll figure out something else. But I can't just stay here when there's even a chance that I can change Burn's vote."

"Then good luck to you," Miss Sue said, "and Godspeed."

"Thank you. Will you tell Gideon where I've gone?"

They promised to do just that.

Elizabeth smiled her gratitude and started following the crowd that was now filing out of the chamber because Walker had adjourned the session.

Now she had to find Jake.

G IDEON HAD TO FIGHT TO GET BACK INTO THE CHAMBER again, but this time it was because everyone else was coming out. The meeting was over, but at least Gideon had some good news for Joe Hanover.

Charlie Brooks was with Joe when Gideon reached them. Charlie was apologizing for having to miss the vote tomorrow but there was simply no way he could get back in time.

"We chartered a train for Charlie," Gideon said, nearly breathless after his exertions.

"What?" Charlie asked in astonishment.

"I should say Senator Sanders chartered it. It will take you directly to the depot closest to your house and wait for you. If your wife is better, it will bring you back to Nashville overnight, and you can be here in the morning for the vote."

"How much will that cost?" Charlie asked with a worried frown.

It had cost almost five hundred dollars, but Gideon wasn't going to mention that. "Senator Sanders paid for it, so you don't need to worry."

"But I can't let him do that. I—"

"Sanders considers it a donation to the Cause. He's an old man. He's determined to live to see ratification, and he thinks this might be his last chance. Don't cheat him out of it," Gideon said.

"Bates is right," Hanover said, slapping Charlie on the back. "Now let's get you to the station."

---

"WHAT IF THE OLD MAN NEEDS ME?" JAKE SAID AS THEY drove out of the city. Their father had hired a very luxurious motorcar, Elizabeth had been pleased to note. It was a red Rolls-Royce Silver Ghost limousine, one of the most reliable motors made. With the windows down, the breeze almost felt cool, too.

"Then he'll be disappointed," Elizabeth said.

"He's very disappointed in you," Jake said, taking her cue.

"Why should he be?"

"Because you haven't made a dime off of this perfect setup."

Elizabeth sighed. "I'm not interested in making money like that anymore."

"Not even to support your precious Cause?" he challenged.

"Why are you trying to make me angry?" she asked.

"For fun. This is going to be a long drive and I get bored easily."

She punched him playfully in the arm, which made him laugh.

"It's going to be pretty late when we get there," he said. "We can't go very fast on most of these roads. The desk clerk who gave me the map told me some of them are gravel."

Elizabeth was glad to note the motorcar had not one but two spare tires mounted on the running boards, just in case. "How late do you think we'll be?"

"I figure it will take us five or six hours to get there. Might not be there until nine o'clock."

"I hope Mrs. Burn doesn't go to bed early. At least it won't be dark yet."

"And what exactly are you going to do when you get there?"

Elizabeth considered the question for a moment. "I'm going to tell her that her son is voting with the Antis, for one thing."

"Will that make her angry?"

"I'm hoping that it does. Then I'm going to offer to take her back to Nashville with us so she can convince him to change his mind for the vote tomorrow morning."

"That means we'll have to drive most of the night to get back," Jake said, not pleased.

"You often stay up all night," she reminded him. "You probably slept half the day today, didn't you?"

He refused to admit that. "What if the Burn woman doesn't want to go?"

"Then we'll figure something out."

"What do you mean, *we* will figure something out?"

"I thought you'd help. You're very good at that sort of thing."

He frowned at her. "Flattery will get you nowhere."

"It was worth a try. Now stop talking. I'm tired, and I'm going to take a nap."

# CHAPTER TWELVE

"S HE DID WHAT?" GIDEON ASKED WHEN BETTY GRAM TOLD
him what Elizabeth had decided.

Getting Charlie Brooks out of the Capitol had been harder
than expected. As soon as the representatives had left the chamber, they had been accosted by groups of both Suff and Anti lobbyists. These avid advocates cornered the poor men in the hallway
or surrounded them on the sidewalks outside. The lobbyists were
even more determined today than they had been yesterday, and
more desperate, too. Neither side could afford to lose a delegate.

But Gideon and Senator Sanders had gotten Charlie on the
chartered train with his promise to return tomorrow, if at all
possible.

By the time Gideon got back from the station, the legislators
had reached the Hermitage Hotel, and the lobby there was buzzing with those trying to convince them to vote one way or the
other.

Now Gideon had discovered that Elizabeth had gone off on
some wild goose chase.

"Elizabeth hopes to bring Harry Burn's mother back so she can convince him to vote for the amendment," Betty explained.

Anna, Freddie and his mother had seen Gideon come into the lobby and made their way over to where he and Betty were talking.

"What's going on?" his mother asked with a frown, seeing Gideon was upset. *Upset*, of course, wasn't the half of it.

"Elizabeth has decided to visit Harry Burn's mother to see if she'll help change his mind," Gideon said. "Is she taking the train all by herself?" he asked Betty.

"She said she had someone to drive her," Betty said.

"Who would drive her?" Gideon asked of no one in particular.

"Jake," his mother said. "Remember, he's pretending to be a chauffeur, so he probably has a motorcar to use."

"He's *pretending* to be a chauffeur?" Betty echoed, obviously confused.

"She means he recently got the job," Anna said with a smile that Elizabeth had probably taught her to use when she was lying to someone. "He doesn't have any experience as a chauffeur, but he is a good driver."

"Yes, that's what I meant," his mother said, playing along like a professional con artist. How had this happened? "He'll take good care of Elizabeth."

"You know him, then?"

"Oh yes, he's . . ." His mother glanced at Gideon for guidance. He shook his head. "He's a dear friend of the family."

"That's good," Betty decided. "She did seem very confident and not a bit concerned about making the trip. She is determined to get Harry Burn's vote."

His mother reached over and patted Betty on the arm. "If it's at all possible, Elizabeth will do it."

But why did she have to go gallivanting all over the state in the middle of the night?

W E'RE NEVER GOING TO GET THERE IF WE HAVE TO KEEP stopping every five minutes so you can water the weeds," Jake said as Elizabeth climbed back in the motorcar after answering a call of nature.

"I can't help it, and we've only stopped twice."

"How close are we now?" Jake asked, snatching the map out of her hands.

"Not very. I just hope we can get there at a decent hour."

"Don't worry. I know how to drive."

"I hope you know how to drive *fast*."

He handed her back the map and gave her an impish grin. "That's the only way I know to drive."

G IDEON AND THE FEMALES HE LIKED TO THINK OF AS HIS womenfolk gathered—except for Elizabeth—in the assembly room along with all the other Suffs from both camps. Charl Williams, the governor's chosen leader of the Suffs, had called a meeting.

"We are all disappointed that we must wait another day for the ratification vote," Miss Williams said, "but we need to ask ourselves why the Antis have delayed it. We can only assume that they are as concerned as we are about losing pledged votes." This brought a round of applause from the hopeful volunteers. "Don't be alarmed because some of our pledged delegates voted for adjournment today, either. Remember, they were weary and hungry because we weren't allowed to deliver the sandwiches we had brought for them. A hungry man is bound to be unreasonable."

That brought a laugh from everyone.

"Victory is near, ladies and gentlemen," she continued. "We will double our efforts from now until tomorrow morning when we can finally celebrate the ratification of the Susan B. Anthony Amendment!"

More cheers followed.

"I have summoned you here to remind you how great our Cause is and how close we are to true democracy in America, where women will have an equal voice with men." More applause. "We cannot rest until that happens, though. We must take another poll by sundown tonight. Find your assigned delegates. From now until the vote is taken, we must keep a close eye on them. Take them to dinner. Take them for a walk or a drive if you can. You may even take them to a moving picture show. Just don't let them out of your sight because we know the Antis will try to bribe or intimidate them if we do.

"We must also be alert in case some of the delegates try to return home. They may decide that being absent for the vote is preferable to supporting one side or the other. We will need additional volunteers to patrol the hotel hallways for possible deserters, and others to watch the train station, because not all the representatives are staying at the Hermitage and those who aren't might slip away unnoticed."

Miss Williams paused for some boos and hissing at such a prospect. Then she gave everyone instructions for signing up if they weren't already officially assigned to a delegate or two. She gave a few more words of encouragement, repeating her belief that they were going to win the final victory tomorrow, and the meeting ended with hopeful cheering.

"I'll gather up the Men's Committee and we'll guard the station and track down the representatives we know are staying in other hotels or rooming houses," Gideon said to his ladies. "It probably isn't a good idea for females to be wandering around the city in the middle of the night."

"No, it isn't," his mother said, "but if Anna and Freddie go together, I think they can safely patrol the halls here in the hotel."

"I'd like to see someone try to get past us," Freddie said, smiling at Anna.

Anna smiled back. "They'll all be here, safe and sound, in the morning."

"And Mother," Gideon said gently, "I know how much you want to help, but I don't think you should stay up all night."

"Sadly, I couldn't if I tried, but I will stay up as late as I can and talk to the delegates who gather in the lobby. And don't worry about Elizabeth. I think we all know she can take care of herself."

"I hope she can take care of Jake, too," Anna said with a grin.

Gideon winced. "And here I was thinking he'd look after her."

They all laughed at that.

Joe Hanover was walking by and stopped. "Mr. Bates, I want to thank you for your help with Charlie today."

"I was glad we were able to do something for him." He could see the women were curious, but he would explain later. "What are you doing this evening?"

"I will be tracking down all the delegates who might be wavering and speaking with each one personally." He pulled a folded sheet of paper from his pocket. "I have a list."

"Can I be of any help?" Gideon asked.

"I don't think so, and I'm sure you'll be much more valuable to Miss Williams." He took his leave.

"That poor man. He looks worn to a frazzle," his mother said. "I hope he gets something to eat, at least."

"And what's this about you helping him today?" Anna asked. "What did you do?"

As they walked over to get in line to sign up for a task tonight, Gideon quickly told the story, minimizing his own role because all he'd done was recruit Senator Sanders, who had used his influence and his own money to hire the special train.

"How awful for Mr. Brooks," his mother said. "I hope his wife will recover, and not just because we need him here tomorrow to vote."

"If only the telegram had been a fake like the others," Freddie said sadly.

"We need to be on guard in case other telegrams arrive tonight," Gideon reminded them. "Tom Riddick will help you check if anyone gets one and wants to leave."

"We know what to do, Gideon," Anna chided him. "Just make sure none of the delegates get on a train tonight."


L IZZIE, WAKE UP."
     Jake's voice seemed to come to her from far away. She didn't want to wake up, though. She was so tired.

"Lizzie, we're here," he said.

That penetrated her fog. Everything came back to her then. She opened her eyes, expecting to see a farmhouse in the waning daylight, but they were in a small country town.

"Where is *here*?" she asked, rubbing her eyes like a child.

"Niota. We just need to find the Burn house."

All the stores were closed, and the streets were nearly deserted. Elizabeth climbed down from the motorcar and looked around. She couldn't find the Burn house if she didn't have anyone to ask.

But she should have reckoned that other males would be as interested in motorcars as Jake was. She could see several tin lizzies parked on the street, but nothing as fine as the limousine that had brought her to this town. At first it was two young boys who came to see it. They were barefoot and dirty from a long summer's day of play, and their eyes were enormous when they took in the magnificence of the Rolls-Royce.

The boys had a million questions for Jake—no one considered for a moment that a female would know the answers—so she patiently waited while he talked about the motor. After only a few minutes, some more boys and then some grown men materialized from the buildings and houses and soon a small crowd had gathered.

After they had expressed their admiration for Jake's fine piece of machinery, Elizabeth asked for their help in finding Harry Burn's house.

"Harry's not here, Miss," one of the men told her. In a town this small, everyone would know his movements.

"I thought he might be in Nashville," she said. "They're having a big vote there, I know. But I need to see his mother. I'm a distant cousin, you see, and I have some news for her."

Good thing Gideon wasn't here. He didn't approve of lying, but this was an emergency.

The men all started giving her instructions at once, but after a minute or two, they allowed one man to be their spokesman. He gave her and Jake, whom Elizabeth had summoned away from the curious children, directions to the Burn house.

In only a few minutes, they arrived at the modest farmhouse. A woman sat on the front porch, writing something on a tablet in the last rays of sunlight.

At least she wasn't in bed already!

Elizabeth glanced at her watch and saw it wasn't quite eight o'clock. A bit late for a visit but not unthinkable.

Jake misinterpreted her sigh of relief. "We would've been here sooner if we didn't have to stop every hour for you. All you did the whole way was sleep and—"

"Even still, we're here earlier than you thought." Elizabeth gave him a glare and pushed her door open. "Mrs. Burn?" she called to the woman who had laid aside her tablet and stood up to greet her visitors.

"Yes, that's me," Mrs. Burn said uncertainly. She was a handsome woman, probably in her late forties with graying hair that had been carefully waved. Since she hadn't been expecting visitors, she wore a plain housedress. "Do I know you? I can't rightly see you in this light."

"No, ma'am, you don't know me. I'm Elizabeth Bates. Mrs. Gideon Bates," she added more correctly. "We're here because of your son."

"Harry's not here, I'm sorry to say. I hope you didn't come a long way for nothing."

"We know he's in Nashville, Mrs. Burn. We've come to see you."

"Me? What for? Don't tell me something's wrong with Harry," she added in alarm.

"Oh no, he's perfectly fine, but we wanted to tell you what's been happening in Nashville."

"You saw Harry, then?" she asked.

"Yes, and I've spoken with him. He seems like a fine young man." That much was true, at least.

"Well, if you've got news about Harry, you better come in. Have you eaten?"

"Not for a long time," Jake said with his charming grin as he exited the motorcar. Elizabeth gave him a dark look, which he ignored.

"Is this your husband, then, Mrs. Bates?" Mrs. Burn asked with just a hint of disapproval.

"My brother," Elizabeth hastily assured her. "Jake Miles."

Mrs. Burn looked relieved. "That explains it, then." She must have heard Jake complaining about her. "Come up on the porch where it's cool. I'll bring you some lemonade in a minute and then rustle up some dinner for you."

"Don't go to any trouble," Elizabeth said politely.

"That would be very kind," Jake countered, giving her a defiant look.

"No trouble at all," Mrs. Burn said with all the graciousness a proper Southern hostess gives to unexpected guests.

When they had both sat down on the porch swing, and Mrs. Burn had gone inside, Elizabeth whispered, "Aren't you going to complain about how long this is going to take?"

Jake used his charming grin again. "Not if she's going to feed us."

Mrs. catt stepped out of her hotel room and saw Gideon coming down the hallway. She waved, and he hurried to her.

"We just got a telephone call from someone who saw a delegate leaving the hotel with a suitcase, Mr. Bates. Can you go after him? They said he used the ladies' entrance, probably thinking no one was watching it."

"Yes, I'll go. Who was it?"

She gave him the name, and he bounded down the stairs instead of waiting for the elevator. The streetlamps hadn't come on yet, so he had to strain to see in the summer twilight. He went down Sixth Avenue, peering into the gloom to catch a glimpse of a man carrying a suitcase. Gideon hoped he could see the man before he reached Church Street, because he might turn down there or remain on Sixth. Gideon didn't want to miss him.

Then Gideon saw him and quickened his step. He had passed Church Street, so Gideon had him in plain sight. He had to actually run to catch up, but as the man heard his footsteps behind him, he stopped. He didn't turn around. He just stopped.

Gideon noticed the hunched shoulders and his general air of defeat. He came up beside the lawmaker. "Good evening, friend."

The man finally turned to look him in the face. "You want me to go back, I guess."

"I understand you're pledged to vote for ratification. I'm sure you know how badly we need your vote."

"They threatened me," he said. "Said they'd ruin my business, start rumors about me if I voted in favor."

"Who is it who threatened you?"

The man shrugged. "I don't know. Some fellow in an expensive suit with a big cigar."

"Do you think a man like that is going to go to your town and set about to ruin you?"

"That's what he said." The man sounded as tired as he looked. No one had been getting much sleep this week.

"Do you think your neighbors would trust a man like that? Do you think they'd believe his lies about someone they've known all his life?"

He thought about this for a minute. "I don't want to think they would."

"And I definitely don't think they would. In fact, I don't think that man or anyone else is really going to do anything at all to you," Gideon said, using all his persuasive skills. "If the House votes to ratify, they won't waste time on you. They'll be looking for ways to win over the woman's vote. And if they vote not to ratify, nobody will care anymore who voted for it."

"Do you really think so?" the man asked. "My wife will be mighty disappointed if I don't vote."

"She'll be even more disappointed if you don't and we lose by one vote," Gideon said.

"Is it that close?" He seemed pained by the thought.

"We think it is."

The man didn't respond. He just stood there, looking sad.

"Come on," Gideon said. "I'll walk back to the hotel with you." He took the suitcase from the man's unresisting fingers and started back.

The man followed after only a moment. "Do you really think my vote will make the difference?"

"Yes, I do," Gideon said. "Everyone's vote will."

W HILE THEY WAITED, ELIZABETH PICKED UP THE TABLET Mrs. Burn had been writing on when they arrived. She had written on several pages, flipping them over the top as she went, and when she had laid the tablet down, she had flipped them all back into place, so the top sheet was visible. The first words on the page were "Dear Son." Elizabeth had scanned the first page when she heard footsteps.

True to her word, Mrs. Burn returned quickly with some lemonade, for which they were very grateful. Elizabeth managed to put the tablet back before Mrs. Burn saw her examining it.

"Now tell me how you know Harry," Mrs. Burn said when they had expressed their thanks for the drinks.

"I'm here as a volunteer for the Suffs," Elizabeth said before Jake could tell some lie she'd have to explain away. "I've been in Nashville for over a week, talking to legislators and trying to win votes."

"I see, and that's how you met my boy. I can't imagine why you're here at my house when he's out there, but we can talk about that while you eat. I'm afraid I don't have anything fancy, but if you give me a few minutes, I'll have something for you."

Elizabeth thanked her and asked her where the necessary

house was so she could use it while she waited. Jake was right. She really was making a lot of trips.

Mrs. Burn cooked up some omelets for them, using fresh vegetables which were probably from her garden, and she toasted some thick slices of homemade bread. She also fried up some bacon and potatoes, the aroma of which reminded Elizabeth she hadn't had any lunch.

"This is delicious, Mrs. Burn," Jake told her. "I can't tell you how much we appreciate it. Lizzie was in too much of a hurry to see you to stop anywhere to eat."

"Now maybe you can tell me why you came all this way over what I know are some very bad roads to see me," Mrs. Burn said.

She was, Elizabeth could easily see, a strong woman. Elizabeth knew she was a widow with four children and a farm to run, which couldn't have been easy. Mrs. Burn may have been a farmer's wife, but she was also obviously intelligent and at least literate. She had been writing a letter to her son when they arrived, after all.

"You probably know that Harry was called to the special session to vote on ratifying the Susan B. Anthony amendment," Elizabeth said.

"Yes, of course, I knew that. I subscribe to four newspapers and a dozen magazines, so I manage to keep up to date with the news," she said in some amusement.

Elizabeth smiled her approval, and Jake nearly choked on his bacon.

"A dozen magazines?" he marveled. "When do you find time to read them all?"

"In the evenings. We have hired men to do the farm work and my girls help with the house, so I don't have to work all the time. I wish you could have met my girls. They're visiting friends this week."

"I'm sorry to have missed them," Elizabeth said. "I've heard you're a suffragist, too."

"I've been one all my life," she said proudly.

Elizabeth couldn't claim such a long commitment, but she at least had been dedicated for the few years she had been involved. "What about your son?"

"Harry?" Mrs. Burn asked in surprise. "He has always supported suffrage, too. He couldn't understand why I, a college-educated former teacher, could not be trusted to vote while our farmhands, some of whom are illiterate, could."

So, Mrs. Burn was not only intelligent but educated. "I've never understood that, either," Elizabeth said. "But if you've been following the news stories from Nashville, you know that things are not going our way."

"I did read about Mr. Candler's speech. He's been tutoring Harry in the law, you know. Such a fine man, and he's been very good to Harry, which is why I could hardly credit the things he said the other day. Unless the newspapers quoted him incorrectly."

"I'm sorry to say they did not. His speech was horrible, and the things he said about Mrs. Catt were appalling."

"Oh dear," Mrs. Burn said, shaking her head. "I've been hoping to read news of something Harry did, but I haven't seen him mentioned anywhere."

"I know Harry must have a lot of respect for Mr. Candler and be grateful for his help," Elizabeth said, testing the waters.

"He does, of course. He wants to be an attorney and have a career in politics, although I keep warning him that it can be a nasty business."

"Then his respect for Mr. Candler might be what is causing him to waver," Elizabeth said.

"What do you mean? Are you saying Harry is wavering in

his support?" Mrs. Burn asked, obviously troubled by the accusation.

"We aren't sure. Many of the legislators have given us their written pledge to support ratification, but Harry won't even give us a verbal one."

Mrs. Burn considered this for a long moment. Jake helped himself to more bacon. He wasn't letting the discussion spoil his appetite.

"As I said, Harry wants a career in politics, and he's running for reelection in a few months. This is a very conservative district, as you can imagine. It's mostly farmers, and they don't tend to be very progressive in their views."

"I see," Elizabeth said. "You think he might be afraid that his constituents will turn against him if he votes in favor of ratification."

"But then he would get women's votes," his mother said with a small smile, "so he might win the election anyway."

"Only if we actually get the vote," Elizabeth reminded her. "When Speaker Walker turned his support to the Antis, we lost some delegates, and when he delayed the vote over the weekend, we lost even more."

"But do you still have enough to win?" Mrs. Burn asked in alarm.

"We can't be sure, because some of the delegates won't commit."

Mrs. Burn nodded her understanding. "Like Harry."

"Yes. I'm sure you read that the vote was delayed until this morning, but after hours of debate, it was delayed again, until tomorrow morning."

"You don't have much time, then," Mrs. Burn said.

Elizabeth drew a fortifying breath. "No, we don't, which is why I asked Jake to bring me here tonight. No one has been able to get your son to declare himself. I am hoping you will agree to go back with us to Nashville tonight to persuade him to support ratification. His vote could make all the difference."

G IDEON SAW HIS CHARGE BACK TO THE HOTEL AND MADE sure he checked back in. Then he escorted the man up to his room and obtained his word of honor that he would be present for the vote the next morning.

Then Gideon made his way to the lobby again, where he had seen his mother still hard at work waylaying delegates. The place was more crowded than ever with Suffs and Antis and legislators and the mysterious men with no identity. A noxious cloud of cigar smoke hovered over everything.

"No, ma'am, I'm not married, but like I told you three times already, I respect my mother and I'll be voting for ratification if they ever let us do it," the young man his mother was addressing said. "Can I go now?"

"Don't drink too much in the Jack Daniel's Suite," she warned. "They're hoping hangovers will keep you fellows from showing up tomorrow."

He was too well bred to say what he was probably thinking, thank heaven. When he had made his escape, Gideon stepped into his place. "Yes, I respect both my wife and my mother, and I'd vote to ratify if I could," he said with a grin.

She grinned back. She looked tired, but he knew better than to mention it. She would go upstairs when she must. "Have we heard anything from Elizabeth?"

"No, and I didn't expect to. I understand this Harry Burn is from a very small town. They may not even have a telegraph office and it would be closed by now anyway."

"It would be amazing if Elizabeth could get his mother to come to Nashville to speak to him."

"It would be a miracle. No one in their right mind would make that trip, especially at night and especially with Jake driving."

Suddenly, the atmosphere in the enormous lobby changed. A man Gideon recognized as a reporter had barged in holding up a long strip of paper evidently torn from a teletype machine and was waving it as he came. The crowd instinctively sensed something had happened, and the buzz of conversation fell silent as everyone turned to see what he had.

He stopped in the middle of the lobby and began to read from the paper in a voice that easily carried to all corners of the room.

"In a surprise maneuver, the North Carolina Senate has voted to postpone consideration of the ratification of the Nineteenth Amendment until the 1921 legislature. The vote was twenty-five to twenty-three to postpone."

All the Antis in the room broke out in cheers while the Suffs groaned at this defeat.

"We already knew North Carolina wasn't going to pass it," his mother said, "but we thought it would at least pass in the Senate."

"But by delaying it until next year, no one needs to vote on it at all," Gideon said, "which means they don't have to offend either side."

"They can even claim they didn't vote against ratification. They were only giving the legislators more time to consider such an important decision, and months from now, it could easily be forgotten," his mother said. "They could do that here, too. If they delay it until next year . . ." She was close to tears. Gideon put his arm around her and hugged her to his side, but he had no words to offer in comfort.

Goodness gracious," Mrs. Burn said. "I couldn't make a trip like that."

"Our motorcar is very comfortable," Elizabeth said.

"Yes, Lizzie slept the whole way here, so it must be," Jake said, leaning back in his chair and rubbing his stomach with great satisfaction.

Mrs. Burns grinned. "That is a very fancy motor you have, young man."

"It's hired," Elizabeth said before he could claim ownership.

"But it is comfortable, and I'm a very good driver," Jake claimed.

Elizabeth didn't contradict him since she was trying to convince Mrs. Burn to come with them.

"It doesn't matter," Mrs. Burn said. "I think I mentioned that I know the roads you'll have to travel, and you'll have to drive all night if the vote is taking place tomorrow. Even if I did go with you, I'd be no good to you when I arrived because of exhaustion. I also can't just up and leave the farm like that."

"But—"

"I'm sorry, Mrs. Bates. I can't go with you. But you are free to tell Harry you spoke to me and that I am looking forward to reading in the newspapers that he voted to ratify."

Elizabeth tried to think of an argument that would sway her, but she couldn't in good conscience ask her to put her health in danger. If she said she couldn't stand the trip, Elizabeth had to believe her. She was already exhausted herself.

"I guess we should be heading back, then," Jake said after a moment of silence. "Like Mrs. Burn said, we have a long trip."

But Elizabeth wasn't ready to give up yet. She just needed a little more time to think. "Let me help you clean up, at least."

She jumped up to help Mrs. Burn, but she suddenly felt dizzy and had to sit down again.

"Are you all right?" Mrs. Burn asked in alarm.

Elizabeth managed a smile as the room gradually righted itself. She realized she was clutching the table to steady herself. "I just got up too fast."

She got up again, more slowly this time, and started to help Mrs. Burn clear the table. "You don't have to do that," Mrs. Burn protested, but Elizabeth kept helping while she tried desperately to think of something she could do.

Jake slipped away to the necessary house, leaving them alone. As soon as they were, Mrs. Burn said, "Does your brother know about your condition?"

"What condition?" Elizabeth asked, confused.

"Then you don't know, either," Mrs. Burn said with obvious delight.

Elizabeth was a little annoyed now. "What don't I know?"

"I strongly suspect that you are expecting."

"Expecting what?" Elizabeth asked, still confused.

"A baby."

Elizabeth gaped at her. "A baby? Why would you think that?"

"Because I've had four and I know the signs."

A small bud of pleasure had bloomed in her chest, but she couldn't let herself believe this. It was just too much to hope for. "What signs did you see?"

"Your brother mentioned how often he'd had to stop for you to relieve yourself. That's a sign. And he indicated you slept almost the entire trip. That's another sign. Then you got dizzy just now for no reason."

"That's not much evidence," Elizabeth said, still afraid to believe.

Mrs. Burn asked her a few more very personal questions, and

Elizabeth realized she had a lot more symptoms. She hadn't even noticed how long it had been since her last monthly.

"And then there's the glow that expectant mothers have. That was really the first thing I noticed," Mrs. Burn was saying.

"I . . . I don't know what to say," Elizabeth said.

"Then I'll say it. Congratulations."

The little bud of pleasure burst into a shower of joy. Elizabeth couldn't wait to tell Gideon.

# CHAPTER THIRTEEN

GIDEON AND THE OTHER MEN FROM THE RATIFICATION Committee were far from alone as they walked the hallways of the Hermitage Hotel that evening. Female Suffs were also patrolling, as were leaders of both political parties and both sides of the ratification debate, along with the mysterious men who refused to identify themselves. Judging from the light spilling out of the transom windows, hardly anyone was sleeping, either, whether they were walking the halls or attending a meeting.

Gideon checked his watch and wondered if his mother was still downstairs. He should probably check on her. Then he rounded a corner and saw Anna and Freddie. They were leaning against the wall and *laughing*!

Gideon hurried to them. "What's going on?"

They needed a moment to compose themselves and even then, they were still holding their sides.

"Oh Gideon, it was so funny," Anna said.

"Although I suppose we should be insulted or at least offended, but really—" Freddie had to stop and choke back another wave of laughter.

"What happened?" Gideon asked, although he was pretty sure he'd be sorry for asking.

Anna took a breath. "We were walking the halls as we're supposed to do."

"We did see one man trying to sneak out of his room, but when he saw us, he went back inside," Freddie said a little shakily. She was still trying to quell her urge to guffaw.

"Then we saw one of those mysterious men from the lobby," Anna said. "He had apparently knocked on someone's door and the man had answered."

"We couldn't see who it was in the room, though," Freddie added.

"We heard the man outside tell the man inside—"

"Who we are sure was a representative," Freddie said.

Anna went doggedly on. "We heard him tell the representative that if he would vote against ratification, he would fix the representative up with some female companionship."

"That's not exactly what he said, but you get the idea," Freddie said with mock solemnity.

"Yes, I do," Gideon said, remembering the phone calls Joe Hanover had gotten from females trying to lure him into a compromising position. This was even worse.

"Then the representative said something—"

"We couldn't hear what," Freddie interrupted again.

Anna gave her an impatient glance. "—And the man in the hall happened to see us."

"We may have gasped when we heard his offer," Freddie confessed.

"That's when he said . . ." Anna's voice broke as a giggle welled up in her throat.

"That's when he said, 'Look, here are the girls now!' and pointed at us!" Freddie said, breaking into gales of laughter again.

Gideon didn't think it was funny at all, but he was glad they did. "What did you do?"

It took a minute or two for them to be able to speak again. "We were outraged," Anna said, although she was smiling too broadly to be believable. "So, we told both men in no uncertain terms we were suffragists, and we were keeping an eye out to make sure men like this didn't try to coerce the representatives."

"The representative stuck his head out for a second to see us, but we still couldn't see who it was," Freddie said.

"Then he slammed the door in the other man's face," Anna said, still grinning. Plainly, they were both quite pleased with themselves.

"What happened to the man in the hallway?" Gideon asked, hoping he hadn't insulted the women any more.

"We told him we were going to report him, so he better high-tail it out of there," Freddie said.

"So, he did," Anna said. "Although he may have just gone to another floor."

"Can you tell me what room this was? I'll check on the representative at least and make sure he's still in our corner."

"How do you know he was in the first place?" Freddie asked.

"Because they wouldn't bother trying to compromise the men who are against ratification."

"Oh, of course. I should have thought of that," Freddie said. She gave him the room number.

Gideon sent the women on their way, wanting to get them out of sight before he knocked on the representative's door.

The man who answered was furious. "I told you I wasn't inter-ested," he said before he got a good look at Gideon. "Oh, sorry, I thought you were somebody else. You're with the Ratification Committee, aren't you?"

"Yes." Gideon introduced himself. "We're patrolling the halls. Two young ladies told me what just happened."

The man shook his head in dismay. "I hope that scalawag didn't insult them again."

"They sent him packing. I just wanted to make sure you're all right."

He sighed. "Except for not getting any sleep. Seems like somebody is knocking on my door every few minutes. One fellow threatened to kidnap me. Then this fellow offered me a woman. Or women as it turned out. If all the Suff representatives are getting this treatment, we'll be falling asleep in our chairs to-morrow."

"I'll make sure everyone on the Ratification Committee knows what's going on. Thanks for your support and try to get some rest," Gideon said, but he was pretty sure nobody would be getting any rest tonight.

ELIZABETH DRIED THE DISHES AS MRS. BURN WASHED, which left her free to think once the shock of discovering she might very well be pregnant wore off. Then it came to her. Would it work? Mrs. Burn seemed cooperative enough, and if she didn't do what Elizabeth hoped she would, well, she could fix it anyway.

"I couldn't help noticing you were writing a letter when we arrived," Elizabeth said. "Is it by any chance to Harry?"

"Yes, it is. I intended to write him last week, but I was so busy, I didn't get to it. I've got a nice long letter almost ready to mail now, but if they're going to vote tomorrow, he might be home before it arrives in Nashville."

"I'm going back to Nashville tonight," Elizabeth said with a grin, "as you well know. I could take it with me and give it to him personally."

"Would you?" Mrs. Burn asked, greatly pleased. "That would be so kind."

But kindness had nothing to do with it.


THE NIGHT WORE ON. SEVERAL MORE REPRESENTATIVES tried to sneak out, and rescue parties went after them and brought them back. They heard that the men assigned to watch the train station also caught a few absconders.

Shortly after midnight, Mrs. Catt sent word that she'd like the men to knock on the representatives' doors every couple of hours to make sure they were still there. Gideon winced at the order, knowing the delegates wouldn't appreciate having their sleep interrupted, but they really had no choice. The Antis were already doing the same thing, only they were either threatening or bribing the Suff delegates to change their votes.

Gideon knocked on one of his assigned doors. The man who answered was annoyed but resigned. This obviously wasn't the first time he'd been disturbed. "Just tell me what you want so I can go back to sleep."

"I'm checking to make sure you're still here," Gideon said. "Some of the delegates have been threatened with kidnapping."

The man's irritation vanished. "You're one of the Suffs, aren't you?"

Gideon had hardly finished nodding when the man disappeared back into his room, but he left the door open, so Gideon waited.

He returned with a bottle of whiskey. "You can take this and get rid of it. One of the Anti stooges knocked a few minutes ago and gave it to me, but I have no use for it and don't want it in my room. I'm a prohibitionist."

"I'll be happy to dispose of it," Gideon said. He would definitely need a drink or two when this was all over. He took it straight to their suite to leave it there because he shouldn't be knocking on doors holding a bottle of whiskey. People would think he was an Anti. He was pleased to see his mother's door was closed. At least that was one less person he had to worry about.

Where was Elizabeth and when would she be safely back here? Anything might happen to them, driving on unpaved gravel roads at night when there was nothing open and all honest people were home in their beds. At least she wasn't alone, although Jake wasn't Gideon's idea of an adequate bodyguard.

Gideon checked his watch and tried to do the math in his head about when he might expect them. It didn't work because he had no idea how long it would take them to drive to Niota and back. That depended on the state of the roads and whether they encountered any misfortune.

At least Gideon wouldn't be lying awake in his bed all night, imagining all kinds of horrors. He wouldn't be lying in his bed at all, and he'd have plenty to keep him busy. If only he could forget to worry.

THE SUDDEN SHUDDERING OF THE MOTORCAR WOKE ELIZA-beth out of a sound sleep where she had been dreaming she was holding a little baby. She couldn't see its face, but she had been so happy. . . .

"What's going on?" she asked groggily as the motor rolled to a stop beside the road. The night was pitch black and there wasn't a building or another motor in sight.

"We got a puncture," Jake said in disgust.

"But we do have spare tires, don't we?" She remembered noticing them.

"Yes, but now I have to change it. Try to stay awake for a little while, at least. You can let me know if you see any wolves about to attack or anything."

"I don't think they have wolves in Tennessee," she said.

"Are you sure?"

"Well, no."

"Then keep watch."

He left the headlamps burning, since they were the only source of light besides the moon and stars. After sitting in the motor for a few minutes, being jostled by Jake's machinations, she realized she finally had a light source so she could read Mrs. Burn's letter to Harry. She couldn't read it in front of Mrs. Burn, it had been much too dark by the time they left the Burn house to read it in the motor and Jake certainly wasn't going to stop just so she could read a letter.

She carefully climbed out of the motor and walked around to the front of the vehicle. The lights were blinding this close up, but she was able to clearly see the address Mrs. Burn had scrawled on the envelope. Fortunately, she hadn't sealed it since it wouldn't be going through the mail.

Elizabeth pulled the pages—seven of them!—out of the envelope and began to read.

IN THE WEE HOURS OF THE MORNING, GIDEON HAPPENED TO be walking down the third-floor hallway when a meeting in Miss Sue's room broke up. He waited while the men and women filed past him. Some greeted him, since he had come to know many of them during his time in Nashville, but none of them were smiling.

Finally, Betty Gram came out. She stopped when she saw Gideon. "Is Elizabeth back yet?"

"I haven't checked our suite in about an hour, but she wasn't there then."

"I hope she's all right, and I hope she's bringing Mrs. Burn with her," Betty said. "Even still, it might not be enough."

"What is the latest count?" The Suffs always discussed the count in their meetings.

"According to our tally, it's fifty to forty-six *against* ratification," Betty said sadly. "Mrs. Catt's people say the same thing."

No wonder no one was smiling. "But you aren't giving up, are you?"

"Never," Betty said with a wan smile. "Just don't let any of our delegates escape."

ELIZABETH HAD FINISHED HER BATH THAT MORNING AND was drying off when she heard Gideon calling her name.

"I'm in here," she called from the bathroom, quickly wrapping a towel around herself so she could preserve just a bit of modesty when she went out to greet him. He didn't wait for that, though. He came right in.

"Thank God you're back. Are you all right?" The desperation in his voice told her how worried he'd been.

"I'm absolutely fine," she assured him.

"You're more than fine," he said, taking her in from head to foot with great appreciation as she stepped into his arms and gave him a kiss. "And this is a much warmer welcome than I was expecting."

"Don't get any ideas. I have a lot of work to do this morning." She glanced at the window, which was rosy with the dawn light.

"So do I, unfortunately, but at least we should both be able to sleep in our own bed tonight after it's all over."

"You don't look like you got to do that last night."

"Hardly anyone did, but we managed to keep a few legislators from sneaking out of town."

"That should help with the vote," Elizabeth said.

She'd expected a smile, but she didn't get one. "A few hours ago, I heard the count was fifty to forty-six *against*."

"Were they counting Harry Burn for or against?"

"I don't know," he said, but he brightened, as if just remembering what she had been up to. "Did you bring his mother back with you?"

She sighed. "No. She said she couldn't make the trip, but she did write him a letter."

"A letter? When did she mail it?"

Elizabeth smiled her triumph. "She didn't. I hand-carried it back. I'm going to give it to him when he's on the House floor this morning."

"Did she tell him to vote in favor?"

"Of course, she did." Elizabeth had made sure of that. "I just hope . . ."

"What do you hope, my darling girl?" he asked gently.

"I just hope it's enough. His mother told me he's running for reelection, and he's worried he'll lose too many votes if he supports ratification."

"But won't the women vote for him if he does?"

She gave him a sad smile and shook her head. "No one knows how women will vote. Not really. Or even *if* they'll vote. I don't think he can count on that."

"What is it he always says to the Suffs?"

"That he will never hurt us," Elizabeth said with a weary sigh.

"Let's hope he means that. Now, how are you feeling? You must have been awake all night. You should try to get a little sleep before the session. It's scheduled for ten thirty, so that doesn't give you much time."

"I don't need any sleep. Jake complained that I slept all the way there and all the way back, although I didn't sleep *all* the way. I feel well rested and ready to go to work. You, however, need to get at least a little rest before heading over to the Capitol."

"If I go to sleep, I'll never wake up. I'm just going to bathe and shave so I'm presentable. Order us some breakfast and after I eat, I'll get back to work."

G IDEON STAYED IN THEIR SUITE ONLY LONG ENOUGH TO wolf down some breakfast. He left Elizabeth and his mother still eating.

Even though the sun was barely up, crowds were once again flooding up the hill to the Capitol. Families were arriving on streetcars with picnic lunches. Farmers drove their trucks, having left their fields for the day. Factory workers swarmed, having been given another day off.

Gideon hurried past them into the Capitol, which was already filling with spectators. He found Joe Hanover coming out of the governor's office on the first floor.

"Any news?" Gideon asked.

"Cox has telephoned the governor several times already this morning. He says American mothers want the League of Nations so Roberts better make sure they get to vote in the next election."

"I guess he's sure women will vote Democratic."

Joe smiled crookedly. "Nobody is sure of anything."

Banks Turner walked by them. The lanky farmer from West Tennessee refused to make eye contact and entered the governor's office.

"He looks like he's been summoned to the headmaster's office to get his knuckles rapped," Gideon said.

"That's exactly why he's here. He's supposed to be one of Roberts's allies, but he's been voting with the Antis for the past few days. Roberts is going to remind him he needs to support the Party."

"I heard we're three votes short," Gideon said.

Hanover nodded. "Charlie Brooks isn't going to make it back, either, in spite of your efforts. His wife is still no better."

"I'm sorry to hear that, for their sake and ours," Gideon said.

Hanover nodded. "At least he didn't desert us voluntarily. The men who were guarding the station are sure no one left by train overnight. If that's true, we should have everyone back today."

"Too bad none of the Antis left town."

"Because no one is threatening them," Hanover replied sadly.

"What do you want our men to do today?"

"I'm sure our illustrious Speaker will want to clear the floor again today, so we'll need you on the doors. After that, who knows what's going to happen? Just make sure no one gets hurt."

THIS LOOKS LIKE A CARNIVAL," MOTHER BATES SAID AS SHE, Elizabeth, Anna and Freddie made their way through the growing crowds from the Hermitage to the Capitol. The sun was shining brightly now, although the air wasn't yet as steamy as it would be later in the day. They all wore their white dresses with purple and gold sashes, the colors of the Woman's Party.

Elizabeth, Mother Bates and Anna all proudly wore their prison pins.

Crowds of people had claimed spots on the porticoes and porches of the Capitol and down the steps and across the lawns. Colorful quilts and blankets had been spread where babies lay and children played. Elizabeth allowed herself to imagine what her own child would look like for just a moment before reminding herself of the serious work ahead. She would keep her secret until that work was finished.

"It's ironic that the Antis had to advertise in the Suff newspaper to get all these people here," Anna said.

"Yes, but so nice for the *Tennessean* to get their money," Elizabeth said.

"I can't imagine why they want these crowds, though," Mother Bates said.

"Probably to intimidate the Suff legislators into thinking everyone in Tennessee opposes the amendment," Freddie said.

Elizabeth nodded in approval. For a newcomer, Freddie had really begun to grasp the politics of the thing. "You're probably right."

Sadly, the Antis may be right, too.

They walked up to the second floor where Mother Bates took Freddie and Anna on up to the gallery while Elizabeth sought out the Woman's Party leaders. She soon located Betty Gram and Anita Pollitzer, who were standing in the hallway, greeting the legislators as they entered the chamber and using the opportunity to remind them of their pledges. Elizabeth started working her way toward them through the growing crowd, and then she saw Harry Burn.

His mother's letter seemed to grow hot inside her pocket, but she couldn't give it to him out here, not amid the mobs of people. Someone would take note. Harry might even forget he had it by the time he made his way to the floor and been accosted by countless lobbyists from both sides.

He was, she noted with a pang, wearing a red rose.

Betty and Anita had stopped him. Of course, they had. That was their job to try one last time. He seemed to say something back to them, but whatever it was, they weren't pleased. Elizabeth slipped in between two Antis who were crowing about the huge turnout. They called her a bad name, but she paid them no mind.

At last, she reached her friends. They both were also dressed in white with the bicolored sashes. Betty wore her prison pin, and Anita had stuck a yellow rose in her hatband.

"Elizabeth!" Betty cried when she saw her. "You made it! Did you have any trouble?"

"Not a bit." Well, hardly any, and they didn't need the details.

"Is Mrs. Burn with you?" Anita asked, looking around for someone who might be Burn's mother.

"I'm sorry to say she couldn't make the trip, but she did send a letter. I have it with me."

They didn't look as pleased as Elizabeth had expected.

"Do you think that will be enough?" Anita asked. "You know how much pressure all the men are under."

"It will have to be. I saw you talking to Burn just now. What did he say?"

"I said, 'We really trusted you when you said you would never hurt us,'" Anita said. "I'm afraid I was a little angry."

"And he said, 'I mean that,' but you'll notice he was wearing a red rose," Betty added.

"Maybe he's just trying to keep the Antis from harassing him," Elizabeth said, but even her skills at lying couldn't make her sound convincing on that score. "At any rate, I'm going to give him the letter as soon as I get inside."

"Even if it does make him change his mind, that still won't be enough," Betty said sadly.

"Gideon told me about the latest count. Do we have anyone at all who might switch?"

"The governor was calling individual Democratic legislators in for a lecture this morning. Maybe he can bring back some of the ones who have strayed," Anita said.

But their lovely faces revealed they had little hope.

"We also don't know what kind of parliamentary tricks the Speaker might pull," Betty said. "He's so good at that."

SINCE THE SESSION HADN'T STARTED YET, RULE #17 WAS NOT in effect, so Elizabeth made her way through the crowd into the chamber. Harry Burn sat in the third row on the left side. A man wearing a red rose was speaking to him and looking very happy. After a few moments, he slapped Burn on the back and moved on.

Elizabeth took this opportunity to step to Burn's desk.

Burn stood up, as gentlemen did when a lady was standing. "I already told your friends—"

"I know, you don't want to hurt us," Elizabeth said with a smile she knew looked sincere. She had practiced it many times. "I just wanted to tell you that I met your mother yesterday."

"My mother?" He looked around as if expecting to see her. "Is she here in Nashville?"

"No, I was in Niota. I went to visit her."

Burn frowned. He obviously didn't believe her, and why should he? The legislators had heard every kind of outlandish claim anyone could make during the past ten days. "Why would you do that?" he asked skeptically.

"Because I know she is a suffragist herself. She told me you are, too."

His cheeks grew pink, but Elizabeth couldn't tell if it was anger or embarrassment.

"Mr. Burn, she wants you to support ratification."

Burn sighed wearily. "I'm sure you mean well, but—"

"She asked me to bring you this letter," Elizabeth went on, undaunted. She pulled it out of her pocket and held it out to him. "She was afraid you wouldn't get it in time if she mailed it."

He stared at it for a moment before accepting it. He must have recognized his mother's handwriting on the envelope. "I . . . Thank you."

"She would especially like for you to read the message at the end," Elizabeth said. "*Before* you vote," she added.

Burn frowned, but he thanked her again. Elizabeth dearly wanted to stand there and watch his reaction to the letter, but he put it, unopened, into his inside coat pocket. Another man wearing a red rose approached and drew Burn's attention. Elizabeth had no choice but to walk away and find another legislator to encourage.

Would he read the letter? Would it change his vote? Had she made that trip for nothing? Would Harry Burn break his mother's heart?

GIDEON HAD NEVER SEEN SO MANY REPORTERS. THEY WERE everywhere, and they seemed to be interviewing everyone from legislators to janitors, knowing that the stories they filed would be appearing on the front page of every newspaper in the country. The *New York Times* had even sent a female reporter, probably in an attempt to please the Suffs.

Mrs. Catt, of course, was back at the Hermitage. She had decided her presence would be too disruptive, so she had not attended any of the legislative sessions, but she was probably still being hounded by reporters over there. The Tennessee Suffs were speaking for the NAWSA and doing a fine job of it. Miss Sue was surrounded, but as usual, she was perfectly calm and giving the press astutely worded quotes. Gideon then saw Miss Josephine Pearson, the Anti leader, who was also holding forth for her share of the press.

Joe Hanover and Tom Riddick were expressing confidence they didn't have any right to feel, while on the other side, Seth Walker was assuring the reporters that today would mark the death of the Susan B. Anthony Amendment.

Gideon caught sight of Banks Turner, who had returned from his meeting with the governor. Now he looked like a boy who had had his knuckles rapped, pale and grim and thoroughly chastened.

"What's wrong with that fellow?" the man next to him asked, nodding at Turner.

Gideon looked over at his brother-in-law. "What on earth are you doing here?"

Jake grinned. "I figured I'd come to see what all the excitement is about."

Gideon couldn't conceal his surprise. Could Jake be maturing finally?

"So, what is wrong with the man you were staring at?"

Gideon shrugged. "He just got bawled out by the governor because he isn't voting the right way."

Jake snorted. "That would just make me dig in my heels more."

Which was exactly what Gideon feared.

"Where are your ladies?" Jake asked.

"Elizabeth will be working the floor, but Freddie and Anna are up in the gallery with my mother."

"I'll go find them, then."

"You won't get a seat," Gideon warned. "It was already packed when they went up."

But Jake only grinned.

ELIZABETH HAD NOTICED THE FLYERS THAT HAD BEEN placed on every representative's desk. Both sides had used that tactic at different times, distributing literature explaining their arguments to the delegates. She hadn't paid these much attention, and most of the men had cleared them from their desks when they sat down, but as she passed an empty desk, she saw "RACE WAR" in the title and her blood ran cold.

She snatched up the paper and began to read. The warnings were dire.

"Except when hurled into political combat with each other by politicians . . . the two races have always gotten along well in the Southern states," the pamphlet read. Elizabeth winced at such a bold-faced lie. "This amendment will not only hurl women into political competition and battle with men, but it will and must involve political warfare between the races." It went on to claim that white men could better represent both females and Black citizens. "The Federal Amendment brings with it race antagonism as well as sex antagonism and the hazard is too great," it concluded.

"The same thing was in the morning papers," Miss Sue said. She had come up to Elizabeth unnoticed as she read.

"It's disgusting," Elizabeth said, crumpling the paper in her hand.

"But effective, and not just in the South," Miss Sue said. "But there's nothing we can do about it now. I'm so glad to see you safe and sound. Did you find Mrs. Burn?"

Elizabeth told her about her trip and that she had just delivered Mrs. Burn's letter to her son.

"Do you know what the letter says?"

Elizabeth smiled. "Of course, I do. It wasn't sealed."

"I hope you didn't read it without her permission," Miss Sue said with a worried frown.

"Would I do a thing like that?" Elizabeth asked. The answer, naturally, was yes, but Miss Sue would never realize that. "I gave Mr. Burn the letter, so we can only hope that it sways him."

Speaker Walker was pounding his gavel in an attempt to call the session to order. It was ten thirty-five on what promised to be a momentous day, one way or the other.

Just like yesterday, Walker ordered that all visitors be removed from the floor under Rule #17. This time the women resisted even more, and the sergeant at arms had to call in deputies to help. Some of the women even came back in after being ejected once, delaying everything even more. The floor was hardly clear, though, because the Senate had adjourned their session and all of the senators had come over to watch what promised to be a dramatic event and they were not ejected. They also didn't eject the reporters. Seth Walker probably wanted his ultimate victory over suffrage accurately recorded.

Elizabeth and Miss Sue were able to squeeze in just behind the brass railing so they had an excellent view of the proceedings.

Finally, they were able to begin. The roll call showed there were ninety-six of the ninety-nine representatives present, the same number as yesterday. Someone new must have arrived, making up for the absence of Charlie Brooks. Elizabeth hoped he was a Suff.

Walker announced that they would resume the debate on whether or not to ratify the Susan B. Anthony Amendment.

The Suffs cheered Representative Miller, who called for the legislators to break from the grip of the special interests who had corrupted the legislature for the past fifty years. Then they hissed when another Davidson County delegate announced that he had had a change of heart and was defecting to the Antis. Anne Dudley would be distraught. This was the sixth of the seven men she had personally escorted to Nashville. The Antis gave him an ovation.

The speeches began as the temperature rose, inside and out. The legislators, after their sleepless night, grew lethargic in the heat. Elizabeth was having a difficult time keeping her eyes open—reminding her of her condition—but surely, she couldn't fall asleep standing up.

The women in the balcony were fanning themselves, and delegates stared off at nothing. Joe Hanover was moving from desk to desk, whispering in the ear of everyone he thought he could influence. Elizabeth kept watching Harry Burn. She hadn't seen him read his letter yet. If he didn't . . .

But at last, during one particularly boring speech which simply repeated all the usual arguments, Burn reached into his coat and pulled out the letter. Elizabeth wanted to shout with joy, but she bit her tongue. She didn't want to draw attention or get completely ejected.

"Burn is reading the letter," she whispered to Miss Sue.

Miss Sue nodded, but she didn't smile. No one was happy about any of this.

After almost an hour, Speaker Walker must have sensed the delegates had reached the limits of their patience. He would know the vote count even better than the Suffs. He had the votes and the time had come to use them. He called Austin Overton to take over the Speaker's chair and stepped down to the floor to be recognized. The room fell completely silent. Everyone knew Walker would have something important planned.

"The hour has come," Walker shouted. "The battle has been fought and it is won. The measure is defeated. Mr. Speaker, I move that the motion to concur in the Senate action goes where it belongs—to the table."

This was exactly what they had done in North Carolina a day ago! Tabling the amendment meant that it wouldn't be considered again until the new legislature—the one being elected in November—met the following year. In effect, ratification would be dead.

The chamber erupted. Suffs were wailing. Antis were cheering. Legislators were thronging the aisles, clamoring to be recognized.

Antis were seconding the motion in droves while the Suffs waved their arms to protest. Speaker pro tempore Overton pounded his gavel, but he could hardly be heard above the din. Slowly, people settled down again, and Overton asked the clerk to do the roll call vote.

Miss Sue had a tally sheet, so Elizabeth didn't bother to keep track, but dozens of others on the floor and in the galleries were keeping their own counts, too. Each time someone voted "nay," the Suffs cheered. When someone voted "aye," the Antis cheered. This made it difficult to hear the next response clearly, so Elizabeth took the job of listening carefully to confirm each vote for Miss Sue.

Elizabeth's heart broke early when Harry Burn voted to table the ratification vote. Plainly, her efforts had failed.

But the count went back and forth. Clusters of delegates would all vote one way and then another cluster would vote the other way. The count shifted, with one side up and then the other, but never by much. Neither side had time to note any anomalies in the voting, but Elizabeth got a jolt when Banks Turner voted not to table. Hadn't he been voting with the Antis up until now? Could something or someone have changed his mind?

When the last delegate cast his vote, the Antis roared their triumph. They had counted forty-nine in favor and forty-seven against. The amendment was tabled, which meant it was dead.

# CHAPTER FOURTEEN

GIDEON DIDN'T HAVE A TALLY SHEET, BUT FROM THE WAY the Antis were shouting and cheering, they must have won the vote. This was a tragedy. His heart sank when he thought of how hard his mother and Elizabeth had worked and how crushed they would be to lose at the last moment. He couldn't see his ladies from here, but women in yellow were weeping everywhere he looked.

Speaker Overton pounded his gavel until the crowd quieted enough that the clerk could read the official results. He announced that the vote was forty-eight to forty-eight, a tie. A tie vote meant the motion to table the amendment had *failed*! Could the Antis' count be wrong?

Now everyone went wild. The Antis were shouting that their tally was right. The Suffs insisted the clerk's tally was official. Practically every representative left his seat and surged to the Speaker's desk, holding up their own tally sheets proving one count or the other.

Soon the Antis were howling and demanding a recount while

the Suffs were claiming it wasn't necessary. Overton was pounding his gavel again, but no one paid him the slightest heed, probably because they couldn't hear it over the clamor. Gideon remembered Joe Hanover's warning not to let anyone get hurt, but how could he even hope to prevent that in this mob?

Overton finally got the attention of the sergeant at arms and told him to force all the members back into their seats. No one wanted to go, of course, but gradually the men began to sit down.

Tom Riddick refused to take his seat. He was still arguing with the Speaker pro tempore that the count was official and didn't need to be repeated. When the sergeant at arms urged him to sit, he snapped, "I have as much right to be in the aisles as Walker does."

Seth Walker had been running up and down the aisles encouraging his delegates to stand fast.

Gideon thought Riddick said something else to Walker, and apparently it wasn't very cordial because Walker instantly turned around and headed back toward Riddick in a way Gideon recognized as the beginning of a fistfight. With the aisles now clear, Gideon broke into a run and jumped between them before either of them could strike a blow.

Others had noticed, too, and jumped up from their seats to grab each man and pull them apart. Riddick's friends were urging him to calm down and take his seat. They assured him the clerk's count was correct, although none of them could possibly be sure. Finally, Riddick sat down, and Walker signaled Overton to do a recount.

"Thanks, Bates," Joe Hanover said as Gideon walked past him on his way back to his post.

Gideon leaned over and whispered, "Did you notice Banks Turner voted no?"

"Yes, and I'm not the only one who noticed." He nodded in the direction of Turner's desk in the fifth row.

Seth Walker had pulled up a chair beside Turner and put his arm around him. He was talking to him urgently but in a voice only Turner could hear. This was very dangerous. Walker could use his power as Speaker to threaten or cajole or both to win Turner back.

"Turner and Walker are good friends," Hanover said with a worried frown. "If he convinces Banks to change his vote . . ."

He didn't have to explain what that might mean.

WHAT DO YOU HAVE?" ELIZABETH ASKED MISS SUE, TRYING to make sense of Miss Sue's tally sheet.

"I'm not even sure," she said in frustration. "And it doesn't matter, does it? The clerk's count is the official one."

"And they're going to count again," Elizabeth said. "Do you think there's any chance we'll win this time?"

"A tie is all we need. We thought the Antis had forty-nine votes, but did you notice, Banks Turner voted no. I don't think anyone else changed sides, so that would explain the tie."

"Harry Burn certainly didn't change sides," Elizabeth said, feeling an unfamiliar lump in her throat that might have been the urge to weep. Uncontrolled emotion was another sign of her condition, but she wasn't going to give in to it here. She would have plenty of time for that later.

"I'm so sorry," Miss Sue was saying. "You tried so hard."

The roll call began, and Elizabeth soon heard Harry Burn repeat his yes vote to table the amendment. Her heart broke all over again. Then she noticed Seth Walker had pulled up a chair beside Banks Turner and put an arm around him.

"Oh dear," she said. But of course, Walker would try to win

Turner back. She could only hope that whatever force had turned him would keep him turned.

This roll call was a little more orderly. After each vote, the clerk would repeat the delegate's name and his vote so there could be no confusion. Miss Sue kept nodding. She had tallied the votes correctly the first time.

Finally, they reached the *T*'s. Tarrant—no. Thronesbury—aye. Travis—aye. Tucker—no. Turner . . .

The chamber fell silent, and it seemed everyone was holding their breath. By now everyone had realized he was the one who had changed sides. All eyes were on Banks Turner, who still sat with Seth Walker's arm wrapped around his shoulders. Suddenly, he shook off Walker's arm and bolted to his feet. "Nay," he called in a loud, clear voice.

The Suffs screamed with joy, and Elizabeth and Miss Sue grabbed each other and started jumping up and down. The celebration was quickly silenced, and the vote continued. Everyone left voted just as they had before. The clerk announced the vote was still tied, forty-eight to forty-eight.

When the Suffs' celebration had died down, Overton announced, "The motion is lost for want of a majority."

More cheers and screams and rejoicing, because ratification was still alive.

But Elizabeth was watching Seth Walker. He had walked away from Turner in a huff, but his fury had died quickly. Now he was striding to the Speaker's chair like a man on a mission. He said something to Overton, who immediately pounded his gavel for silence.

"I now call the vote to concur with Senate Joint Resolution #1, ratifying the Nineteenth Amendment."

It took only a moment for everyone to realize what this meant. Once again Walker had exercised his skills at parliamentary

procedure to foil his opponents. He had lost the vote to table—
and therefore kill—the motion on the amendment, but he had
also finally and definitively gotten an exact vote count of who
would support it and who would not. He didn't even need Banks
Turner's vote. A tie was as good as a majority because, like the
motion they had just considered, a tie would defeat the amendment equally well.

The Antis were jubilant and the Suffs groaned their despair.

Joe Hanover was roaming the aisles like a madman, stopping
to grab a man's arm or slap him on the back, whisper some words
of encouragement in his ear, and then moving on to the next one.
The representatives looked weary and a few actually looked
frightened. What threats had they received? Elizabeth was certainly frightened. If they lost here, they had little chance of winning in any of the remaining states. Suffrage could be dead for
another generation.

The roll call began again. Anderson—yes. Bell—yes. Bond,
Boyd, Boyer, Bratton—all no. "Burn . . ."

This time Elizabeth didn't hold her breath. She just braced
herself for another disappointment.

"Aye."

He said the word so quickly and calmly that for a long moment, no one seemed to notice he had changed his vote.

Or had she heard him wrong because she wanted this so badly?

Elizabeth looked at Miss Sue whose pencil hadn't moved
from Harry Burn's name even though the clerk had called more
names since then.

Elizabeth felt frozen. Had that really happened?

"Did he say aye?" Elizabeth asked.

"He did," Miss Sue replied, just as astounded.

"I guess this is what he meant when he said he would never
hurt us."

A ripple of awareness went through the chamber as others gradually realized what Burn had done. Slowly a buzz of voices started in the gallery as people began to speak of it to one another and soon that buzz grew into a roar that filled the chamber. The Suffs rose to their feet and cheered, exultant and triumphant. Elizabeth and Miss Sue were screaming along with them.

They drowned out the clerk's voice, so the vote had to stop until order could be restored, but no one needed a rose anymore to identify what side they were on. All the Suffs were grinning broadly, and all the Antis were in despair.

"We'll still need Banks Turner," Miss Sue said.

"Yes, a tie won't help us," Elizabeth said, craning to see where he sat.

They had to wait through almost the entire alphabet for Turner's vote. Elizabeth's stomach was in knots by then. Seth Walker and his cronies had been glaring at Burn as if sending him silent threats. Now they turned those glares to Turner. He would have to be a brave man to withstand that.

As the clerk's roll call approached the $S$'s, Seth Walker walked over to stand beside Banks Turner again. He was whispering in his ear, every muscle tense. What could he say that would win Turner back? Any number of things—bribes or punishments, favors or betrayals. Turner sat like a stone.

The clerk had reached the $T$'s. Tarrant—aye. Thronesbury—no. Travis—no. Tucker—aye. Turner . . .

The whole room had fallen silent, but Turner made no response.

Everyone was staring at Turner now. His face had twisted into what must be an agony of indecision, as Walker continued to whisper urgently into his ear.

"Mr. Turner," the clerk called again.

Again, Turner made no reply. Joe Hanover stood at his own

desk, his face pale, his expression horrified. Elizabeth thought she might faint, but then she remembered to breathe. Still, she glared at Turner, willing him to speak.

"Mr. Turner," the clerk called a third time, and a third time Turner did not respond.

This time the roar from the galleries was the Antis who knew that without Turner's vote, ratification would fail. Walker straightened and fell silent, his work complete.

The clerk went on with the roll call, but it was almost over now. Miss Sue had even stopped keeping a tally any longer. They all knew how this would end. Elizabeth took Miss Sue's arm and they leaned into each other for support. This time Elizabeth didn't fight the tears that threatened. Other women were sobbing all over the chamber.

The roll call ran down to the *W*'s. Finally, the clerk called, "Walker," and Seth Walker added his nay vote to the list. The count was tied without Turner's vote. Ratification was dead.

This time the Antis surged to their feet, but before they could so much as shout, Banks Turner stood up.

Everyone froze in place. What was he doing?

Turner was a thin man of about thirty and unprepossessing. He had lost most of his hair on top, and his prominent forehead was dotted with sweat, but Elizabeth thought he looked a bit noble standing there with all eyes on him once again.

Turner raised his voice so everyone could hear. "Mr. Speaker, I wish to be recorded as voting aye."

Silence fell as the shock of it reverberated through the chamber.

Then Anne Dudley's shriek pierced the air, launching a roar of celebration that shook the statehouse to its foundations. People clapped and shouted and whistled and stomped their feet. Those who had room actually danced while those who didn't simply jumped up and down with delirium. Women were weeping again, but this time for joy, and men everywhere were also shedding tears.

They'd won!

G IDEON WAS ALSO SHOUTING AND CLAPPING, BUT HE HADN'T forgotten his duty. He still kept watch over the chamber floor for any hint of violence. Many here would not be happy about the results, and they might take out their anger on someone else.

The clerk hadn't even had a chance to read the final count, although everyone knew that Banks Turner's last-minute vote had given the Suffs the majority.

The Suffs were mobbing Joe Hanover as if he were the winning pitcher of the World Series, and he was beaming. He tore off his yellow rose and threw it up to the gallery. The Suffs up there had pulled out hundreds of tiny yellow flags and were waving them. They started pulling off their flowers and tossing them over to rain down on the representatives below. In response, the other delegates threw their flowers back up.

It was bedlam.

Still, Gideon saw Seth Walker fighting his way to the Speaker's chair. Overton wasn't even banging his gavel because he must have realized restoring order now was hopeless. He looked down in despair at the real Speaker, who was shouting something up at him. Gideon stepped forward so he could hear.

"Mr. Speaker," Walker was shouting. "I want to change my vote from nay to aye."

A chill went down Gideon's back. Walker certainly had not had a sudden change of heart. He was doing this for a reason.

"And," Walker continued, "I wish to move for reconsideration."

Gideon knew hardly anyone had heard this. Half of them were

too caught up in the celebration and those who weren't couldn't hear it because of the noise. He knew what it meant, though. Only those who had voted in favor of a bill could call for a reconsideration. Now Walker would have three days to try to change at least one other vote and hold a recount to kill ratification at last.

P OOR MRS. CATT," MISS SUE WAS SAYING, OR RATHER SCREAM- ing, to make herself heard. "She's sitting back at the hotel and wondering what on earth is happening."

"Surely, she can hear the cheers," Elizabeth said.

"But she won't know which side is cheering."

"I'm sure someone has gone to give her the news," Elizabeth said. "We'll have to cable Miss Paul immediately. She must be agonizing over this."

Someone had started singing, "My Country, 'Tis of Thee," and Elizabeth and Miss Sue joined in.

Anita and Betty had been on the other side of the chamber, and now they had made their way over to where Elizabeth and Miss Sue were singing. The women all hugged one another, laughing and crying at once over this great victory.

But when the song died away, people in the galleries started getting restless, and someone yelled down that Harry Burn was a traitor. Others joined him, hurling down insults and accusations that he had been bribed or worse. Burn would not be safe here much longer.

G IDEON HEARD THE INSULTS BEING SHOUTED AT BURN from the galleries. Burn was obviously in danger. If Gideon was supposed to prevent violence, this would be a good place to start.

As Gideon approached Burn, he could see that Burn had reached the same conclusion.

"Mr. Burn, I'm Gideon Bates. My wife is the one who brought you your mother's letter this morning."

Burn's eyes grew wide with surprise. "She's an amazing lady. Your wife, I mean."

"Yes, she is, and I'm sure she doesn't want any harm to come to you." He glanced up at the galleries where Antis were now leaning over to better shout at Burn. "Let's get you out of here."

Gideon led Burn into the clerk's room, which opened onto the chamber. The window was open to catch what air was available. Gideon looked out. "It's quite a drop from here."

Burn looked out, too. "I think I can use the ledge to make it to the next window. It opens into the library, I think."

"Are you sure?" Gideon wouldn't want to chance it.

Burn grinned boyishly. "Yes, I'm sure." This must be a big adventure for him. Gideon helped him climb out the window. He started scooting along the narrow ledge to the next window.

Gideon hurried out. People were beginning to leave the building.

Joe Hanover stopped Gideon. "They're threatening Harry Burn," he said, glancing up at the churning galleries. "The governor just ordered the sergeant at arms to protect him. Did you see where he went?"

"He's gone out the window in the clerk's room into the next window. I'll make sure he gets away safely."

Joe nodded and Gideon hurried out of the chamber and down the hall to what did turn out to be the library. Burn was just coming in through the window.

The librarian was quite surprised. Apparently, this never happened.

"Sorry," Burn murmured to the startled man.

Gideon heaved a sigh of relief and followed Burn down the wrought-iron spiral staircase that served only the library. So far, no one else had seen them.

On the first floor, the crowds were filing out. Some were joyous and some were angry, but none of them paid Burn and Gideon much attention. Gideon saw the sergeant at arms scanning the crowd.

"That fellow is looking for you." Gideon nodded in the direction of the sergeant at arms. "The governor ordered him to guard you."

"I don't need him," Burn said, still grinning. "I've got you as a bodyguard."

The two men slipped behind the sergeant at arms and quickly closed the distance between the Capitol and the hotel. There Gideon saw Burn safely to his room. The Antis would certainly continue to vilify him, but at least he was safe for now.

E LIZABETH DIDN'T FIND MOTHER BATES, ANNA AND FREDDIE until she had worked her way back to the Hermitage. The lobby was packed with celebrating Suffs and bitter Antis who kept insisting the battle wasn't over. The only way she found them was because Jake was with them and was able to see over a lot of the other people and find her in the crowd.

*Jake?* Weren't they supposed to pretend they didn't know him?

Elizabeth told Miss Sue and the others she would join them in Miss Sue's suite in a few minutes and worked her way through the crowd to where Jake was waving.

"Oh, Elizabeth, we did it!" Anna exclaimed.

"Or should we say *you* did it," Mother Bates said. Everyone had to hug her and exclaim over their victory.

"What about me?" Jake asked, pretending to be insulted when no one hugged him. "I drove her."

"Yes, Jake, you were very helpful, but Harry Burn's vote alone wouldn't have done it," Elizabeth said modestly.

"And neither would Banks Turner's vote," Freddie said. "We needed both of them, so we're very glad you went to see Mrs. Burn."

"Jake told us all about your adventure," Mother Bates said.

Jake leaned over and stage-whispered to Elizabeth, "I didn't tell them about the pirates. I thought that would scare them."

This made Anna and Freddie laugh and Mother Bates roll her eyes.

"Mrs. Burn is a delightful lady," Elizabeth said, remembering what Mrs. Burn had told her about her condition. How long could she keep her secret?

Mother Bates sighed. "I can't believe it's all over."

"It's not," Elizabeth said with a pang.

"What do you mean?" Anna asked with a frown. "We won the vote."

"Seth Walker has done it again. You probably couldn't hear him with all the noise. We certainly didn't, but on the walk back to the hotel, we heard from some of the representatives that Walker changed his ratification from no to yes."

"But that's wonderful," Mother Bates said. "Another vote to our majority."

"That's true as far as it goes. He gave us the fiftieth vote, which makes it a true majority of the entire House's ninety-nine members. No one can challenge that kind of majority. But changing his vote also enables him to move for reconsideration, which he has also done."

"Reconsideration?" Freddie asked. "What does that mean?"

"Just what it sounds like," Elizabeth said sadly. "Miss Sue explained that anyone who votes in favor of a bill can move to have that bill reconsidered and voted on again."

"Does that mean they could overturn the original vote?" Anna asked in surprise.

"That's exactly what it means, and Walker probably thinks it's possible with the vote so close. He only needs for one of our men to go home to accomplish his goal of overturning ratification."

"That hardly seems fair," Jake said, looking more disturbed than she'd expected. She actually hadn't expected him to care at all.

"Not giving women the vote in the first place wasn't fair," Mother Bates said. "Somehow I don't think the Antis care about that."

Someone put a hand on Elizabeth's shoulder. She looked up in surprise and found her husband smiling down at her. His smile wasn't joyous, though. It even looked a little sad. He knew all was not well.

"Did you hear what Seth Walker did?" she asked him.

"I heard him do it. The Men's Ratification Committee is meeting in an hour. Miss Sue and Mrs. Catt have asked us to guard the hotel hallways again tonight so no one leaves. They think Walker will try to take another vote at the session tomorrow morning if he manages to get some Suff delegates to leave town."

"How many nights can you go without sleep, darling?" Elizabeth asked in dismay. "You've got to get some rest."

"I'll sleep when this is over," he said with a smile. He seemed proud to be helping and Elizabeth couldn't deny him that. "And maybe I can get a nap this afternoon."

"But Walker could keep this up for weeks," Mother Bates protested. "Sooner or later, he'll have the right number of votes."

"He only has three days to call for a reconsideration vote, so it won't go on for weeks, Mother. Don't worry, we're going to arrange shifts for the men so they can get at least a little sleep."

"I'm meeting with Miss Sue and the other Party members in a few minutes," Elizabeth said.

"Then Anna and I should get some rest so we can help guard the hallways tonight, too," Freddie said.

Anna laid a hand over her heart. "I don't know if I can stand the suspense for three more days."

"Of course, you can," Jake said. "You're one of the toughest women I know."

Anna gave him a fond smile, and everyone else gaped at him.

"What?" he asked, annoyed at their surprise.

"It's just that you're not usually very kind," Elizabeth said.

"I wasn't being kind," Jake said as if she had insulted him. "I was just stating a fact." Before anyone could question that, he turned to Gideon. "Put me on your list. I'll help patrol the hotel, too."

Elizabeth must be dreaming. What had come over her brother?

"Won't your father object?" Mother Bates asked.

Jake shrugged. "I don't have anything to do tonight."

Did that mean he had something to do tomorrow? And what was it? Fortunately, Elizabeth was too busy to care.

MISS SUE'S SUITE WAS ALREADY HUMMING WITH ACTIVITY when Elizabeth arrived a few minutes later. Betty Gram was just leaving to send Alice Paul a telegram to give her the happy news. Miss Sue was preparing her remarks for the press. Others were discussing shifts for patrolling the hotel.

"Some of the representatives are already saying they want to go home. They miss their families. Their businesses are suffering, or their farms are neglected," Anita told her. "We can't let a single one of them go."

"But if the Antis want to leave, good riddance," Elizabeth said.

Betty soon returned after sending the telegram to Miss Paul. "I just found out the Antis have started sending those phony telegrams again, the ones where they claim someone's loved one is sick and they have to return home immediately," she reported. "They were coming in while I was in the telegraph office."

"I hope everyone knows by now that these aren't necessarily real," Elizabeth said.

"I hope so, too, but that isn't the worst of it. The telegraph operator told me the Antis are spreading the word that every representative who voted in favor of ratification should receive at least a hundred telegrams of protest. Apparently, they had already set this up in case they lost the vote."

That would make any elected official take notice, especially if they were already worried about reelection.

"We need to make sure all our delegates know this is all just a ploy by the Antis," Elizabeth said.

Women were dispatched to find the delegates and warn them.

The women worked through the afternoon, making schedules and dispatching volunteers to help corral straying delegates. Dinnertime came and went without notice. Miss Sue composed a full report for Miss Paul. Miss Sue also received dozens of congratulatory telegrams as the day wore on and the word spread across the country. She had just gone down the lobby to meet with some reporters when a young woman came into the suite. She was smartly dressed and had her hair stylishly bobbed. She carried a portfolio clutched to her chest.

Elizabeth had never seen her before, and she looked rather uncertain. "May I help you?"

"Are you Miss White? They told me this was her room."

"Miss White is speaking to the press at the moment, but you can come in and wait if you like."

She glanced at the women who were poring over lists and taking notes. "Are you all with the Woman's Party?"

"Yes." Elizabeth introduced herself. "Are you a Suff?"

"Oh yes, and my mother, too."

"Did you come to volunteer?"

The young woman bit her lip. "No, I . . . I have something very important to show Miss White, though."


G IDEON DID GET A SHORT NAP THAT AFTERNOON, BUT HE was afraid it had only made him groggier. He was walking the hallways but more slowly than he had the night before. At least he only had to remain on duty until three o'clock in the morning. Then someone would relieve him.

He had volunteered for Harry Burn's floor because he wanted to make sure the young legislator didn't receive any unwelcome visitors. He'd had quite a bit of coffee to revive him earlier and now he was feeling the need to relieve himself of it. He saw the light was still on in Burn's room, so he knocked, identifying himself so Harry would open the door.

"I'm glad to see you," Burn said. "Are you my guard tonight?"

"For the first half of the night. I was wondering if I could use your bathroom."

Burn grinned. "Sure. Help yourself." As Gideon came in, he added, "The first thing I did when I got back here to my room was telephone my mother. She was awfully glad to hear I'd voted for suffrage, and she sends her regards to Mrs. Bates."

Gideon smiled with pride and thanked him. Then he hurried off to take care of business, but while he was in the bathroom, he heard someone else knocking on the door. Gideon winced when Burn let whoever it was in. Who would be calling on him? Gideon moved silently to the bathroom door and opened it a crack so he could hear without being seen, just in case.

"You're wasting your time," Burn was saying, "if you think you can get me to change my vote."

"Hear me out," another man said. Gideon didn't recognize the voice. "We know what happened. We know Joe Hanover bribed you to change your vote."

"What?" Burn exclaimed, obviously flabbergasted. "He did no such thing."

"Oh yes, he did," the man said, and several other voices confirmed it, which told Gideon they had sent a delegation to intimidate Burn. "Hanover pulled you into a coatroom right before the vote."

"Dragged you in by your lapels," another voice said. "Roughed you up a bit, too."

"No, he didn't," Burn said, but the first man raised his voice to talk over him.

"Then he promised to make you the biggest man in Tennessee and pay you ten thousand dollars in cash."

"None of that happened," Burn insisted. "I changed my vote of my own free will."

"No, you didn't, and this did happen," the first man said. "We have sworn affidavits here from witnesses who saw it all."

Gideon heard some papers rustle, so he must be showing the documents to Harry.

"Now, you can attend the session tomorrow and vote with the Suffs," the second man said, "but if you do, we will publish this whole story in tomorrow afternoon's *Banner*. Your reputation will be ruined in the entire state, and you'll never be elected to anything again."

"Or," the first man added, "you can leave town and forget all of this."

"Speaker Walker is going to call a vote tomorrow," the second man said. "If you're there and vote with the Suffs, you'll read all about yourself in the afternoon newspapers."

They made a few more threats and a couple of the men told Burn how he was betraying the South. Then they left.

As soon as Gideon heard the door close, he stepped out of the bathroom. "Who was that?"

"It doesn't matter who they were. Did you hear?"

"Yes." Gideon studied Burn's young face, which was now a lot paler than it had been a few minutes ago. Both the Suffs and the Antis had threatened to reveal the names of those who had pledged to their respective causes in order to keep them in line, and then accused one another of blackmail. This, however, really was blackmail. "What are you going to do?"

Burn shook his head. "I don't know what I *can* do. I think they really would set out to ruin me, but how can I go against what I believe?"

"Give me a minute to think." Gideon's mind was racing. He knew a little about blackmail from the time Elizabeth had helped one of her friends who was a victim, but they didn't have time to run an elaborate con to set this right. Harry would have to decide what to do by morning.

Before Gideon could come up with any plan he thought would work, someone knocked on the door yet again.

"I'll get it this time," Gideon said, heading for the door. He wasn't going to let Harry face down his enemies alone this time, but the person standing there was the last person he expected to see. "Elizabeth, what are you doing here?"

"I could ask you the same thing," she said with her beautiful smile. How could she be getting more beautiful? He had no idea, but he knew it was true.

He stepped back to admit her and then noticed she had a young woman he didn't know with her. He nodded and she smiled weakly as she passed him.

"Good evening, Mr. Burn," Elizabeth said. "I'm sorry to call so late, but I have some important information for you." She turned to the young woman. "This is Miss Sally Foster. She is a stenographer." Elizabeth introduced the two men, who expressed their pleasure at making her acquaintance. The poor woman looked very apprehensive.

"Elizabeth, what—"

"If you give me a minute, I'll explain," Elizabeth said. "Perhaps we could sit down."

When the men had seated the ladies in the easy chair and the desk chair, Burn sat down on the bed and Gideon leaned against the wall.

"As I said," Elizabeth began, "Miss Foster is a stenographer. This afternoon she was summoned to the hotel to take down some statements and type them up." Elizabeth gave Burn an apologetic smile. "I'm afraid these witnesses had a very nasty story to tell about you being bribed by Joe Hanover, Mr. Burn. Miss Foster heard them bragging about how they would use these statements to force you to change your vote."

Gideon and Harry exchanged a surprised glance.

Elizabeth smiled like a cat who'd gotten the cream. "Sally, why don't you finish the story?"

Miss Foster smiled shyly, obviously a little proud of herself. "Well, I took down what they said and typed it up, but I knew it was all hokum."

"How did you know?" Gideon asked. His legal training demanded he ask the question.

"Because I was in the gallery this morning and didn't see anything untoward. I didn't tell them I was there, of course. I just typed up the pages and delivered them. But . . ."

A glance at Harry told him the poor boy was past speech. "But what?" Gideon asked.

"But I made copies. I thought Miss Sue White or Mrs. Catt might want to know what they were doing."

"She came to Miss Sue's suite and told me her story," Elizabeth said. "I knew Mr. Burn would want to be warned about what they are doing. I imagine they're planning to publish this ridiculous story or at least threaten to in order to get Mr. Burn to change his vote."

"Yes, *blackmail* him into changing his vote," Gideon said. Elizabeth nodded. She would be remembering their previous experience with the awful crime. "They were just here and threatened to publish it in the *Banner* tomorrow afternoon if he didn't leave town or change his vote."

"But what can we do about it?" Burn finally asked. "We know it's hokum but—"

"Oh, I think we can figure out exactly what to do about it, Mr. Burn," Elizabeth said. "We just needed your permission."

# CHAPTER FIFTEEN

Gideon and Harry Burn escorted Miss Foster out of the hotel to take care of the blackmail business. Elizabeth was tasked with finding Joe Hanover and telling him what was going on. As the hour had grown later, the halls were haunted by staggering men who had spent too much time in the Jack Daniel's Suite. Luckily, Hanover was in his room hosting a meeting of several other Suff leaders. He stepped out into the hallway and closed the door behind him when Elizabeth told him she had a message for him from Gideon.

His expression darkened when she told him about the plot against Harry Burn. "Now it all makes sense," he said. "A group of them came to see me earlier and warned me if I didn't stand down on my defense of suffrage, they had documents proving I had bribed Harry Burn and they would publish the whole plot in the newspapers."

"The *Banner* is Edward Stahlman's paper, so I'm sure he would love to print a story like that, vilifying the Suff leaders. Fortunately, we have Luke Lea and his *Tennessean* on our side."

Elizabeth told him of their plan to foil the blackmailers.

By the time she had finished, he was smiling. "And luckily, the *Tennessean* is a morning paper. This is genius."

Elizabeth simply smiled. She knew it was, but gloating wouldn't be seemly. "Now you can make your plans accordingly," she said.

He thanked her profusely, both for the help and for letting him know.

Elizabeth went off to find some of the Men's Committee members to tell them Gideon had left his post for more important duties so they could send someone else to cover for him.

E LIZABETH HAD HAD A GOOD NIGHT'S SLEEP BECAUSE SHE had eventually found herself nodding off over her lists, and Miss Sue herself had sent her off to bed. Keeping her condition a secret was going to be a problem if this went on much longer. She wanted to tell Gideon first, but they had hardly had a moment to themselves since she had visited Mrs. Burn.

Mother Bates was up early and had ordered breakfast. She had been asleep when Elizabeth got back to their suite, so she knew nothing about their adventures of the night before. She had ordered breakfast when she heard Elizabeth get up.

"Did you ask them to bring a newspaper, too?" Elizabeth asked, trying to sound nonchalant.

"Oh yes. I wanted to see how Luke Lea and his people reported on the victory yesterday."

Someone knocked on the door. Elizabeth answered, expecting it to be their breakfast, but it was Anna and Freddie, and they were almost as excited as they had been yesterday after the ratification had passed.

"Have you seen the papers?" Anna practically screamed, holding up one of them.

"Not yet," Elizabeth said as they burst into the room.

"We couldn't believe it," Freddie exclaimed. "Look at this."

The story was spread across the front page of the *Tennessean*.

"What is it?" Mother Bates asked, jumping up to snatch the paper from Anna.

"The Antis tried to blackmail Harry Burn into changing his vote," Anna said.

"They had people swear they had seen Joe Hanover offer him ten thousand dollars and anything else he wanted," Freddie said. "They warned both men that if they didn't stop fighting for suffrage, they would publish the statements these phony witnesses had made and ruin them."

"But the stenographer who transcribed the statements knew they were fake," Anna said.

"And she is a Suff!" Freddie cried triumphantly.

"So, she took the story to Luke Lea," Anna said.

"Who is also a Suff," Freddie said, in case they didn't remember.

"And he published the truth in his paper!" Anna concluded triumphantly.

"What is all this screaming about?" Gideon asked blearily from the bedroom door. He hadn't shaved or even combed his hair, although he had thrown on enough clothes to be decent.

"The story is on the front page," Elizabeth told him, taking the newspaper from his mother's hands and giving it to him to see.

"Very nice," he said, examining it. "They did promise it would be front page news."

"You already knew!" Anna said in exasperation.

Gideon just smiled, but Elizabeth said, "Gideon escorted the stenographer to the *Tennessean* offices last night."

Freddie and Anna drooped a little, but they soon recovered. "Isn't it nice to win for a change?" Anna decided.

"We beat them this time, but we don't know what else they might have planned," Gideon said. "Seth Walker is a master of manipulation, and he probably still has something up his sleeve. But you're right, it's certainly nice to beat them at their own game for once."

"At least Mr. Walker won't be calling for a vote this morning," Mother Bates said. "After this story, surely every suffragist will be in his seat ready to vote for suffrage again."

EVERY DELEGATE WHO HAD BEEN IN THE CHAMBER YESTER-day was in his seat again today when the roll was called. The galleries had cheered for each of their heroes as they entered the chamber earlier, the Antis for Seth Walker and the Suffs for Joe Hanover, Banks Turner and Harry Burn. But Seth Walker looked a little subdued after the blow Luke Lea's *Tennessean* had struck that morning. Even Herschel Candler, the senator who had fought so hard to defeat ratification, had been disgusted by the attempt to smear his protégé, calling the charges the Antis planned to make against Harry Burn "ridiculous."

As soon as the roll call was over, Harry Burn stood up and asked for a point of personal privilege. Then he handed a piece of paper to the clerk.

"That will be a copy of his speech," Miss Sue said. She and Elizabeth were once again just behind the rail after having spent some time before the session encouraging their legislators. "He'll want it accurately printed in the record."

Then Burn began to speak. "I desire to resent in the name of honesty and justice the veiled intimidation and accusation regarding my vote on the suffrage amendment as indicated in certain statements, and it is my sincere belief that those responsible for their existence know that there is not a scintilla of truth in them." He paused while his supporters cheered. "I want to state that I changed my vote in favor of ratification first because I believe in full suffrage as a right; second, I believe we had a moral and legal right to ratify; third, I knew that a mother's advice is always safest for a boy to follow, and my mother wanted me to vote for ratification."

Elizabeth wanted to cheer for that, but she didn't want to draw attention. She did hear a few claps from the gallery and knew it was her crew paying tribute. Miss Sue gave her a nudge and a big grin.

"Fourth," Burn continued, "I appreciated the fact that an opportunity such as seldom comes to a mortal man to free seventeen million women from political slavery was mine; fifth, I desired that my party in both state and nation might say that it was a Republican from the east mountains of Tennessee . . . who made national Woman Suffrage possible at this date, not for personal glory but for the glory of his party."

Harry Burn received an ovation from the Suffs and jeers from the Antis, but the jeers were half-hearted. They all knew Burn's honest statement would only increase his stature going forward.

Seth Walker didn't even try to bring up reconsideration that morning. Plainly, he hadn't been able to move a single suffragist. At least not yet. The meeting soon adjourned until the next day.

THE DAY WENT BY IN A SERIES OF MEETINGS AND MORE PA-trolling to make sure none of the delegates left town. The evening was quiet at the Hermitage, though. The Antis were having a "Save the South" rally at the Ryman Auditorium, featuring all the best Anti orators, starting with Seth Walker, so every Anti was there, cheering on their leaders.

Elizabeth was reading about it the next morning while the three of them breakfasted in their suite. "Walker praised the men who signed their names in the 'blood of the South' to keep this a 'white man's country and a white man's government,'" she read aloud in disgust. "As if that's what Woman Suffrage is all about."

Gideon looked up and shook his head. "I always wonder if these Southerners are really concerned about a race war or if they just use that as an excuse because they want to keep their women in subjugation, too."

"It's difficult to tell, isn't it?" his mother said.

"Oh dear," Elizabeth said, having continued to read silently. "Walker also said he has persuaded several legislators to join the Antis and he now has enough votes to overturn ratification."

"He must be lying," Mother Bates said. "All politicians lie, don't they?"

"A lot of them do," Gideon agreed, "especially when they're in a tight spot, and Walker certainly is."

"Do you have any idea who might have switched sides?" Mother Bates asked her.

Elizabeth wracked her brain. "I would have said none of them would change now. They're all heroes, although I know they've been flooded with telegrams excoriating them for their choice. We've even nicknamed them the Sterling Forty-Nine."

"So, Walker is probably lying," Gideon said with a certainty he couldn't possibly possess. He was only trying to cheer his ladies, but Elizabeth loved him for it. "Oh, did I tell you? The Antis have been sending people to Mrs. Burn's house, trying to get her to say she never wrote that letter to Harry."

"And what did she say?" Elizabeth asked, feeling a little queasy.

"She was outraged and informed them she most certainly did. Harry told me all about it when I took him to the other hotel."

"Why did he move to another hotel?" his mother asked.

"He couldn't stay here anymore. People were pounding on his door all day and all night. We didn't think he was safe."

"He probably wasn't," Elizabeth said, very glad for the change of subject. "I guess the only way to find out if Walker really has turned some votes is to go to the Capitol. Miss Sue will want us to check with all our assigned legislators before the session starts."

G IDEON'S MOTHER WAS GOING TO THE CAPITOL LATER WITH Freddie and Anna. Jake, it seemed, had duties elsewhere, so this morning Gideon and Elizabeth walked to the Capitol together. He was still to guard the doors and Elizabeth would be lobbying the delegates until the session began.

Once again, he was struck with how beautiful she was, as if she were glowing.

"You look lovely this morning," he said, patting the hand she had tucked into the crook of his arm.

"I thought I looked lovely every morning," she replied with a grin.

"I should have said you look *especially* lovely this morning. This lobbying business seems to agree with you."

She smiled mysteriously, but before he could ask what she was thinking, she said, "You seem to be enjoying yourself, too. I think you like all this cloak-and-dagger business."

"It has been sort of like a moving picture, hasn't it? All danger and suspense and close escapes."

"Let's hope Seth Walker was lying and we escape again today."

He had nothing to add to that.

Gideon escorted Elizabeth to the chamber, where she joined

Miss Sue and the others who were already at work. Gideon then found Joe Hanover, who looked even more haggard than usual and maybe even a little desperate.

"What's wrong?" Gideon asked.

"Charlie Brooks, you remember, he's the one who left because his wife was sick? Well, she's no better and he hasn't come back yet. Now Tom Dodson has got word his baby is dying."

"And it's true? You've checked?" Gideon asked, his stomach clenching.

"Yes, it's true. He's determined to get home, but if he leaves, we'll be short one vote and Walker will—"

"Where is Dodson? Is there a late train he can take? Or maybe we can charter one for him like we did for Charlie."

"He's already left for the station. He was gone before I even knew about it."

"I'll see if I can find Newell Sanders, and we'll try to catch Dodson before his train leaves."

Senator Sanders was more than happy to charter another train if it would secure suffrage. He and Gideon and a few other men raced to the station. The departure whistle for Dodson's train was already sounding, but Gideon and the others jumped on different cars to search, scanning every seat to find their man.

Dodson must have seen Gideon and immediately stood up. "What is it?"

"We need you to stay for the vote. Walker claims he has shifted several delegates. We don't know if it's true, but if you aren't there, he won't even need to. We'll lose in a tie."

Dodson's eyes filled with tears. "I know, but they said my baby is dying. I have to go."

They both had to grab a seatback to keep from falling when the train lurched into motion. The conductors were calling, "All aboard!"

"We can charter a special train for you. You can leave as soon as the vote is over, and it will get you home even faster than this one will because it won't make any stops."

"Are you sure?"

"I'm positive. Will you come back with us?"

Dodson hesitated for a long moment as the train inched out of the station. Then he reached up, grabbed his bag and said, "Let's go."

The men jumped off the moving train to the cheers of their comrades.

"You take Dodson back," Senator Sanders said to Gideon. "I'll make arrangements for the charter. We'll get you home, son. Don't worry."

Dodson thanked him profusely and then went with Gideon and the other men back to the Capitol.

H AVE YOU FOUND ANYONE WHO IS WAVERING?" ELIZABETH asked Betty Gram when they encountered each other on the chamber floor.

"Not a soul. If anything, they seem more determined than ever to support ratification."

Elizabeth smiled at that. "Could Seth Walker have been lying when he said he had the votes?"

"It seems very likely," Betty said with an answering grin.

They both turned at the sound of activity near one of the doors. Gideon was escorting one of the representatives into the chamber and, oddly, carrying a suitcase. They were both being greeted enthusiastically by Joe Hanover, who suddenly didn't look quite as haggard as he had earlier.

"What has your husband done now?" Betty asked slyly.

"Something heroic, I'm sure."

Many people were doing heroic things that morning. One of the legislators who was a schoolteacher had been threatened with the loss of his job if he voted yes. Today he was protectively surrounded by a group of Governor Roberts's supporters that included the state superintendent of schools. They were sending a silent message that the Antis didn't like a bit.

And Harry Burn and Banks Turner were wearing yellow roses today.

Elizabeth and her friends moved behind the brass rail when Speaker Walker called the session to order. Elizabeth thought he looked a bit pale and not nearly as confident as a man with all the votes he needed. After the opening proceedings were accomplished, Walker surprisingly tried to adjourn the meeting until Monday.

"He needs more time," Elizabeth whispered. "He doesn't really have the votes."

"But he thinks he can get them by Monday," Miss Sue said with a frown. "Remember how many votes we lost the last time they postponed the vote over the weekend."

The clerk started the roll call vote on the motion, but the Suffs held fast. The motion to adjourn until Monday failed by the exact count as ratification had passed.

The Suff legislators then gleefully moved to adjourn until the next day, Saturday, and that passed, again by the same margin.

"This means if he can't get the votes by morning, the three-day time limit will be up and ratification will be official," Miss Sue said.

The Suffs in the galleries cheered and then broke into song. Singing patriotic songs, they filed down to the first floor where they stopped to serenade Governor Roberts in thanks for his help, however belated. Then they proceeded down the front steps and out onto the lawn, still singing.

Elizabeth had found Gideon in the crowd and hugged him. Kissing in public would be too shocking, but there was plenty of time for that later. They strolled hand in hand across the state-house lawn and back to the hotel while Gideon told her about his escapade at the train station.

"And Dodson left as soon as the vote was over and is now on his way home," he concluded just as they reached the Hermitage.

They found Mother Bates, Anna and Freddie in the lobby. Tears of happiness were running down their faces, and they were not alone. The Suffs were finally starting to believe ratification would survive even the Antis' dirtiest tricks.

The lobby was full once more with Suffs and Antis eyeing one another suspiciously while the Suffs celebrated and the Antis seethed. The roar of excited conversation filled the massive room to its vaulted ceiling, but then they heard a man shouting over the din, and everyone paused what they were doing to look.

Elizabeth had been holding Gideon's arm, and she felt him tense, ready to rush to someone's rescue, but suddenly he relaxed, and when she looked up, he was smiling as he stared in the direction of the disturbance.

Then she was finally able to make out what the man was shouting.

"Federal agents, make way please. Federal agents. We have a prisoner."

"What on earth?" Mother Bates said.

Elizabeth didn't have to ask. She had been expecting something like this.

"Federal agents, make way," the man continued to shout as he moved through the crowd. He was wearing that shabby suit again, and he had three other men, also in shabby suits, with him. They all wore shiny gold badges of some sort pinned to their lapels, and they were escorting a tall, distinguished-looking man with silver hair, whose hands were clasped in front of him. He was wearing handcuffs.

Handcuffs. Nice touch.

The tall man was nodding to certain people in the crowd. "It's just a misunderstanding," he was saying to whomever might be interested. "It will all be cleared up with a few telephone calls."

Elizabeth was happy to see Lon McFarland, that cowardly senator who had abstained so he wouldn't have to take a stand, pushing his way through the crowd to see what was going on.

"Smith, what is all this?" he demanded.

"It's federal business, sir. Please step back," Jake said in a voice even Elizabeth thought sounded like a federal agent would sound.

"It's nothing," the Old Man said with a practiced smile. "I'll have this cleared up in no time and be back here in time for dinner." He somehow managed to look both confident and a little worried at the same time. He was a master.

"Make way," one of the men with Jake said, guiding the Old Man through the onlookers who had pressed even closer for a better view.

"Oh, Mr. Smith," Mother Bates said with just the proper amount of dismay as he passed. "This looks very serious."

"Not at all, ma'am, not at all," he assured her before being shoved into motion again.

Elizabeth gaped at her in amazement. Mother Bates had just made people who knew about the Old Man's "business opportunity" think she had been conned as well. Mother Bates merely shrugged as if to say "All in a day's work." She had successfully shielded them from any suspicion that they or the Suffs might have been involved. Gideon might be appalled, but at least he wasn't saying anything.

When Jake and his minions had escorted the Old Man out of

the hotel, conversation instantly began again. Elizabeth looked around and she could easily tell who had invested in the Old Man's scheme by their pale faces and worried frowns. None, she noticed, had voted for ratification. She didn't know if she was pleased by that or angry because that meant the Old Man hadn't kept his promise to help them get votes. At least she didn't have to feel badly because he had cheated one of theirs.

"You girls don't look surprised," Mother Bates said to Freddie and Anna, who exchanged a sly glance.

"Jake warned us," Anna admitted. "They have an official-looking motorcar outside. They're probably going straight to the station."

"And no one will ever know what happened to Mr. Robert Smith," Freddie said with mock solemnity.

"Oh, Jake said to tell you he's sorry, but he doesn't think the Old Man got anything from the men you suggested," Anna added.

"Or from the ones we suggested, either," Freddie said. Did she look disappointed? Elizabeth would have a talk with her when they got home.

"I gave him Lon McFarland, so I'll make sure he gives a donation to the Party," Elizabeth said. "What do we do now?"

"What we did yesterday, I guess," Gideon said. "The Men's Committee is meeting, and I suppose we'll be patrolling the hotels and the train station as usual."

"Then Freddie and I will be resting this afternoon," Anna said.

Elizabeth was very much afraid she would be, too, but only because her body was going to demand it. She only hoped Gideon could get some sleep as well. "I'll check with Miss Sue to see what the Suffs are going to do, if anything."

"I'm sure the Antis will also be meeting, trying to come up with some new plan," Mother Bates said.

"But what can they do if all our men stand firm?" Anna asked.

"They can try something we haven't thought of, but it really seems that the tide is turning in our direction," Elizabeth said.

FRIDAY NIGHT WAS MUCH QUIETER THAN THE PREVIOUS nights, Gideon noticed as he walked the hallways. He didn't even hear any telephones ringing, which had been a frequent sound on previous nights when the Antis had called Suff representatives through the night to threaten them and interrupt their sleep.

He had just checked his watch. It was nearing three o'clock in the morning and his shift was almost over. He was strolling down the hallway on the seventh floor and noticed a light in the transom over Miss Pearson's door. He knew the Anti leaders had met earlier, but that meeting was long over. Maybe Miss Pearson simply couldn't sleep.

But then her door opened, and she stepped out, fully dressed and even wearing a hat. She startled when she saw Gideon.

"Have you come to escort me?" she asked with a frown.

"No, ma'am. I'm guarding the halls to make sure no one deserts," he informed her with a smile.

"You're a Suff, then," she said in disgust.

"Yes, I am," he said proudly. He could have said more but it would be wasted on this woman who had devoted her life to defeating Woman Suffrage. But he couldn't help being polite. "I hope you aren't planning to leave the hotel alone at this time of night."

"What I'm doing is none of your business, young man. Now get out of my way."

She brushed past him, heading for the elevators.

What on earth was going on?

He strolled farther down the hall and stopped when another door opened. This time it was a man carrying a suitcase. He also expressed surprise at seeing Gideon.

"Didn't mean to scare you," Gideon said. Ordinarily, the sight of a man with a suitcase was a call to action. They couldn't let a single Suff representative leave town. But this man was an Anti. An avid Anti.

"You didn't scare me," the man said with a frown. "What are you doing, lurking around my room?"

"I'm not lurking. I'm patrolling the halls. May I ask where you're going?"

"No, you may not."

"It seems like an odd time to be checking out of the hotel," Gideon observed blandly.

"What makes you think . . . ?" he began and then realized he was carrying a suitcase. "It's none of your business when I check out of this hotel."

"No, it isn't," Gideon agreed, having gotten confirmation of his suspicion.

The man grunted and brushed past Gideon on his way to the elevator, which had already carried Miss Pearson away.

Gideon was trying to make sense of this when the man scheduled to relieve him came out of the stairwell.

"I just saw Miss Pearson and one of the Anti delegates leaving their rooms," Gideon said. "The man had a suitcase."

"Our men are reporting that all over the hotel. We're not stopping them, of course. If they leave town, they can't vote, which is good for us, but where are they going? And why?"

Gideon tried to remember what he knew about parliamentary procedure. His brain was foggy from lack of sleep, but he finally recalled something. "Quorum," he said.

The other man frowned. "Quorum?"

"Yes, the House can't conduct business unless at least half of the elected members are present. They may be trying to break quorum by sending all the Anti delegates away."

THAT WAS EXACTLY WHAT THEY WERE TRYING TO DO, AS Gideon found out the next morning. The volunteers who had been guarding the train station reported that twenty-five Anti delegates had boarded a special L&N train in the middle of the night and left for Alabama. If they were out of state, they couldn't be called upon to vote. But not enough of them had left.

Gideon was in the chamber doorway, watching for any trouble, when Speaker Walker called the session to order on Saturday morning. Forty-nine Suff representatives were still present because even though they had lost Tom Dodson, Charlie Brooks was back. His wife was getting better. Only eight Anti delegates were present along with Speaker Walker, but together, that made a quorum. If breaking quorum had been the Antis' plan, they had failed. Saturday also marked the time limit of Walker's ability to call for reconsideration.

Some Tennessee suffrage women celebrated the lack of Antis by surging onto the floor and seating themselves at the missing Anti legislators' desks. Gideon saw Elizabeth, once again standing just behind the brass railing, clapping as Miss Sue joined them.

Tom Riddick stood up and gleefully moved that they table the motion to reconsider the ratification vote. Seth Walker protested, but the Suffs overruled him. Methodically, they went through the procedure of tabling the motion and finalizing the procedural steps reaffirming the ratification and sending it to Governor Roberts for his signature.

When they were done, the galleries erupted into pandemonium as great as that when the bill had passed three days ago.

Finally, it was done! People streamed down from the galleries to congratulate the Suff delegates. Gideon found Elizabeth in the crowd and threw his arms around her, lifting her off her feet to swing her around while she laughed happily.

"We won!" she cried.

"Yes, we did, at last."

Nearby, someone rang the miniature Liberty Bell that had been placed in the chamber days ago. At last, women had their political freedom.

"Not everyone will be happy about this, though," Gideon said, setting her on her feet again. "We should probably leave tonight. I really need to get back to work, and I don't want you and my mother and the others here if trouble breaks out."

"I know the Antis are planning 'indignation meetings' in every district whose representative voted for suffrage, starting with Harry Burn's district," Elizabeth said. "That will be awful. Poor Harry."

"Poor all of them, but there's nothing we can do to help now. The locals will know best how to deal with it, and as soon as Governor Roberts signs the bill, there's nothing they can do anyway."

"I'm sure they'll try something, but you're right, we should go home. We've done all we can here."

Mother Bates, Anna and Freddie found them in the crush and even Jake—who, as a "federal agent," had decided to stay and see the final drama of suffrage play out—was there to help them celebrate with jumping up and down and a little dancing.

AFTER TAKING A PULLMAN CAR BACK TO NEW YORK ON SATurday night, which meant Elizabeth got little sleep, she nearly slept the clock around on Sunday, waking only twice to eat. Gideon fretted, but she explained she was just worn out from all the excitement. She didn't have the energy to tell him the whole truth just yet.

Gideon returned to the office on Monday, and Elizabeth spent the day reading the newspaper accounts of the battle in Nashville. The Antis had wasted no time in fighting back, though. They filed an injunction immediately to prevent Governor Roberts from signing the bill, but Gideon assured her the Suffs would win that legal battle in a day or two. Still, it was a troublesome development.

Elizabeth was alone in the parlor when Gideon came home from work.

She hurried out to greet him with a kiss. "Were they very happy to see you at the office?"

"Deliriously. I'm afraid we're going to have to have Mr. Devoss for dinner to make up for my absence, though."

"Good. He can congratulate your mother for her victory," Elizabeth said. "Come in and sit down. I have something to tell you."

"I hope it's not bad news about the ratification. I know the Antis have taken it to court but I'm sure—"

"No, it isn't about that, and let's not talk about ratification for a little while."

She could see he was intrigued, and she smiled mysteriously. He glanced around the parlor. "Where's Mother?"

"At a committee meeting. The Party is planning a celebration for New York City."

"Then we're alone?" he said, perking up a bit. "Maybe we should go upstairs."

She laughed at that. "In a minute. I need to tell you something first."

He sank down on the sofa and coaxed her into his lap. "All

right but be quick." He pulled her in for a kiss so she couldn't say anything for a few minutes.

Finally, she broke away and said, "You may have noticed I've been sleeping a lot."

She watched the emotions play across his face until it settled into a worried frown. "Are you ill?"

"No, not at all, but there is a good reason why I'm sleeping a lot. I'm sleeping for two."

He was still frowning. "Two? Who else would you be sleeping for?"

"I don't know yet. We won't meet him—or her—for a few more months."

"What . . . ?" he began. This time his frown was puzzled, but she watched as understanding dawned on his handsome face. "Are you . . . Are we going to have a baby?"

"Yes, darling, at last. I haven't seen a doctor yet, but Mrs. Burn said—"

"Mrs. Burn? Harry's mother?" he asked in surprise.

"Yes, Harry's mother. She noticed some, uh, symptoms and, well, she made me realize it was true. Oh, darling, are you happy? I'm very happy."

"I am," he assured her. "I am." He proceeded to show her just how happy he was by kissing her thoroughly.

"And this will mark the real end of my career as a con artist," she said when they paused to catch their breaths.

Gideon frowned thoughtfully. "Did you say *this* will mark the end?"

"What do you mean?"

"I mean that as far as I know, you haven't done a con in over a year. Unless . . ."

"Unless what?" she asked. She looked very innocent, she knew.

"Unless you did one in Nashville."

This amused her so she smiled. "What could I have done there?"

"I confess, I've been wondering and . . . Well, Mrs. Burn's letter. Did she really tell Harry to vote for ratification or did you, uh, add a little postscript to it?"

She wanted to tell him the truth. Or did she? A woman with secrets is so much more interesting. She smiled her mysterious smile again. "My darling, do you really want to know?"

He thought about it for a long moment, and then he said, "No, I don't think I do."

"Good," she said. "But you can be sure I won't be doing any more cons. A mother can't be going around taking money from people."

"Even for a good cause?" he asked with a grin. "Don't tell me you wouldn't help a friend if they needed it."

"Well," said Elizabeth, "maybe then."

# AUTHOR'S NOTE

I HAVE WANTED TO WRITE THIS STORY EVER SINCE I FIRST came up with the idea for the Counterfeit Lady Series in 2011. I became interested in the Woman Suffrage movement when I was researching the early twentieth century and happened to read *Jailed for Freedom* by Doris Stevens. This amazing book provided the research for the first book in the series, *City of Lies*. Later, I read *The Woman's Hour* by Elaine Weiss, which tells the thrilling story of how Tennessee became the thirty-sixth state to ratify the Nineteenth Amendment. This book proved to be a gold mine of information about this momentous event, and I owe Ms. Weiss a debt of gratitude.

The first question I'm sure you're going to ask is, "Did all of this really happen?" The answer is a resounding YES. Almost. As far as I know, no one was trying to con the legislators at the Hermitage Hotel, although how would we ever know? Also, Elizabeth and her crew weren't really there because—and I hope this doesn't come as a shock to anyone—they didn't really exist.

However, almost everything they did participate in did happen, although to someone else.

Yes, Harry Burn's mother did write him a letter, and he did receive it on that Wednesday morning just before the session started, but she had mailed it, and it was delivered to him by a page after it arrived at the Capitol. If you do an internet search for "Harry Burn letter" you can see the actual letter and envelope which are stored in the East Tennessee History Center as part of the McClung Historical Collection in Knoxville, Tennessee. You will notice that Mrs. Burn asks Harry twice in this letter to vote for suffrage.

It is a long, newsy letter, written in pencil on lined tablet paper, and on page two she says, "Hurrah and vote for suffrage and don't keep them in doubt. I noticed Chandlers [sic] speech. It was very bitter. I've been waiting to see how you stood but have not seen anything yet." Then again, at the end of the letter, just above her signature, she writes, "Don't forget to be a good boy and help Mrs. Thomas [sic] Catt with her 'Rats.' Is she the one who put rat in ratification? Ha!" Did someone encourage her to add the second admonition? Not that we know of, but let's just say it could have happened!

When I was studying the letter, I noticed that it was postmarked in Nashville at 2:30 A.M. on Tuesday, August 17, although Harry did not receive it until around 10:00 A.M. on Wednesday, August 18. If the Antis had allowed the vote to take place on Tuesday, as originally planned, Harry would not yet have received the letter. Would he still have changed his vote? Would the amendment still have been ratified? We will never know.

Harry Burn did face a lot of backlash from his vote, and he did escape from the Capitol that day just as I described, only without Gideon's help. Later he gave the speech in the chamber exactly as I described, and he gave five reasons for changing his vote, only one of which mentioned the letter from his mother. The Antis did hold an "indignation" meeting in his district and campaigned vigorously against him, but he won reelection and had a long, successful career in public service.

Governor Roberts was not so lucky. He lost the election. As you probably guessed, Governor Cox also lost his election for president to Warren G. Harding who, oddly enough, attracted a lot of the female vote. Sadly, he wasn't the honorable man Seth Walker imagined.

The Old Man's con is based on a real enterprise run by a Chicago lawyer, George Remus, during Prohibition. He bought fourteen distilleries and obtained permits to produce medicinal and industrial alcohol. And yes, back in the early twentieth century, doctors did prescribe alcohol as a remedy. Drugstores would carry it and use it to fill the prescriptions. After Prohibition became law, doctors wrote many more prescriptions to thirsty patients. Drugstores also began selling phony prescriptions to those who didn't want to bother seeing a doctor. Then they just started selling liquor out the back door to anyone who wanted it. Remus produced much more liquor than he was authorized to, and eventually the authorities caught up with him. He had made millions, but he lost it all. You have to admit he was clever, though.

The Antis continued to fight against Woman Suffrage for a few more years. They filed an injunction immediately, as I said. Governor Roberts was finally able to sign the bill on the following Tuesday and sent it special delivery to Washington. There U.S. Secretary of State Bainbridge Colby signed it in the early morning hours of Thursday, August 26 with only his secretary as witness. The Antis still kept up their legal maneuvers, but women were allowed to vote in the November 1920 elections except in two states that refused to change their voter registration deadlines in time to accommodate the new law. It wasn't until the

Supreme Court ruled in 1922 that they brought an end to the Antis' efforts to nullify the Susan B. Anthony Amendment.

Sadly, women weren't able to purify politics, and the amendment didn't immediately grant women all the rights of men. That fight is still going on, over a hundred years later. The National American Woman Suffrage Association and the National Woman's Party never mended their differences, and each felt they had not received the proper amount of recognition for the parts they played in the Cause. Alice Paul continued to fight for women's rights for the rest of her life. Carrie Chapman Catt founded the League of Women Voters and worked for international Woman Suffrage after the Nineteenth Amendment passed.

The Hermitage Hotel is still going strong, and now the street running beside it is named Anne Dallas Dudley Boulevard. Their website features an article about the part the hotel played in ratifying the Nineteenth Amendment.

So, the answer to all your questions, is, "Yes, this really happened." Sometimes truth is stranger than fiction.

Please let me know how you enjoyed this book. You can sign up on my website to receive notices when my new books are released so you don't have to miss a single one! You can contact me at victoriathompson.com or follow me on Facebook at Victoria .Thompson.Author or on Twitter @gaslightvt.